PRAISE FOR

Here are some of the over 100,000 five star reviews left for the Dead Cold Mystery series.

"Rex Stout and Michael Connelly have spawned a protege."

AMAZON REVIEW

"So begins one damned fine read."

AMAZON REVIEW

"Mystery that's more brain than brawn."

AMAZON REVIEW

"I read so many of this genre...and ever so often I strike gold!"

AMAZON REVIEW

"This book is filled with action, intrigue, espionage, and everything else lovers of a good thriller want."

AMAZON REVIEW

THE FALL MOON
A DEAD COLD MYSTERY

BLAKE BANNER

Copyright © 2024 by Right House

All rights reserved.

The characters and events portrayed in this ebook are fictitious. Any similarity to real persons, living or dead, is coincidental and not intended by the author.

No part of this book may be reproduced in any form or by any electronic or mechanical means, including information storage and retrieval systems, without written permission from the author, except for the use of brief quotations in a book review.

ISBN-13: 978-1-63696-017-3

ISBN-10: 1-63696-017-0

Cover design by: Damonza

Printed in the United States of America

www.righthouse.com

www.instagram.com/righthousebooks

www.facebook.com/righthousebooks

twitter.com/righthousebooks

DEAD COLD MYSTERY SERIES
An Ace and a Pair (Book 1)
Two Bare Arms (Book 2)
Garden of the Damned (Book 3)
Let Us Prey (Book 4)
The Sins of the Father (Book 5)
Strange and Sinister Path (Book 6)
The Heart to Kill (Book 7)
Unnatural Murder (Book 8)
Fire from Heaven (Book 9)
To Kill Upon A Kiss (Book 10)
Murder Most Scottish (Book 11)
The Butcher of Whitechapel (Book 12)
Little Dead Riding Hood (Book 13)
Trick or Treat (Book 14)
Blood Into Wine (Book 15)
Jack In The Box (Book 16)
The Fall Moon (Book 17)
Blood In Babylon (Book 18)
Death In Dexter (Book 19)
Mustang Sally (Book 20)
A Christmas Killing (Book 21)
Mommy's Little Killer (Book 22)
Bleed Out (Book 23)

Dead and Buried (Book 24)
In Hot Blood (Book 25)
Fallen Angels (Book 26)
Knife Edge (Book 27)
Along Came A Spider (Book 28)
Cold Blood (Book 29)
Curtain Call (Book 30)

ONE

"You remember the Redfern case?"

Dehan spoke to the bacon on her plate as she cut into it, frowning. I leaned back comfortably, holding my coffee cup halfway to my mouth.

"Sure, it was Bob Lindsey's case just before he got shot." I scratched my chin. "Six, seven years ago? Couple killed in their home on Ellis Avenue, few doors down from the Glory of Christ church, as I recall. Daughter disappeared, presumed killed too. Bobby died. The shooting was unrelated to the case. Case went cold." I sipped my coffee. Outside, birds were singing in the warm, summer Sunday morning. "You want to look at that case?"

She shrugged and pulled a face at the same time. "I was always curious." She eyed me while she wiped her mouth with her napkin. "I have a feeling about that case, Stone. It was seven years ago this fall . . ." She tapped her temple with her finger. "And it's still up here. I don't know why we never looked at it." She took the same finger and wagged it at me. "There is more to that case than meets the eye, and you knew it at the time. I could see it, writ large on your ugly face."

"Thanks."

"Your face isn't ugly. Don't get sensitive. You know what I'm saying."

"Yeah, it caught a lot of people's attention at the time. But what can I tell you? It wasn't my case. They hit a dead end..."

"He got shot."

"That didn't help. What's your point, Dehan?"

She laid her knife and fork across her plate, picked up her cup, and frowned into her coffee.

"There was more to that case than that couple getting stabbed to death. I was interested at the time, but I was a rookie. I wish I'd been your partner back then. We should have taken the case. There were threads that were never followed. I knew you were thinking back then that the case should never have gone cold."

"How could you know that?"

She smiled. "I was aware of you."

"Really? Back then?"

"Sure, you were this wiseass, smart-ass with a bad attitude who had a kick-ass record for solving hard cases."

"So it was all about the ass?"

"You know it."

I shrugged and then followed up with a nod. "It's true, I did think that at the time. Bobby's partner . . ." I thought for a moment. "Sanchez. He kind of sat on it for a while. Then it went cold. I had cases of my own..."

"You know what?" She frowned. "There were aspects to the case I often thought could have made it a federal case."

I was surprised. I thought back, trying to remember. It had been six years ago and the details were hazy. "I'm not sure, Dehan. I can't think of anything offhand that would take it out of the purview of the NYPD and bring it within the jurisdiction of the bureau... Talk me through."

She poured herself more coffee. I held out my cup and she refilled mine too. Then she sat back, holding her cup in both hands, her eyes became abstracted, and she started to recite from memory.

"Karl and Christen Redfern, 2163 Ellis Avenue, first-floor apartment. Occupied by them and their daughter, Amy. Sometime between the night of Saturday the twenty-second and the small hours of Sunday the twenty-third of September, 2012, somebody entered their apartment and killed Karl and Christen. His body was found in the kitchen. He had been stabbed in the right kidney, once, with a long, broad, sharp blade, probably a kitchen knife. He was then stabbed in the heart, through the fourth and fifth intercostals. However, bleeding from the kidney had been profuse, whereas he had bled little from the heart, suggesting the wound to the heart was perimortem.

"Christen was killed in their bed while she was sleeping. There were between fifteen and twenty stab wounds to the heart. It was hard to be precise because the area was so damaged and badly lacerated, the ribs themselves had been fractured and broken. Bruising, pre-, peri-, and postmortem, was extensive. She also had bruising to the face, and other parts of her body, suggesting the attack went on some time while she was dying, and after she was dead.

"Amy Redfern was not found at the house, or anywhere else. No trace of her has ever been found."

She sipped her coffee and set down her cup with care, like she was centering her ideas on the tabletop. She went on:

"Of note are the fact that the prints found at the scene were predominantly Karl's and Christen's, Amy's, and her boyfriend, Charlie's. That is to be expected, but there were no prints that were attributable to a killer on the kitchen knives, the surfaces, or the victims themselves.

"One large kitchen knife was found in the drying rack by the sink. There were no traces of blood or fingerprints on it. Normally, when crockery or cutlery is washed, some prints are found, but this knife had been polished clean. The blade was consistent with the weapon used to kill both of the Redferns and was probably the murder weapon."

I grunted. "Do I remember correctly that the lock had been

very crudely forced? Hadn't the wood been hacked away from the latch with some kind of blade, like a screwdriver?"

She nodded. "That's right. And, final point of interest, both Karl and Christen had cannabis, coke, and alcohol in their systems."

I gazed out the window, across the living room, wondering why we couldn't spend Sunday morning like normal people, going to the park, or driving out to the country. But the case was coming back to me, and I had to admit, it was interesting, and had intrigued me at the time. Absently, I said, "No motive ever became apparent either, did it?"

"Nope."

She stood and walked over to the window I'd been looking out of and stood with her hands in the back pockets of her jeans, gazing at the street. After a moment, she turned and sat on the sill.

"There was no cash found in the house, which may or may not be significant. According to neighbors, they struggled to get by and spent whatever disposable income they had on booze and drugs, mainly weed." She shrugged. "If I were going to burglarize a house, I would not have chosen theirs. You wouldn't need to go very far to find a better candidate."

I watched her lean down and grab her bag from beside the sofa. From it she pulled a case file, gave me a guilty grin, and brought it to the breakfast table. I sighed and reached for it as she handed it to me.

"Dehan, it's Sunday. The day even God kicked back and put his feet up."

"I know, Stone, but I started rereading it and it got under my skin. What happened to that girl? You know what I mean. I know you do."

I opened the file and she lifted out the crime scene photos till she found the photographs of the two bodies, his in the kitchen, slumped on the floor in a dark pool of blood, and hers facedown on the bed. We both studied them for a minute. Then I smiled to myself because I knew she was thinking the same as me.

"What struck me back then was that he was attacked initially from behind, and though it wasn't expert, it was efficient: a single, disabling stab to the kidney, and as he turned and collapsed, another to the heart."

She looked at me and nodded. "I know..."

I went on, "But the attack on Christen was totally different. It's savage and frenzied, delivered with enough force to break bone..."

She was nodding as I spoke. "So you're thinking that Christen was the actual target. He got Karl out of the way, went into the bedroom, and let rip."

I nodded. "Yeah, it's possible, isn't it? There can't be much doubt that she was the focus of real rage, and he wasn't."

She scratched her head, then tied up her hair. She looked in her cup, put it down, and glanced out the window. I watched her do all that, frowning, and she grinned at me.

"You want to go see the scene?" I raised a skeptical eyebrow and questioned her with it. She said, "The landlord wants to sell it, so he's keeping it vacant. I called him. I told him we probably wouldn't come today, being Sunday an' all, but that, you know... we might."

I stared at her a moment.

She went on, "He said that would be fine, so long as we don't scare away potential buyers... Are you mad?"

"No. I love examining crime scenes on my days off. It makes such a change from what I do the rest of the week."

"You're mad."

"No! No, really. It's obviously got under your skin, so let's go scratch that itch."

I stood, and she stared at me, then smiled. "See? That's why I married you out of four billion men."

"Flattery, Dehan, will get you exactly..."

"Everywhere with you. Everywhere..."

"Exactly. Everywhere. Let's go."

I pulled on my jacket and gathered together keys and phone.

It was a warm, quiet Sunday. The birds were busy in the plane trees doing whatever it is that birds do when they won't stop chattering. I tossed Dehan the keys to my old, burgundy Jaguar Mark II and made my way to the passenger door.

"Least you can do is drive me, as you're making me work on my day off."

She caught them left-handed without looking and unlocked the car. "Quit griping, I'll make it up to you."

I climbed in and slammed the door. "Damn right you will. Exactly what did you have in mind?"

She fired up the old bruiser and sniggered. "I'll buy you a new pair of slippers, and a pipe."

I scowled at her. "I don't wear slippers, Dehan, and I don't smoke a pipe."

She pulled out and accelerated toward Morris Park Avenue. "And I'll get you a comfy old cardigan to go with them."

"Take a hike. This is the thanks I get: mockery!"

She'd started laughing. "Then you can sit Sunday mornings and watch the sports and get mad at the news."

It was a fifteen-minute drive from Haight Avenue to Ellis Avenue, but it was Sunday, the roads were empty, and Dehan was driving, so we did it in ten. All the way she sniggered, and I made a careful study of the shop fronts.

2163 Ellis Avenue was a slightly dilapidated, rust-colored clapboard house with nice big bay windows on the ground floor and the upper floor. It also had a nice porch with five stone steps leading down to the sidewalk and a white wrought iron railing that looked as though it had recently been painted. A large sign had been attached to those railings, advertising the house for sale.

We climbed the steps to where a small, brown awning protected the front door from rain and sun and studied the two mailboxes and the two bells on the entry-phone. Both bells had a faded, misted window where you could put a card with your name on it. They were both empty. Dehan had phoned the landlord from the car to let him know we were coming. Now she pressed the bottom bell and a tired voice said, "Yeah . . ." like he'd figured we thought life was barely worth living, and he was agreeing with us.

"Good morning, sir, this is Detective Dehan of the NYPD. I called about ten minutes ago . . ."

"Yuh . . ." He made it sound like it was a shame she called about ten minutes ago, but there wasn't much he could do about it. The door buzzed. I pushed it open and stood back for Dehan to go ahead, then followed her into a handsome, well-proportioned hall with an ugly, beige carpet and a broad, mahogany staircase climbing the left-hand wall. On the right, there was a large door which opened, as the street door closed, to reveal a small man in big brown pants and a big colorless cardigan. His face looked as tired as his voice had sounded. We showed him our badges. Dehan spoke.

"Mr. Bernstein? I am Detective Dehan. This is my partner, Detective Stone."

He looked at us curiously, then his eyes smiled.

"Sure. I know. Come in." It was all said with the kind of resignation that you buy into because they persuade you it's a virtue. By the time you realize it's not, it's too late, because you've already resigned yourself to it. He walked away from us into a large, bright room that ran the full length of the building. He spoke as he walked, in small, tired steps.

"It was my sister's house. She died. Everybody dies. Sooner or later. But it's still a surprise when they do." After a moment, he added, "I never thought she would ever die."

On the right as we stepped in was the bay window. Ahead there was an open fireplace with a black, marble hearth. Against the opposite wall there was an old, leather sofa that had once been expensive, before it was donated, and two armchairs that hadn't. They all sat around an unattractive coffee table that was pretending to be pine but failing to convince.

On the left, the area that had once been a dining room was now a kitchen-diner, with a long, fake mahogany table running sideways across the room. In the far wall, there were two doors which I figured were the bedrooms. Mr. Bernstein had his ass against the dining table and was watching us.

I said, "You remember the Redferns?"

"Oh, yes. They died too, but for different reasons. My sister died of old age. She was very old." He shrugged in a way that suggested he found a certain pleasure in the self-evident, and added, "Old enough to die."

I asked, "What were they like?"

"Sad. The daughter was sweet, a bit neurotic. He used to beat them, of course. I guess enough of that could make you neurotic, right? They drank a lot. But one tries not to pry. Would you like me to leave while you do your *Monk* thing?" He smiled and held out his hands in front of him as though he was lining up a shot for a camera.

Dehan smiled and nodded. "We'd appreciate that."

"I'll be down the road. You have my number."

The door closed behind him, and a moment later, the sound from the street swelled a second before being cut off when that door was closed too.

TWO

We stared at each other a moment, not aware that we were staring, but somehow sharing our thoughts. I pointed at the kitchen. "You're Karl."

She nodded and went over to the sink, talking over her shoulder. "He was making coffee, right?"

I went to the door of the apartment. "Yeah, and this is one of the things that always unsettled me. If you're in the kitchen, making coffee, how come you don't hear me peeling the wood away from the latch?"

She thought about it for a moment. "There are two possible answers to that, and they might both apply. First, both Karl and Christen are stoned out of their minds. So while our killer was cutting through the wood, Karl might well have been stood here watching the kettle boil, communing with the fairies and giggling to himself."

I gave my head a little twitch and asked, "Or?"

"Or Karl might have been as unconscious as Christen when the killer came in. He needed to pee, most likely got hungry and thirsty—you know how it is . . ."

"No."

"Maybe the breaking of the latch was what woke him and he didn't realize it. So he gets up *after* the killer broke in."

I made the face of a person who is not satisfied. "Okay, so you're in the bedroom. Go in the bedroom . . ."

"Which one? I don't remember."

"Have a look."

She peered through both doors and turned to face me. "Okay, that one on the left is Amy's."

I nodded.

"This one on the right is bigger and has the en suite."

I waved her through the door and I called out to her as I went through the motions of busting the latch.

"Okay, so I break in, meanwhile you fall out of bed, stagger to the toilet. I hear you moving about, I hear you flush, so I hide . . . where?"

I looked about. She appeared in the bedroom doorway. I glanced at her and went on. "I guess I flatten myself in the corner, beyond the dining table. The light switch is over in the kitchen, so he hasn't switched it on yet and it's still dark. Now you move to the kitchen . . ."

She crossed the floor into the kitchen and began to move around like she was making coffee. I moved around the dining table and crept up behind her, stopped, and sighed noisily.

"See? There are too many problems with this theory, but the big one right now is this." She turned to look at me and she was nodding, like she already knew what I was going to say. I went on anyway. "Did you notice in the crime scene photos where the block with the kitchen knives was?"

She pointed at the surface behind her. "The obvious place, by the cooker."

"So to get the kitchen knife to kill you with, I have to go *past* you without being seen, and then come *back* behind you, to stab you in the kidney."

She shrugged one shoulder. "It's possible the knife was not in the block. It may have been on the table."

I shook my head. "Even so, that's just part of it; what nagged at me from the start was, *I already have a weapon*. I just used it to hack away the lock. Why do I wait for you to get all the way across to the kitchen, get a mug, get the instant coffee from the cupboard, spoon it into the mug, switch on the kettle, *and only then* grab the knife and stab you in the back—all that instead of stabbing you right from the start with the tool I used on the door? What have I been doing all this time?"

We stared at each other for a moment. "After that point it works fine," I said. "You're about to pour the water onto the coffee, I come up behind you, stab you once in the kidney, you turn as you go down and I stab you once in the heart. But how and *for what purpose* I got hold of the kitchen knife is not clear. That period from entry to stabbing, that does not satisfy me at all."

She nodded. "I agree." She mimed killing Karl, stabbing him in the heart on the kitchen floor, then looked over at the bedroom. "So at that point, he moves quickly to the bedroom door. There is enough light from the kitchen for him to see that Christen is lying on the bed. We don't know if she was facedown or not to begin with. She took a hell of a beating. But she winds up facedown and that's when he goes into his frenzied attack with the knife. Then he returns to the kitchen, thoroughly washes the knife, leaves it in the rack, and goes."

"But that brings us to the other problem."

"Amy."

I nodded. "Amy."

"The crime scene report said the room was in a mess . . ."

"The room *was* in a mess," I said. "But it didn't look as though it had been turned over or ransacked. It just looked like the room of a young woman who doesn't clean up often. It was like her parents' room." I shrugged. "The sheets on the bed were dirty, there were dirty clothes on the floor, dirty underwear. There was a bowl of cereal under the bed that had gone moldy, an ashtray on the bedside table that was brimming over. A lot of the butts were joints. There was, apparently at least, nothing essential missing, other than her cell and her purse."

She pulled out a chair, sat, and rested her elbows on the table. "So either she wasn't here when the killing happened, or she was here and left with the killer."

"Both of those scenarios beg questions." I raised my thumb as number one. "If she wasn't here when the killing happened, why didn't she come back at some stage? Her closet was full of clothes, all her books, her iPod; as far as they could tell at the time, everything she possessed except her phone and her purse were in her room. And in six years she never showed up, never phoned, never contacted anybody..."

Dehan spread her hands. "But likewise, if she left with the killer, was it voluntary or involuntary? The very fact that she never took any of her stuff suggests she hadn't planned for it and she wasn't leaving of her own free will, right?"

I nodded. "Yeah, it does."

"So, what I am thinking, Stone, is that he has abducted her, and he has either kept her against her will or, more likely, he has killed her and dumped her body somewhere."

I shoved my hands in my pockets and moved across the room toward the two big windows. An afternoon breeze shifted the dappled shade on the blacktop. A hint of the approaching fall tinged the light with copper. I spoke aloud, staring out through the glass at the street. "Whatever it was, that was one messed-up motive. The focus of his attack is the mother. He beats her, then stabs her fifteen or twenty times, all in the heart. That's *a lot of focus*, all on her heart, and then he takes the daughter, without a struggle." I turned. "He lets her take her cell and her purse, and then he kills her. I have a lot of trouble understanding what is motivating him."

Her form was slightly hazy in the half-light, staring down at the tabletop. "I know," she said. "I agree. But that's what it looks like he did, right? So what that means is that there are bits missing from the picture. There is something that connects the mother, the daughter, and the killer in a way that makes sense of the killer's rage and his decision to abduct Amy."

"You've decided she was abducted?"

"That's putting it a bit strong, but I am pretty sure of it. *I'm having trouble making sense of any other explanation.* If she'd run, she would have called for help, or called the cops. If he'd killed her here, there'd have been a body, or blood, or signs of a struggle..."

"And you think you know what this missing piece is?"

She sighed, made a doubtful face, and got to her feet. "Maybe. Let's say I have a hunch that I know the kind of area where we might find it. You done here?"

I nodded.

"Good. C'mon, I'll buy you an ice cream in Central Park."

"In Central Park..."

"Sure. It's Sunday. We go to the park. Live a little." She went and opened the door, holding it for me. "See, that's the problem with you, Stone. It's always work, work, work. My father would have told you: 'Son, take a rest on the Sabbath.' He was a wise man."

I sighed, shook my head, and followed her out to the car.

We drove twenty-five minutes to Manhattan. All the way, she talked about everything you could possibly imagine talking about in the short space of twenty-five minutes, while I thought about the crossword I'd been planning to do, drinking lemonade in the backyard.

We dropped the car near the corner of East 106th and crossed 5th Avenue at a slow lope. We found the Conservatory Garden gate and went in among the lawns and the trees around the Harlem Meer. There, we stopped at the kiosk. I told her I didn't want an ice cream and she ordered two vanilla cones, then slapped me on the chest with the back of her hand. "C'mon, loosen up. Have some fun. When was the last time you had an ice cream, *pendejo*?"

THE FALL MOON | 13

I smiled and after a moment asked her, "Do you know what *pendejo* means, Dehan?"

"What do you think?" She put money on the counter, took the two cones, and handed one to me. She started licking as we started to walk. "My mother was Mexican. All her family are Mexican. Of course I know what it means. It means asshole, idiot, dickwad. It's a serious insult in Mexico, but the way I use it, it's not. It's like, 'Hey, asshole,' 'Hey, *pendejo*.' It's like a term of endearment."

I shifted my fingers to avoid the drips of melting cream. "It means pubic hair."

She raised an eyebrow at me.

I went on. "You call somebody a *pendejo* and you're calling them a pubic hair. So what's this hunch you have?"

She switched eyebrows, sighed, and returned to her cone. "Jeez . . . So, all that time ago, when I was a rookie, I never got the chance to talk to you about the case. It wasn't my case, you were kind of this senior, forbidding guy who was always busy; plus, now you've mellowed a bit, but back then you had this real bad attitude. And I was just . . . you know . . . a rookie. Then, by the time I'd screwed up enough courage, Bob got shot, Sanchez took over and sat on the case. It went cold . . . So, I never got to discuss it with you and I don't know if you were aware of it."

"Aware of what?"

We were following the path along the water, and I was wondering if I could drop the cone in and make it look like an accident.

"Six, almost seven months before Karl and Christen were killed, sometime in March, he was badly beaten and put in hospital."

I stopped and stared down at her, aware that she had said something important but not aware why. "By whom?"

She grinned and started walking again. "Whom? It kills me when you say that. I always wanted a partner who said things like 'whom' and quoted Conan Doyle. 'Eliminate the impossible, Dehan...'"

I caught up with her. "Dehan! What has got into you today? Who beat him up?"

She shrugged, still grinning. "He refused to testify, said he didn't see who it was, but it seemed like a big coincidence, you know what I mean?"

"Wait a minute, slow down." I stopped again. My hand was covered in melted cream and I switched the cone to my other hand so I could lick my finger. "How did you find out about this . . . ?"

"What can I tell you? I liked the case. I was curious. You going to eat that?"

"No."

"Why didn't you just say?" She took it from me and started licking it. "We had a stabbed homeless guy, and a son of a bitch who beat his wife to death." I crouched down to wet my finger in the meer. She went on talking. "I'm not saying they weren't important. Everybody's life is important, I get that. But they weren't exactly sudoku either. Plus, my partner was a real asshole. I'm not a feminist, but every damn word out of his mouth was about my ass or my boobs."

I stood and we started walking again.

"So I took an interest in the Redfern case and I started snooping around. I'm good at snooping around. You know? Looking at the angles . . . ?" She did a little duck and dive and stuffed the last of my cone in her mouth. "So I figured maybe I should find out a little about Karl and Christen. Maybe it was a ghost from their past that came and bit them in the ass."

I nodded. "Yeah, I had wondered that."

"Yeah, I figured. Then Bob got shot, and Captain Peralta didn't want to know when I asked her if I could take the case." She shrugged. "So I put the word out with a couple of informants. I wanted to know who put Karl Redfern in hospital."

"And?"

She stopped and narrowed her eyes at me, poked me gently on the chest with her finger. "See? Like me, you think it's going to be a big revelation, open up the case." She shook her head and looked past me at where the midday sun was sparkling on the meer. "Adolfo Davila and Mateo Bonilla, from the Bronx. Both members of the Chupacabras."

I frowned. "Did you talk to them?"

She shook her head, still gazing out at the coppery water. "Both dead."

"Both dead . . . ?"

She thrust her hands in her pockets, hunched her shoulders, and turned slowly on her heel to start walking again. "You're going to ask me how and when."

I fell into step. "Mm-hm . . ."

"They were shot point-blank down by the fish market on Hunts Point. Nine-millimeter hollow points. One each to the chest, then one each to the head when they were down."

"An execution."

She stopped and wagged a finger at me. "An execution, but note, not execution *style*." She shook her head. "Every badass kid from a 'hood' all across the U.S.A. who watches TV can't wait to get out on the streets with his new nine-millimeter Taurus and kill some poor schmuck 'execution style.'" She held out her hands like she was holding a gun and snarled, "Git on yo' knees, mother focker! *Bam! Execution style!*" She started walking again. "But this wasn't execution *style*. This was . . . *efficient*. They didn't see it coming. *Bam! Bam!* One each in the chest. Then he confirmed the kill. No waste of time, no waste of ammo. No evidence."

"Shells? Slugs?"

"The four slugs. No shells."

"When?"

"The night of the twenty-sixth to the twenty-seventh of August, 2012."

"Less than a month before Karl and Christen."

"And neither Karl nor Christen owned a gun."

I crossed the path on slow feet and sat on the bench that runs along the gardens opposite the lake. She came and sat next to me. I had my elbows on my knees, but she was leaning back with the ankle of her right leg on her left knee.

"And what you're trying to do is show that these four murders are connected, and tie them to the Chupacabras."

She sat forward and leaned gently against me. "Let's take it one step at a time, partner. I am not *trying to show* that they are connected. They are connected, because the guys who got killed at the fish market are the same guys who put Karl in hospital; that right there is a connection. What I want to show is that these are parts of the same crime. There are other connections, some are more obvious, others are more subtle."

I frowned at her. "You been working on this on your own, without telling me?"

"Not exactly, but I have looked at it from time to time."

"Huh . . . Okay, tell me the more obvious connections."

"Drugs."

"Karl was a user, mainly weed . . ."

"Yeah, but also him and his old lady liked to snort when they could afford it."

"Okay, and the Chupacabras are major dealers. But that is tenuous at best, Dehan."

"I know, but tenuous as it is, it is a damn sight more substantial than Bob's best lead at the time. Am I wrong?" She didn't wait for an answer. She knew she was right. She bulldozed on. "Now listen to this. The one thing that stands out about the killing of Adolfo and Mateo is the efficiency, right? The focus."

I nodded.

"Now go back to the killing of Karl and Christen. There is no frenzy with Karl, it is cool and efficient, and note: one quick stab to a vital organ to incapacitate, and then confirm the kill with a stab to the heart. *Exactly* the same as Adolfo and Mateo. Then, he goes in to Christen and he goes crazy, but he goes *focused* crazy. Remember, the ME said he had never seen anything like it."

"I remember. That struck me at the time."

"Fifteen or twenty blows, in rapid succession, all within a radius of four inches. Focus. I *know* it's not a lot, Stone, but you can smell it as clear as I can, this is the same killer."

I puffed out my cheeks and blew.

She shrugged. "Besides, it is all we got."

I nodded. "Which is probably why the case went cold. What do you suggest? The Chupacabras are not going to talk to us."

"What do *you* suggest?"

I made a face. "You won't like it. It has nothing to do with the angle you're looking at."

She shook her head. "You don't know that and neither do I because none of this makes any sense right now. Hit me."

"The boyfriend."

She blinked a few times to show her lack of enthusiasm. "Charlie."

"Charlie. He disappeared at the same time, remember?"

She shrugged. "I know, it *looks* significant. It's a hell of a coincidence, I agree, but at the time, Bob and Sanchez ruled him out."

I nodded. "They did, but still, that's where I would start."

"How? He disappeared."

"His mother. We go and talk to his mother."

THREE

We went and had an absurdly expensive lunch first, and then I insisted on taking in the Rubin Museum of Art, a place I had been threatening to take Dehan since we'd been married. She was always keen to explore different ideas and cultures, and I was pretty sure she would love the place, but that Sunday her comments on the Tibetan Buddhist Shrine Room were, "Uh-huh . . . ," her observation on the Gateway to Himalayan Art was, "Mm-hm . . . ," and her thoughts on Art and Politics in Tibetan Buddhism were, "Huh . . ." So after an hour, I suggested perhaps we could come back some other time, after we had spoken to Pamela Albright, Charlie's mother. She'd nodded with conviction.

"Yep, I'm down with that, Stone."

"Dehan, you owe me a Sunday."

"You got it, boss."

It was five thirty by the time we pulled up outside Pamela's large, handsome brownstone on East 127th. Two tasteful brass lamps flanked the large, highly polished mahogany door, and a large brass disk housed the original 1920s bell. A glance through the bay windows showed a number of what looked like genuine antiques. Unlike Amy's parents, Charlie Albright's mother was not poor.

Dehan rang the bell, and after a couple of minutes, the door opened. The woman who opened it was a bottle blonde, slim and well dressed, of average height and probably in her early fifties. She had once been attractive, but now relied on too much makeup and perfume to hide what age and alcohol were doing to her skin and her breath. Her smile suggested I could pour her a drink and Dehan could go play with the traffic. Dehan showed her her badge instead.

"I am Detective Dehan with the NYPD, ma'am, and this is Detective Stone. Are you Pamela Albright?"

She fingered a string of pearls at her neck. She didn't seem sure whether to be belligerent or accommodating and settled for incredulous as a compromise. "What on Earth does the NYPD want with me?"

I said, "We were wondering if we could ask you some questions about your son."

Her eyebrows shot up and she took half a step back. "*My son? Now? After six years?*"

I smiled understanding at her and said, "We run a cold-case unit out of the Forty-Third Precinct, Mrs. Albright, and we're taking another look at Charlie's case."

She frowned at me with slightly unfocused eyes, then turned to Dehan. Her frown was deepening. "What can you possibly hope to learn after all this time?"

I answered again. "We are not sure, but it is possible that Charlie's disappearance is related to another case. It's too early to say, but it might be a lead. May we come in?"

She considered us both a moment, then stepped back without saying anything.

The difference with the Redferns' house was striking. The layout was pretty much the same, with the broad staircase climbing the left wall of the substantial entrance hall, and a door on the right leading to a spacious, sunny living room and dining room. But where the Redferns' house had been mauled and mutilated, and chopped into apartments without thought to its elegant proportions and size, Pamela Albright's house had been left intact, and had preserved all of its nineteenth-century elegance.

White was obviously the thing with Pamela Albright. Her drapes were white, the walls were white, the heavy, calico armchairs and sofa were white, and the rugs on the floor, presumably to break the monotony, were cream. Both fireplaces, in the living area and in the dining area, were white marble, and the heavy dining table and the six chairs that surrounded it were also white.

She gestured us to the two overstuffed chairs and lounged on the sofa between us, angled slightly into the corner so as to look at me. Dehan sat back, discreetly put her cell on record, and pulled a notepad and pen from her jacket. Pamela pulled a cigarette from a pack beside her on the sofa and lit up with a gold lighter that looked like a Cartier. She inhaled deeply, watching me through hooded eyes.

I said, "What can you tell me about Charlie's relationship with Amy?"

"Amy?" She made an ugly face, with her very red mouth drawn down at the sides. "She was a pretty little thing. A bit of a hippie. Sweet and polite, little piece of nothing, really." She breathed in sharply through her nose and her lids concealed her eyes for a moment. "You see, Charlie had a problem."

Dehan glanced at her. I waited a moment, then asked, "What kind of problem?"

"He was severely dyslexic, and dyspraxic. He was very bright. Many dyslexic and dyspraxic children are. But it also made him socially very awkward. He had huge difficulty relating to other children, and though we wanted to send him to Gerald's prep school, he didn't make it. It was terribly humiliating for Gerald."

Dehan said to her notebook, "Gerald?"

"My husband. He died when Charlie was just six."

Dehan raised an eyebrow at her notebook. "Aged six, he had already humiliated his father. Put that in your Oedipal pipe and smoke it."

Pamela turned bodily to scowl at Dehan, who focused hard on making notes on her pad. I said, "So he went to public school?"

"I had little choice," she said coldly. "With Gerald gone, I went to pieces. He was my rock, my strength. He was a banker, you know? He made sure the house was paid for and we had a generous income, but it was the loss of that strength, his presence, you understand?"

She frowned at me, as though I might not understand. I nodded to reassure her that I did, so she went on.

"My family rallied at first, as did his, but people are fickle, Mr. Stone, aren't they? When they see that you are mourning in your own way, not in theirs, or at their pace, they grow impatient. Poor Charlie grew very attached to my mother and my sister after Gerald left, and he missed them when they went too."

Dehan looked at her sharply and raised an eyebrow. "They . . . *went*?"

"Back to Miami."

I scratched my chin. "So all of this must have aggravated Charlie's dyspraxia."

"Of course, the stress and the anxiety played havoc with him. I often wonder if I could have done more to help him. I should have done more, I know . . ."

"But it sounds as though he was able to relate to Amy."

She leaned forward. "She was the *only* person he could relate to. It was distressing. Her parents were these hippie types . . ." She paused, gazing at the window. "They weren't really even interesting enough to be hippies. They didn't bake lentil bread or grow pot or anything like that. They just didn't wash very often, and he, the father, had his hair matted into long strands. I think he did it intentionally. She seemed inoffensive enough, the mother, Cristina . . . ?"

"Christen."

"Yes, that's it, but I didn't like Charlie going over there. I always worried he'd catch something. And I'm sure the other parents used to look at her and Charlie and call them the odd couple."

"So they were friends for a long time."

"From the beginning. She was a sweet child, like a little fairy. White, white skin, little white face with blue, blue eyes and platinum hair. Skinny little arms and legs, always dressed in clothes that somebody had passed on, so they never quite fit. Sometimes she'd go into school and her face hadn't been washed, or nobody had brushed her hair. So Charlie would ask me if she could come home after school, and he would wash her face, or insist that we give her a bath, and comb her hair for her. He cared for her as though she were his own sister."

"He had no other friends?"

She sucked on her cigarette, drew the smoke down deep, and spoke with little clouds puffing from her mouth as she crushed the butt in the ashtray. "She was the only one who didn't torment him. She was nice to him, and they stuck together. Soon the other kids learned to leave them alone. By the time she was ten or eleven years old, I think she spent as much time here as she did at her own place. They used to play that I was going to adopt her. Poor child. Perhaps I should have."

She laughed and I smiled. She swung her legs off the sofa and stood.

"I can feel dehydration threatening. Can I offer either of you a drink? I am sorely in need of a gin and tonic."

We told her she couldn't, and she made her way with the careful grace and dignity of a habitual drunk to a collection of bottles on a sideboard in the dining area. She spoke as she built the drink. "Of course, I imagine that they started experimenting with sex in his room. And I wasn't sure *what* to do about that. I mean, he was so shy, and so awkward to talk to. If I had attempted to broach a subject like that with him . . ." She laughed out loud as she returned to the sofa and sat. "A child of that age can get pregnant, you know."

Dehan had put down her pen and was frowning hard at Pamela. "So what did you do?"

"I had Fettuccini..."

I shook my head. "Fettuccini?"

She laughed again. "Oh, her name is Fernanda, but it seems to me such an absurd name for a woman that I call her Fettuccini. She is the woman who does for me. She's been with me for years, God love her. I had her go to the clinic and get leaflets and things, and a box of condoms, and I had her leave them all in his room. The poor child never got pregnant, so it must have worked."

A silence fell on the room. My mind went back to the filthy bedroom Bob had found six years ago, the dirty sheets, the unwashed underwear on the floor, the closed drapes and the fetid air, the moldy cornflakes under the bed. I tried to see it all in the context of this little fairy, the sweet little hippie with Charlie bathing her and combing her hair.

I drew breath. "So, did they have plans? Were they in love, engaged, planning to live together, get married...?"

She pouted and spread her hands. "I don't know. *Obviously* they didn't do well at school. They barely scraped into community college. I don't even remember what they were studying. He was studying IT, I think. They didn't really care, as long as they were together. That was the big thing for them. She might have been studying English literature, I honestly don't remember. They both loved poetry, and they used to read *The Lord of the Rings* to each other. Oh, and she was a Christian, always talking about early Christianity, Jesus, and Antioch. My *God*, it was tedious. But they never shared their plans with me. We didn't discuss things as a family. They decided and I paid."

I sat forward, with my elbows on my knees and my hands clasped, as though I were praying. "Pamela, by the time they disappeared, was she spending more time here than at home, would you say?"

"God, yes. She was practically living here. He used to sneak her up to his room at night, thinking I didn't notice. In the end, she was spending days on end here before going back home for a day, two at the most, then coming back here. Can't say I blamed her."

"And the day he disappeared . . ."

Her face became drawn. "It's all a bit of a blur, to tell you the truth. It was very traumatic."

"I can imagine, but if you can help us to go over it again, we may be able to find out what happened to him, even . . ." I shrugged and left the words hanging.

She gave a dry little laugh. "He ain't coming home, Detective Stone. I don't know what got into him, but he ain't coming back." She sighed, pulled another cigarette from her pack, and lit up. Smoke trailed from her open mouth. "He came home late on the Saturday night. I remember that. He was alone. I was already in bed. But next morning, I asked him where Amy was. He said he didn't know."

I said, "Did that strike you as unusual?"

She waved her cigarette in the air. "He was always so surly and sullen. Never gave me a civil answer. I thought nothing of it. I do remember it had been a very hectic weekend. It seemed everybody was coming or going or tramping in or tramping out . . ."

"So she was here part of the weekend. Was she here Saturday?"

She rolled her eyes, groaned, then laughed. "Like I say. It was a chaotic weekend. People coming and going." She raised an eyebrow at me. "I haven't always been single, you know." She sighed when I didn't smile. "I am pretty sure she was here, on and off on Saturday, but what time she left, or came back . . ." She spread her hands. "Sorry. I'm a bad girl."

Dehan made a question with her face and showed it to me. I ignored it and asked Pamela, "You said you're sure Charlie isn't coming back. Where do you think he is, Pamela?"

She sucked on her cigarette, and I saw a small tremble. I saw tears in her eyes, and she shook her head, reaching quickly for a handkerchief to dab at her nose. "I think he's dead." She shrugged. "I wasn't the best mom in the world, but I wasn't the worst. I never hurt him. Never even smacked him when he was small. He always had everything he wanted. This was a home for him and for Amy. If he was alive, he would have called. He would have called to say he was okay." She gave a sudden, wet laugh. "He would have called to ask for money."

The laugh died away. She tapped ash even though there was none on the tip. "I don't know what happened that weekend. But whatever it was, it was bad. And I know it cost poor Amy her life, and I think Charlie went shortly after. Maybe he couldn't be without her. That's possible."

I thought about that. It was certainly possible, but it was also unlikely that in six years, his body wouldn't have shown up somewhere. I put my hands on my knees and made to stand, but then stopped and frowned at her, dabbing at her nose with her handkerchief. I smiled. "Change of season, gets you every time."

She returned the smile with a small laugh. "Oh, no. I'm fine. It's just the talk, it has brought it all back."

She still had the handkerchief to her nose. I glanced around the room, looking for the box. I didn't see it. I said, "Do you still do it? It's an expensive habit."

She kind of collapsed, sighed, and laughed all at the same time. "You are determined to drag me through the mire today, aren't you, Detective Stone? I did *a lot* of it at one time. It has a way of making you feel invincible and indestructible. It also has a way of making you crazy and burning a hole right through your bank account. After Charlie disappeared, several friends performed what I believe is known as an intervention on me. They made me see that if I had not been out of my mind all weekend, I might just have been able to save Charlie. So I stopped." She held up her glass of gin and tonic. "This I am hanging on to until Charlie comes home. If he ever does, I'll jack it in."

I nodded a few times. "Who sold you the coke, back in the day?"

"Oh my god, really?" She thought for a moment. "His name was... *Felix*. We were never what you'd call friends, but he was at all the parties and he supplied to *a lot* of people. I mean, we were not the crème de la crème of New York society, but we were on the fringe, he had some pretty influential clients, and he was making a great deal of money."

"You still in touch?"

"No! And I *really* don't want to be."

"Don't worry." I smiled. "I don't want you to be either. Who can we talk to about tracking him down?"

She thought about it for a minute, then shook her head. "I don't know. I really, honestly, don't know."

Her eyes were big and wet and scared, and I didn't push. I stood. "Thank you, Pamela. You have been very helpful. We'll let you know if we get any news. We'll see ourselves out..."

As we stepped into the hall, I glanced back and saw her at the dresser in the dining room again, mixing herself a strong one.

Dehan took the stoop three steps at a time and stood looking at my burgundy beast. I followed, she tossed me the keys, and I went around to the driver's side. She leaned her chin on her arms on the roof and stared at me. I said, "What?"

She frowned and her voice was serious. "I have ruined your Sunday, and I think the least I can do is cook you a sirloin and get you a bottle of wine. You deserve it."

FOUR

It was dark. She was sitting at the wooden garden table we had on the back porch, and the flames from the barbeque were washing her face with flickering orange light. Her long, black hair was tied in a knot behind her head, she was holding a glass of wine, and she was frowning at the flames.

I had beside me a plate with two large steaks on it, which I had doused with oil and sprinkled with coarse Maldon sea salt. There is nothing else you need to do with good steak, except place it over red-hot coals. I refilled my glass and watched her a moment, thinking, not for the first or last time, that I was a very lucky man indeed, and spoke:

"You realize that next Sunday, you will be my slave. I plan to do absolutely nothing while you cook, iron, see to my several and various needs..."

She nodded absently. "Yes," she said, and then, "I am giving your brain a rest, Stone. While you cook the steak, I am thinking for you."

"Really...?"

She leaned back, stretched out her long legs, crossed at the ankle, and narrowed her eyes at me.

"Karl and Christen Redfern were buying dope, and when they could afford it coke, from Mr. X. Fact."

I dropped the steaks onto the barbeque. There was an explosion of oily flames. I stepped back, sipped my wine, and nodded once. "Fact."

"Pamela Albright was buying coke from Felix, at the same time. Fact."

I nodded.

She went on. "The night the Redferns were killed, there was a lot of activity at the Albright house: Charlie and Amy left and returned several times, and we know that Pamela was stoned much of that time."

"Okay."

"So let me speculate with those facts. Let's say that Mr. X and Felix are one and the same person." I made a face that said I didn't like it, but she pointed her finger at me and said, "Wait! Don't talk. *He* deals direct with the almost crème de la crème of New York who hang around Pamela and her crowd, but *one of his minions* deals with Karl and Christen."

I grunted and flipped the steaks. She went on.

"Chances are Felix would never even have heard about them, if it wasn't for the fact that Charlie was forming a bridge. He brings Amy and her parents into Felix's world. And Felix starts to see her—Amy—around. Now, you've seen the photos from the file, Amy was cute; peculiar, but cute: vulnerable, a little hippie, pixie, fairy type. A lot of guys go for that. So I am thinking that maybe Felix takes a fancy to Amy. He likes her because she is shy, retiring, submissive, and he is one of your alpha male, coke-fueled ego freaks."

I was nodding. "Okay, that is both feasible and interesting, but where does it take us?"

"Where does it take us?" She stretched out a little longer and laced her fingers behind her head. "It takes us to a possible connection between Felix and Amy's parents. Does he try and make a move on her? Karl and Christen tell him to take a hike and leave their little girl alone. As a warning, he has Karl beaten up and put in hospital. They continue to oppose him, so he kills them."

The steaks were beginning to singe in the intense heat. I took them off and set them on the plates, which I placed on the table, and removed the tinfoil from the bowl of French fries I had made earlier. Dehan sat up and smiled at the food.

"See, this is why I married you, Stone."

I ignored her and sat.

"Okay, it gives us a very tenuous link between Felix, drugs, Amy, and the Redferns. But it's full of holes, Dehan. And the biggest hole of all is, why does he need Karl and Christen's blessing to have Amy? The real obstacles would be either Charlie or Amy herself. Besides which, we don't know if this Felix has any connection with the Chupacabras, and remember, the two boys who put Karl in hospital were from the Chupacabras gang."

I cut into my steak. She was already chewing and spoke with her mouth full.

"Somph, dash is de firsh ting be neechoo fime ow."

"That's the first thing we need to find out? I agree." I frowned. "You know? I've been thinking and, granted we're not vice, but I have to say the name 'Felix' doesn't ring any bells for me."

She nodded, cutting her steak, then gave a Latin shrug. "It was six, almost seven years ago, but I have to agree. Felix isn't a name that leaps out at me. He may have been using a false name among his almost crème de la crème friends."

"Maybe."

We ate in silence for a short while. When she'd finished, she sat back and offered me a satisfied smile and drained her glass. Then she collected the plates and took them into the kitchen.

I looked at the moon hanging over my backyard. It looked fat and smug, smiling the same smile Dehan had just shown me. It was waxing, turning from orange to silver. A cool breeze touched my face and I realized I might have had one too many. The sound of Dehan's heel made me look up. She had a frosted bottle of tequila in her hand, a lemon, and two shot glasses. I made noises of distress, but she ignored me and poured two shots, then sliced the lemon with her pocketknife. After that, she did the whole salt, lemon shot thing.

I shook my head.

She leaned forward with her elbows on the table and raised her thumb as number one.

"Drugs." Then she raised a finger each for the next two words. "Christen, Amy." She reached for the bottle and scowled at my glass. "Drink, for cryin' out loud! Apply some *cojones*, partner! I'm working alone here."

I sighed and knocked back the shot. She grinned and refilled. "That, my friend, is the heart, soul, and essence of this case: drugs, Christen, Amy."

I leaned on the table, did the salt, lemon shot thing, and shook my head. "Wrong, I'll tell you what the heart of this case is. Dyslexia and dyspraxia. Amy was as dyslexic and dyspraxic as Charlie. Dyspraxics have a feeling that they don't belong. They feel isolated from the world. Charlie and Amy found each other, recognized each other, and came together, and that is what is at the heart of this case." She stared at me for a long moment, then nodded. On an impulse I reached out and refilled our glasses. "But I agree with you, drugs are key, and so are Amy and her mother. Maybe the case has two hearts and two souls. C'mon, last one."

We did another shot. She squeezed her lips, trying to suppress a belch, failed, and grinned. "Are you chickening out because tomorrow is Monday?"

I shook my head. "I never chickened out of anything in my life, Carmen. I just don't want you falling asleep at payback time."

As I said it, she refilled our glasses. "One for the road," she said.

"There is no road," I replied.

She held up her glass to me and began to sing. "*Caminante no hay camino, se hace camino al andar, golpe a golpe, verso a verso . . .*"

I laughed. "What's that?"

"Antonio Machado: walker, there is no path, the path is made as you walk, blow by blow, verse by verse . . ."

"You, my friend, are quoting poetry at me. You are getting drunk."

"Sometimes you have to be reckless, because there is no time to be careful. I had a friend who used to say, 'Sometimes you just have to be Irish, because there is no time to be Greek.' In a moment, Stone, we will have lost this moment. Forever. Tell me some poetry, *now*!"

We knocked back the shots, she refilled our glasses, and I wondered what the hell I had got myself into. She was still grinning.

I said, "Okay, one of my favorites. 'The rain it falleth on the just, and also on the unjust feller, but mainly on the just, because, the unjust took the just's umbreller.'"

She laughed noisily and slapped her thigh. We knocked glasses and tossed them back. As she set her glass down again, she said, "You're one of the good guys, Stone. Always thought so. Now, tell me a real poem and we'll go to bed."

I looked for the moon, but she had snuck overhead while I wasn't looking, and was now raining silver light on the table from above. The barbeque had burned down and the bottle of tequila was almost empty. I drained it into our glasses.

"Funny day," I said. And then, "I shall be telling this with a sigh, somewhere ages and ages hence: Two roads diverged in a wood, and I—I took the one less traveled by, and that has made all the difference."

She nodded. "Robert Frost. You're a good man, Stone. Robert Frost is good. You took the road less traveled, and that's why I love you. Take me to our bedchamber."

FIVE

I AWOKE LATE, AT SEVEN THIRTY, WITH LESS OF A hangover than I deserved, but enough to make me uncomfortable. I carried it into the bathroom, where it survived a shower, toweled myself dry, pulled on some clothes, and stepped out onto the landing, wondering why Dehan was already up. What greeted me was the smell of coffee, bacon, and hot bread rolls, the clatter of knives and plates, and the creak and slam of the oven door. They were sounds that should have been reassuring, but somehow weren't. Especially as, above it all, I could hear Dehan's voice yammering on the phone, sounding vaguely like she was selling insurance. I peered into the kitchen.

She had her cell wedged between her shoulder and her ear. She had a tea towel over the other shoulder, a pot of coffee in her right hand, and a spatula in her left. On the cooker, bacon was frying in one pan and four perfect eggs were sizzling in another. In a basket on the side, there were four hot rolls fresh from the oven. She was talking. While she talked, she pointed at things that I had to do.

"No, the name was definitely Felix . . ." (*Take the coffee.*) "What can I tell you? I can tell you what I'm telling you. That's all I got . . ." (*Wait! And the rolls!*) "What I hear is he's a smooth operator. You know what I'm saying? Working the fringes of the

Manhattan glitterati..." (*Come back for the cups.*) "He's going to all the parties, making connections..."

I carried the coffee and the hot rolls to the table. It was set with plates, butter, and marmalade. No cups. I could still hear her talking.

"Felix, yeah, Felix, like the cat. This is six or seven years ago. But I am guessing he was around before that..."

I returned to the kitchen, eased past her, and collected two cups. She had the bacon on the plates and she was scooping the eggs out too. Suddenly she erupted. "*Me cago en la puta madre que parió al hijo de la gran puta! Goddamn it!*" She slammed the pan on the cooker and threw the spatula in the sink. "How stupid am I? Tell me that! Please! *How stupid am I, Al? Jesus!* That's it! Of course it is! Thanks... What...? Nonono! No, you've been real helpful. Email it to me, will you? I didn't mean to scare you." She laughed. "Thanks, pal."

She hung up and handed me a plate. I took it and said, "Good morning, Dehan. What's going on?"

She shook her head at me and made for the table. "How could I have missed that?"

"I don't know. It's a mystery." I followed.

She sat and pointed to the chair opposite. "Sit!"

I sighed softly, sat, and poured myself a large cup of very black coffee. When I had eaten one of the eggs, half the bacon, and a hot roll, I said, "What did you miss, Dehan?"

"Finally! Mr. Grumpy is awake! Not Felix—you must have distracted me with all that tequila and poetry—not Felix," she said and waved an eggy knife at me. "*Félis!* Feliciano! Feliciano Camacho, brother of Julio Camacho..."

I sat back in my chair and nodded. "Oh... now that makes a lot of sense," I said. "Julio Camacho. The 'godfather' of the Chupacabras."

"Exactly. El Patron. It was playing on my mind all night, you know? While you were snoring, I was thinking. 'What a stupid name, Felix. Who's called Felix anymore? And a dope dealer? A dope dealer called Felix? No way.' So I was up at six and called the Forty-First, they're on Longwood. They cover the whole Hunts Point Longwood area."

"I know where the Forty-First Precinct is, Dehan."

"Right. 'Course you do. So I got them to put me through to the head of vice."

"At six a.m."

"Yeah. Well, he came in at eight. Shut up. So he says to me, 'No way, not in New York.' High-end, low-end, he knows all the gangs in the five boroughs and he doesn't know any Felix. Then he says, 'That area? Where we are talking about? That is Chupacabras territory.' And I'm thinking, that name came up before..."

"Adolfo and Mateo, who put Karl in hospital. They were members of the Chupacabras."

She ignored me and carried on talking. "So Al says to me that six years ago it was run by the two Camacho brothers. One of them, he can't remember his name, was not so important and eventually retired. Julio was the bad boy, he was running the show, and now he's the *patron*. Like you said, the godfather." She stopped, nodded a few times, shook her head. "Then, when he said that, I remembered—*hijo de puta!* How could I be so stupid? Not Felix, *Félis*!"

"You know where he retired to?"

She started eating again. "Not far. New Jersey. Englewood. I figured we could go and pay him a visit. Al at the Forty-First says he's an upstanding pillar of the community now. He made his fortune, now he's trying to whitewash it. If we take it easy, don't come on too strong, don't threaten him, he might be willing to cooperate."

I broke a roll and mopped some egg. She went on. "So I figure, what we're looking for here is the link that ties Adolfo and Mateo to Feliciano, and then to the Redferns." She sighed and spread her hands like I had asked a stupid question. "Obviously the link is that Adolfo and Mateo and Feliciano were all in the Chupacabras. But we need something tighter than that . . ."

I nodded and chewed a while. "Yeah, I guess. But I think we need to be pretty open-minded about what that link might be, Dehan. Because so far I can see two things clearly: one, there *is* a link; two, it is a link that doesn't make any sense at all right now."

She drew breath.

I spoke quietly. "Don't talk for a minute. I am willing to bet that as we start digging up the threads that tie these people together, we're going to find they lead us off to places we did not expect to go."

She shrugged. "Maybe." She reached over for the coffeepot and refilled her cup. "But you know how it is, Stone, once drugs are involved, things get pretty predictable."

"Twenty stab wounds in an area of four inches is not predictable."

She grunted.

We washed up together and by nine thirty, we were thundering down the Bruckner Expressway toward New Jersey. We crossed via the George Washington Bridge and turned north along the Palisades Interstate and into the leafy suburbs of Englewood.

Feliciano Camacho's house was a grotesque sage-green building that couldn't decide if it wanted to be a Spanish hacienda or a Rococo palace. It failed at both. It was set back from the road behind a large wall with a crescent drive running between two open gates guarded by four iron eagles. The whole place was surrounded by a superabundance of pine trees, maples, planes, and chestnuts that were in the first stages of turning from green to russet and orange.

I pulled into the drive, stopped in front of an oak door that would not have looked out of place on a medieval castle in Disneyland, and climbed out. The door opened before we reached it, and a guy in an Italian suit with a wire in his ear, shades over his eyes, and a bulge under his left arm stepped out to meet us. His face managed to ask us who the hell we were and tell us he didn't give a damn who the hell we were, all in one look without a single expression.

I ignored the look and said, "I'm Detective John Stone, this is Detective Dehan. We're here to see Feliciano Camacho."

"You got an appointment?"

It was Dehan who answered. "Why are you asking stupid questions? Who told you to ask stupid questions? Did Félis tell you to ask stupid questions? Huh? Did anybody say to you, 'Hey, dumbass, go outside and ask stupid questions'? No? Nobody told you to do that? Good. So get the fuck inside and tell your boss Detectives John Stone and Carmen Dehan are here to see him. Or does he need your permission to see us? Dumbass!"

He looked at her resentfully and muttered, "Wait here," then turned and went inside.

I blinked at her a few times. "If we take it easy, don't come on too strong, don't threaten him . . . that was your strategy?"

She looked away and shrugged. "Appointment! Do we have an appointment? What is he, a dentist?"

The door opened again and the reservoir dog stepped out with his tail between his legs and jerked his head at us. We followed him inside, where he led us through more architectural mayhem: over terra-cotta floors, among Greco-Roman statues, through Tudor arches, and down adobe corridors past Arabic gardens and neoclassical colonnades, to another Disney oak door upon which he knocked and then pushed.

We stepped through into a large library-cum-study. The walls were occupied, floor to ceiling, by dark-wood bookcases. Some had glass-paneled doors, and all were filled with sterile, dust-free, unread hardbacks. The floor was covered in a burgundy Wilton carpet, there was a nest of Chesterfields around an open fireplace, and, to the left of the door as we entered, there was an oak desk big enough to launch a squadron of B-52s. Standing behind it, looking vaguely confused, was a big man in his early fifties. He was dressed in an amber, double-breasted suit, and his hair was gelled into spikes, making him look as though he'd been terrified and then sneezed on by something large and sticky.

Dehan pulled out her badge and showed it to him. "Detective Carmen Dehan, this is Detective John Stone, NYPD, are you Feliciano Camacho?"

He frowned at the badge and then at Dehan. "Just tell me, do I need my lawyer?"

"No."

He looked past her at his boy and said, "*Vale,* Dixon, *váyase.*"

Dixon left, and Camacho spread his hands, laughing softly, looking gently nonplussed. "I am Feliciano Camacho." He gestured at me. "You are Detective Dehan and he is Detective John Stone. Why are you in my house? What does the NYPD want with me?"

"Not much, actually, Feliciano."

He liked the sound of that and gestured toward the Chesterfields by the fireplace. "Shall we sit? Can I offer you coffee?"

We said we didn't want coffee, but we sat, and he went straight in with a thinly veiled warning.

"Detective Dehan, I am sure that you are aware, as many people are, that there is a period in my past where I walked a dangerous path, where the line between good and evil was . . ." He nodded a few times, like he was trying to think of a really good word. In the end he came up with, "Blurred—to say the least! A lot of people paid a high price for my wild ways. But that is all behind me now, all of my business interests today are legitimate, and I have influential friends in law enforcement and in the bureau who will vouch for me."

His smile was amiable and smooth, but his eyes said he wanted to gut us like fish and barbeque us for his dogs. Dehan smiled. "We are not interested in you, Feliciano. We heard already, you are a pillar of the community these days, so we thought we'd drop in and see if you can help us out a bit."

"If I can, I would be pleased to."

I said, "Do you remember Amy Redfern?"

He looked at me like I gave him a headache. "Amy Redfern? I don't know anybody with this name. Should I remember her?"

Dehan shook her head. "Not necessarily. How about Charlie Albright?"

His eyes became abstracted. He looked up at the ceiling above Dehan's head. "Albright . . . Yeah, I remember Pamela . . . ah! Yes, her son was Charlie. Am I right? Yeah, I remember. But he was . . ." He shrugged and spread his hands, as though mentioning his name was somehow absurd. ". . . nothing. He was nobody." Then he smiled, snapped his fingers, pleased with himself. "Oh, yeah! Yeah, his girlfriend! She was a little, skinny thing. They were both like little ghosts. You know? Like little bits of mist." He laughed at his own inventive simile. "She was Amy, I remember. My memory ain't so bad, huh? But I did not *know* them. I knew Pamela, I knew some of Pamela's friends. The kids were there sometimes, in the background. We went to a lot of crazy parties, a party almost every night. You know the stupid stuff you do when you are young."

I said, "That was only six years ago."

He raised a finger. "It ended six years ago. For me. It started long before that. And believe me, Detective Stone, I did a lot of growing up in the last six years. I am fifty-two now!" He turned back to Dehan. "To be honest with you, Detective Dehan, I am surprised that you are asking about these kids." He gave a self-deprecating laugh. "I knew a lot of people back then that you might be interested in, but these kids?" He shrugged and shook his head. "They was nothin'."

She offered him a weary smile, overworked cop to wise, reformed villain. "You know how it is, Félis. Nine-tenths routine, going through the numbers and ticking the boxes, one-tenth following leads that go nowhere. Now, how about Amy's mother, Christen Redfern? Did you ever meet her?"

"I have no idea who she is. Was she a friend of Pamela's?"

"I don't know. That is pretty much what we are trying to find out. Aside from the relationship between Amy and Charlie, was there any connection between the Redferns and Pamela's crowd?"

He sat back and crossed one expensive leg over the other. "I can tell you that I, personally, never met anybody called Christen Redfern. I can also tell you that Pamela was the poorest person in that group." He narrowed his eyes and made a face that was oddly reptilian. "We were moving in circles of leading TV producers, influential bankers, celebrities . . ." He held up both hands. "Okay! We are not talking Chris Hemsworth, Leonardo DiCaprio, but *names,* for sure. Big names. So Charlie and Amy . . . *poof*!" He waggled his fingers in front of his face to suggest something evanescent, then laughed.

Dehan disguised a flash of irritation with a lame smile. Before she could speak, I asked him, "Mr. Camacho, did either Charlie or Amy ever approach you . . ."

He frowned like the word was new to him. "*Approach* me? I'm not sure what you mean."

I offered him a rueful, lopsided smile. "Well, neither do I, exactly. Did either of them ever engage you in conversation, discuss your business with you . . . ?"

He gave a soft grunt and stared at the ceiling again. I stared at it with him. It was paneled in oak, like the rest of the room, and I decided that if it hadn't been in that house, it would have been a nice ceiling.

"Yeah." He said it suddenly, as though he had surprised even himself. "Yeah, Charlie approached me once. I can't remember exactly . . ." He turned to Dehan. "You have to remember, off the record . . ." He glanced at both of us in turn. "We are off the record, right? Are we off the record?"

"We're off the record."

"I was making sometimes ten or fifteen K in a night. Sometimes more than that, at the peak, when things were good. So this little piece of shit comes to me . . ." He half laughed and half sighed. "I gotta be nice to him because Pamela is helpful to me, right? She gives me some respectability and she connects me with important people, and this is her son. But he is asking me some shit about..."

He stared around the room, like he'd lost part of his sentence and he didn't know where he'd put it. Finally, he spread his hands and shook his head.

"I don't know! I don't even know. Probably I wasn't even listening, you know what I'm saying? I was thinking about something else, and this kid is wasting my time, talking to me."

I scratched my chin. "This could be important, Mr. Camacho. Some vague idea about the general purpose of the talk? Was he asking for something? Offering something...?"

"No, no, no. No, he was asking for something. You know, I got the feeling he wanted me to supply him, and he was going to sell. He was telling me some long fockin' story about his girlfriend's dad, and he wants to get coke for him or some shit—forgive my language—you know? It makes me mad just remembering it." He shook his head. "So I'm thinking, this piece of shit wants me to supply him. He wants to break into some territory—I don't know where her and her dad live, right?—is he gonna maybe start a turf war, with *my fuckin' merchandise*, just because this emaciated piece of shit wants to play bad boy?"

"Stupid kid."

"Right?"

"So how did you handle it?"

"Well, I don't want to upset Pam, but I want to put a scare into the little motherfocker; for his own sake, you hear me? So I told him go talk to my boys."

There it was. I didn't look at Dehan. I nodded and smiled, like I had grudging admiration for his street wisdom. "That sobered him up a bit?"

"I have no idea!" He leaned forward and laughed. "He vanished from my mind. *Poof!* A short while after that, the whole scene broke up. I was getting tired anyhow, wanted to move on, do other stuff. I'm thinking of putting money into movies, you know that?"

Dehan made a face of surprised interest. "Really? So what was that, about six months later?"

He tipped his head on one side. "Yeah, about that."

I said, "Adolfo and Mateo?"

He looked at me sharply.

I said again, "Adolfo Davila and Mateo Bonilla? They were your boys, the ones you sent Charlie to?"

His eyes narrowed and told me he was still dangerous. "Yeah. How'd you know that?"

"I didn't. I was asking."

Dehan asked, "They died, right?"

He took a while to answer. "Yeah, they died. It all happened about the same time. You know what? Suddenly I am not comfortable with this conversation. How's about you tell me why you're asking me these questions. Or maybe, you know, you just get the fock out of my house? I have been courteous, and hospitable, and I have offered you coffee, and now you're springing surprises on me about Adolfo and Mateo, and talking about killing people. You know what? I'm not comfortable with that."

I sighed. "We are just trying to find Charlie and Amy, Mr. Camacho, and we are trying to trace their last movements before they disappeared..."

"So you thought you'd pin it on me. You were never able to pin anything on me before, so you thought you'd try and pin this on me now, right?"

"Wrong. All we want is a few facts." I glanced at Dehan. She gave her head a small shake. "Either way, Mr. Camacho, we've taken up enough of your time. You've been very helpful."

We stood. He remained sitting, examining us one after the other. Finally, he stood too. "Don't come after me. I'm clean. I changed my life. I'm making amends for the wrongs I committed. You understand what I am telling you? Don't come after me."

Dehan leaned toward him, offered him a chilling smile, and placed her finger on his chest. "Right now, Félis, I have absolutely no interest in you. Keep threatening me and all that might change. Let's be polite. We'll do our jobs, and you keep doing your good works, and making peace with your god. Deal?"

He nodded and unexpectedly held out his hand. "You have a card? A cell where I can contact you? Maybe I can find something for you. I want to keep relations good, you understand?"

Dehan stared at him a moment, then shrugged, reached in her jacket, and pulled out a card. He took it, examined it, and put it in his pocket. Then he pressed a button on the mantelpiece above the fireplace. The door opened and Dixon the Reservoir Dog put his head in.

"*Si, Jefe?*"

"Show Detectives Dehan and Stone out. They're leaving."

SIX

We came to the intersection of Sage Road and Sylvan Avenue. The light was red, and I stopped. We were surrounded by woodland on all sides. Desultory cars demonstrated the Doppler effect down the avenue. The big old engine under the Jaguar's hood rumbled. We hadn't spoken since we'd left Camacho's house and the silence persisted now.

The light changed to green. I glanced in the mirror. There was nobody behind me. I chewed my lip. Dehan said, "You going to go?"

I glanced at her and after a moment turned south onto the avenue. "Talk me through it." She drew breath to answer, and I started talking instead. "I said this would happen." I glanced at her. "Remember? I said this would happen when we found the connection. Well, here it is. We have the connection. Charlie approaches Camacho. He wants a little action. It's what he's grown up with, it's what he knows. Camacho is probably the 'go-to' guy for his mother, so it is logical he will go to him for help. Right?"

I looked at her. She nodded. I went on. "But like Camacho said, who is this kid? A nobody. He doesn't listen to him. He doesn't even want to think about him. So he sends him away to his boys, to scare him, to teach him a lesson. Logical. Expanding into a new geographical area is a big deal. You may have to kill people. Like he said, you might start a turf war. You need to know who you're going up against, and you need somebody you can trust and rely on, heading up the operation. Charlie is none of those things. Logical. Right?"

"Right."

We had come to the bridge and I turned onto it. We picked up speed, high above the water, toward Manhattan. The wind battered at us, and I had to raise my voice.

"So do the boys give Charlie a scare? Do they do what's expected? No, not exactly. Instead they do the unexpected and beat seven bales of crap out of Amy's father, and put him in hospital for the better part of six months. They know Charlie is off-limits because Feliciano is friends with his mother, so instead they throw a scare into him by putting Karl in the emergency ward. Logical?" I shrugged. "Maybe. But now . . ." I shook my head. "Six months later, Karl comes out of hospital, and Adolfo and Mateo get executed . . ."

She had been using her whole body to nod for a few seconds. Now she said, "We need to get the date he was released."

I said, "Fine, but really it makes no difference. Hear me out. At first glance it looks like one of two things happened: one, Karl got out and executed Adolfo and Mateo. But Karl had no priors for anything more serious than a domestic disturbance, much less murder or assault with a deadly weapon. Add to that the fact that he was fresh out of hospital, must have been weak, and that those guys were killed in a highly efficient, professional manner, and that scenario begins to look very improbable. *Not* logical."

"Okay . . ."

"*Then*, second thing, a short time later, Karl and Christen get murdered. And so, probably, do Charlie and Amy. Punishment from the Chupacabras for having killed two of their boys? At first glance, again, it would seem logical, until you remember that Feliciano Camacho had no idea who Amy and her parents were.

Again, *not* logical." She drew breath, but I cut across her. "And if you are going to suggest Karl was working with another gang, that doesn't hold water either. Why would he get in bed with the very gang whose turf he was planning to invade?"

She was quiet, staring out the window. The river moved across her aviators and the breeze whipped her hair across her face. After a while, she shifted in her seat and turned to face me. "So, if it wasn't Karl and it wasn't somebody else . . ." She spread her hands, revealing the absurdity of the proposition.

I ignored it and said, "Bob must have got Amy and Charlie's financials, phone records . . ."

"Sure, but they are a dead end. They stop the day of her parents' deaths."

"You've examined them? How long have you been looking at this case?"

She shrugged. "You know . . . on and off . . ."

"You could have told me. We're a team, remember? We work cold cases. Let's look at those records."

"Sure, they're in my desk. But I just told you . . ."

"Humor me. I have a hunch."

She gave me an insolent smile. "You still get hunches at your age?"

"Yeah. I get all kinds of things at my age that I shouldn't get."

She raised an equally insolent eyebrow. "Yeah? Like what?"

"Molested by younger women with no sense of decency or propriety, for one."

She made a grating noise in her throat which I figured was a laugh. After a moment, she wagged a finger at me. "I know what you're thinking. You're thinking maybe they are not dead." She nodded a few times. "You are thinking that maybe they escaped. And you want the bank records and phone records to see if there is some clue, in the weeks running up to Karl's death . . ." She pulled a face and shook her head. "Large withdrawals of cash for stashing, phone calls out of state, unexplainable payments . . ."

I smiled at her. "There is something missing. Everything we

have seen is . . ." I spread my hands. "Valid. It is part of the picture. But it is not adding up to the whole picture. There is something important missing. Charlie's behavior is odd. He goes to Camacho looking for help. Camacho puts him onto his boys and that's the last we hear about that. Charlie does not pop up on any radar selling dope. He just returns to his status quo for six months and then vanishes. There is something there, something about Charlie that we are not seeing."

She nodded. "Yeah . . . Yeah, I agree." She thought a moment longer. "How about you go through Charlie and Amy's records this afternoon? Meanwhile, I want to take a closer look at Adolfo and Mateo's activities in the weeks leading up to their death. Later we can compare notes, see if there are any coincidences that might confirm or deny they were engaged in some kind of activity together."

"Sounds like a plan." I turned it over in my head, then asked, "You hoping to connect Adolfo and Mateo to Arizona or New Mexico?"

She looked at me sidelong, then nodded. "I guess that's the idea."

We picked up the Bruckner Expressway and I drove for a while, sucking my teeth. Finally, I asked the question that had been playing on my mind. "What makes this case so different, Dehan? There must be a hundred cases you can pick up that, with time and patience, will connect the Chupacabras with Arizona or New Mexico and ultimately Mexico and Sinaloa. What is it about this case that has been playing on your mind for almost seven years?"

She began to shrug, like there was no special answer, but the gesture died and she turned away, to look out the window. She stayed like that until we were approaching the turnoff for Soundview. Then she exploded into a torrent of words.

"You're right. How many deals get struck every year? Must be thousands. How many shipments from the border to New York? Many hundreds. And any diligent Fed or cop, working the system the way it's supposed to be worked, should be able to trace a supply line from a Manhattan party to a cartel across the border in Mexico—and close that source down; the way El Chapo was closed down, the way Escobar was closed down, and others . . ." She sighed noisily, shrugged her shoulders, and spread her hands in a gesture of helplessness. "So that the next guy can step into the boss' shoes, take over the operation, and start all over again. The boss is dead, long live the boss!"

By now I was frowning. "What are you saying?"

She made a noise like a raspberry. "The cartels and the gangs are living, breathing infections, Stone. They are like metastasized cancers, with tumors running from Mexico and Colombia all the way to Boston and Seattle. And El Chapo, Pablo Escobar, Zambada, they are just tumors in a body wracked by cancer. You cut out one, and another grows in its place. Because the whole organism is sick. And we, you and me, we can't do anything about that. But we can do something about people. Karl, Christen, Charlie, Amy . . . They are not anonymous, they are people. Individuals who suffered an injustice. A really bad injustice. And they were forgotten because every day, this world deals more and more in big, anonymous generalities."

She turned to look at my face as we peeled off onto Soundview and I slowed to turn onto Story Avenue.

"And somewhere along the way, between the New Order, the Mexican wall, the U.S. government, the DEA, the FBI, and the NYPD, Christen, Karl, and Amy, and a million other *individual* human beings, fell through the cracks: got tortured, raped, and murdered. Each one had a mother, a father, a family. Each one suffered as a person—not a statistic, class of person, or a demographic." She shrugged. "I just decided I wanted to do justice, for Christen and her family."

I pulled into the parking lot opposite the entrance to the station and killed the engine. I sat awhile drumming my fingers on the steering wheel, and she sat staring out the window. After a moment, I asked.

"Did you think this had something to do with Mick Harragan?"[1]

She offered the trees outside a rueful smile. "No. It was long after Mick had gone. But yeah, I was on a mission back then. I don't know what reason Sanchez had for sitting on the case, but it was clear to me that there was a connection with big money, maybe big corruption, and I guess I saw myself in Amy to some extent." She turned to look at me, and there was anger in her dark eyes. "People talk about tragedies, but nobody looks at the kids who are also victims of these tragedies. Amy, Charlie, they were just trying to get by, be together, find some happiness, and these parasites and predators, these bastards, destroyed them because they happened to be in the wrong place at the wrong time."

I nodded. "Okay." Then I smiled. "Justice only makes sense when it's for the individual. When it is delivered by anonymous institutions to anonymous masses, it becomes politics. I get that." I hesitated a moment. "But stay objective, okay? Amy is not Carmen Dehan. It's a different story."

"I know." She shrugged and smiled. "You asked. That's all."

Inside, Dehan went to our desk. I grabbed some polystyrene coffee for us and settled to work my way methodically through Amy's and Charlie's bank and telephone records from six years before. I had one question I needed to answer: Were they dead, or still alive?

---

1. See *An Ace and a Pair*.

SEVEN

Outside, the shadows were growing long. Dehan stood abruptly, walked away, and came back ten minutes later with a paper bag full of croissants and two cups of real coffee from the deli on the corner. She put the stuff on the desk, dropped into her chair, stared at me, and said:

"What?"

I helped myself to a croissant, pulled over the cup, and sipped. "How do you know I have something?"

"It's on your face. Spill it."

I sighed. "The records go back a year before Amy and Charlie disappeared. I was mainly interested in Charlie, because at the time Bob didn't really look at Charlie. They were focused on Karl and Christen."

"Okay."

"So I started at the beginning and two things struck me: one, there is practically no activity in his account, and two, he received a regular payment of one thousand dollars on the first day of each month. I called Pamela and asked her about it. She said it was an allowance that she gave him."

She nodded. "I heard you. Nothing surprising so far."

I leafed through a couple of pages, talking as I did so. "Every month he withdraws between five and seven hundred dollars in cash, leaving a balance of between five and three, obviously. Now, six months before he disappears, this begins to change."

She leaned forward, frowning. "Good, how?"

"At the beginning of March, a couple of days after the money is deposited, he withdraws practically all of it, including everything that has accumulated over the months, a total of three thousand four hundred dollars, leaving only five bucks in his account. He then does the same thing every month for the next six months: almost immediately after the deposit, he withdraws everything."

I glanced at her and sipped my coffee. She was looking smug. I went on.

"That made me curious. So I had a look at Amy's records. Obviously she had no monthly allowance from her parents, but she did have sporadic payments from occasional part-time jobs. Sometimes the payments were cash, sometimes they were deposits from her employers. It looks like she never held a job for more than three months, but she usually had a job of one sort or another.

"So she makes a few cash withdrawals every month, pretty much what you'd expect, and then, six months before she disappears, she starts withdrawing everything, every month, just like Charlie." I spread my hands. "This can only mean one thing . . ."

"They knew they were in danger."

"They were planning to run. The question is, did they make it? They were smart enough to use cash—no credit cards and no debit cards—so they have not left an electronic trail."

She looked smug. "I think they made it." She rummaged on her desk. "I was going through the property that the Redferns left. Most of it was claimed by Christen's sister, Ingrid . . . um . . . Njalsen. Ingrid Njalsen. Did you know that?"

"No. What do you mean, most of it? Who claimed the rest of it?"

She grinned. "That's the point. I had a hunch, I still get them too, and checked the DMV for cars registered to Charlie Albright,

Amy Redfern, and Karl and Christen. It was a long shot, but it was worth a try, right? You never know how something like that will pay off. And whadd'ya know? The rest of it turns out to be a silver 2000 Chevy Impala, and it was never claimed. It was never reported stolen. It was never found. It never showed up. But the interesting thing is, Stone, neither did the keys."

I flopped back in my chair, scowling. "How the hell was this missed?"

She shrugged and spread her hands. "Beats me. I guess it was established and agreed right from the start that the murder was not part of a robbery. So the focus was never on missing property. And, putting it bluntly, Bob and Sanchez just plain missed the fact that the Redferns owned a car! So the assumption at the time —their assumption, the chief's assumption, and *my* assumption —was that Amy had been abducted and/or murdered. Whether they owned a car simply wasn't relevant. Plus, there was nothing in the apartment to even *suggest* they owned a car." She shrugged again. "And, like I said, the sister never reported it missing."

"The disappearance of a car is *very* relevant to an abduction or a disappearance. Where does the aunt live?"

She scrabbled through bits of paper, talking as she did so. "N-J-A-L-S-E-N, that's an old Icelandic spelling. Did you know that? It's Christen's maiden name. Ingrid never married. She lives in the family home in . . ."

My memory was creaking into action. I vaguely remembered there had been a sister. "Midwest? Illinois? No . . ."

She nodded. "Iowa. Town called Garrison."

"Garrison. We need to go and talk to her."

She ripped a croissant in half, put most of it in her mouth, and said, "Be meeff choo challchoo dge cheeff . . ."

We stared at each other while she chewed. I said, "We need to talk to the chief?" She nodded and grinned.

We climbed the stairs to the deputy inspector's office and knocked. On his command, we entered, and he smiled with pleasure as we stepped in and closed the door.

"Carmen, John, how can I help you? What are you working on at the moment?"

He gestured at two chairs, and we sat. Dehan sighed. "The Redfern case, sir."

His eyes narrowed at the ceiling. "Karl and Christine . . . ? Seven years ago . . . ?"

"Christen, yes, sir."

"And how is it proceeding?"

She looked at me. I said, "Well, sir, Dehan unearthed what may prove to be a very important clue. It seems the Redferns owned a car. That was not established at the time. No papers or keys, or anything of relevance to the car was found in the apartment, and Christen's sister, Ingrid Njalsen, the Redferns' sole heir, never reported the car as missing when she took possession of the property. So until today, we had no idea there was a car."

He nodded. "That is quite important. Talk me through it."

"Well, sir, we also discovered that Amy Redfern . . ."

"The daughter whose body was never found."

"Exactly. She and her boyfriend, Charlie, had been stashing away money for the six months prior to their disappearance."

"Oh, indeed?"

Dehan took over again. "So we think it's important that we go and speak to Ingrid Njalsen. The fact that she never reported the car as missing suggests she might have known where it was and didn't want it found because her niece had it."

"The youngsters fled in it. I see. So where is this Ingrid Njalsen?"

"In the village of Garrison, Iowa."

He sighed rather noisily. "Can you telephone her? Or Skype? I hear a lot of people are doing that these days."

Dehan blinked several times very quickly, then grinned. "No, sir, phoning is probably not a good idea. The idea is to turn up without warning, unexpectedly . . ."

"Catch her by surprise and rattle her . . . Yes, I see. I suppose you'll want to fly . . ."

I shook my head. "We can drive, sir. It's about fifteen hours, three five-hour shifts, save the department some cash and you can add it to our Christmas bonus."

He laughed like I was joking and told us he expected us back in a couple of days. "And please, don't get lost and wind up in California."

We reciprocated by laughing like he was joking and told him we'd head right back as soon as we had spoken to her.

On the way down the stairs, Dehan spoke to me over her shoulder. "You figure fifteen hours?"

"I-80, fifteen hours, maybe a little more." I looked at my watch. "If we make an early start, we'll arrive in time for dinner. You want to pack? I'll try to find a hotel..."

She had her phone out. "I'm on it. You drive, I'll book. And put out a BOLO on the Impala. I'll call the sheriff and let him know we're coming. What do you reckon, eight tomorrow evening?"

I shook my head, and as we stepped out into the warm, copper afternoon I said, "No, don't do that. These are tight communities, and we don't want her alerted in any way that we're coming. We'll talk to her in an unofficial capacity. If she's uncooperative, then we'll approach the sheriff."

She made a skeptical face. "You sure about that, partner?"

I nodded as I opened the door to the Jag. "We have too much to lose if we go by the book."

She shrugged and climbed in. As we accelerated onto the Bronx River Parkway, she said, "Okay, there are no hotels in Garrison. The nearest place is the Cobblestone, eight miles away, in Vinton."

"That'll do. I doubt we'll be there more than twenty-four hours."

We had an early dinner and an early night, and next morning we were up at five, dumping our bags in the trunk. The slamming doors made a desolate echo in the predawn street and we sat a moment, cocooned in the close darkness of the car, while Dehan took a pull of coffee from the flask. I fired up the engine and we pulled away, out of the sleeping street, toward Iowa and the small town of Garrison.

We drove in silence until we had crossed the Harlem and the Hudson, we had left the Jersey suburbs behind, and we were pushing deep into the outer darkness toward the Midwest along the I-80. Then Dehan inched around in her seat and frowned at me, fingering strands of hair from her eyes.

"So, talk me through this, Stone. There are lots of pieces that seem to kind of connect but actually don't; for instance: we have Karl's and Christen's death, a seriously brutal murder by somebody we agree seems to have had a special hatred for Christen, right?"

"Yeah."

"And we have Charlie and Amy, for six months, preparing to make a run for it . . ."

"Apparently."

"Okay, *apparently* preparing to make a run for it. That suggests that they knew there was some kind of danger, something bad was going to happen. Did they warn her parents and get ignored? Did they just withdraw into themselves and keep it a secret? That troubles me, but it's a side issue; for now let's just say that it looks like they knew something bad was coming, and they prepared for it. They may or may not have warned her parents.

"Meantime, there is the question, did they cause this to happen? Remember, it is just six months earlier that Charlie approached Camacho and asked about getting into the business, and Camacho, directly or indirectly, had his boys put Karl in hospital. So is there a trigger around this time? Is that—itself—the trigger? Is that what scares them into making plans to run? But if it is, why did they wait six months?"

Sleeping houses shrouded in limpid amber light slipped past outside. I sighed. "Something strikes me about that. When Charlie approached Feliciano, if he was approaching him about getting into the business, that meant he had already decided he needed to increase his income—significantly and at a high risk."

"That's true. And we have to assume Adolfo and Mateo were instructed to say no, and that's why they put Karl in hospital..."

I nodded. "But it starts to get confusing. First of all, if they put Karl in hospital, it means that they saw him as Charlie's partner or even senior partner. So, if he was involved in the plan to go in with the Camachos and spread their turf, and got put in hospital for it, why was he not just as aware as Charlie of the coming threat?"

I glanced at her. She was nodding. I went on.

"More than that, why *was* there still a threat? The Camacho boys give Karl a beating and put him in hospital, after telling him, 'Stay out of our business.' So he does, he stays out of their business. Charlie stays out of their business too. Neither Charlie nor Karl was known to the NYPD as a trafficker. So why, after six months, after he comes out of hospital, do they suddenly decide to kill him?"

"And how did Charlie and Amy know, six months in advance, that they were going to have to run?"

I shook my head. "It really doesn't make a lot of sense." I gave a small laugh, more in frustration than humor. "Leaving aside the fact that the threat, all along, was to Karl and Christen—in particular Christen—not Charlie and Amy."

She was quiet for a long while. Outside, in the dark passing world, the buildings were becoming more sparse and the woodlands more dense and abundant. Then she shook her head. "No, Stone. That can't be right. It's simple logic. If you flee, it's because you perceive a threat. It's that simple."

I nodded. "I can't argue with that."

"So the next logical step is to conclude, inescapably, that they were aware of a threat."

"Okay. I like these baby steps."

She ignored me. "But they were aware of a threat that *we* are not aware of. And that leads us irresistibly to the conclusion that the threat to Karl and Christen was not the same as the threat to Charlie and Amy."

I didn't answer. There was no answer. The logic was flawless. The logic also meant that we had barely progressed an inch, unless Ingrid was able to help us. What had happened to Charlie and Amy was still unknown, and all we had on Karl and Christen was pure speculation.

We stopped at midday outside Cleveland and had lunch at a roadside diner. We drank a couple of gallons of coffee and then Dehan took over the driving. Her driving, like everything else about her, was urgent, direct, and to the point. She stayed closer to 100 MPH than she did to the speed limit, but she was safe, never took risks, and was always cool and in control.

We didn't discuss the case. There was nothing more to be said until we had some concrete evidence. We chatted sporadically about nothing much and the hours ground by slowly. The landscape was increasingly flat and unremarkable.

Finally, at shortly before seven that evening, we passed Iowa City and turned north on the 380. At Cedar Rapids, we turned west again onto the Lincoln Highway and eventually, at shortly before eight p.m., we turned onto 24th Avenue, and drove through endlessly flat country, on an endlessly flat, straight road, under an endless blue-white sky, for thirteen miles, until at long last, we came to the small town of Vinton.

The Cobblestone was a large, gabled building standing at the center of a large parking lot. We checked in, dumped our bags, wandered into town for a burger, and collapsed into bed at ten thirty. As I drifted into sleep, I could still feel the road speeding beneath me.

EIGHT

Over breakfast the next morning at seven forty-five, I suggested to Dehan that nine a.m. might be a good time to go and see Ingrid Njalsen. She had shaken her head vigorously, draining her coffee at the same time, and got to her feet. She was like a thoroughbred with an adrenaline syringe up her backside.

"Country folk!" she said loudly. "Also: Scandinavians. All that cold, snow and ice. It gives them a tough, vigorous constitution and makes them rise early, for their saunas. Come on, Stone. Git yer ass in gear. We'll be there by eight."

So I too had drained my coffee and got to my feet, realizing too late that she had my keys.

Eight miles and six minutes of flat land, vast horizons, and sunshine later, we rolled into Garrison. Garrison is a small town that looks like a large, industrial farm. Broad fields and copses of tall, copper trees surround and encroach on the houses dotted with enormous steel silos, barns, and tractors. We cruised past rickety clapboard houses in green and white and red that had been placed and built more in obedience to the needs or whims of the builders than the arbitrary grid system that had mapped out the roads: a system that fit people into towns, rather than towns around people. Here and there, there were bits of sidewalk, but over time, trees and other imperatives had replaced them with roots and beaten tracks.

Ingrid Njalsen's house was at least a hundred and fifty years old. It stood at a crossroads at the center of town and gave the impression of being two large, white clapboard houses joined in the middle by a small cottage. It was set back from the road, amid a large area of lawn, flanked by chestnut trees and copper birches. A stone path led to four broad steps that climbed to a wooden veranda. Beside the house, there was an American flag flying on a tall pole, and sitting on the steps, watching us, was a small black-and-white dog.

I scanned the area for a twenty-year-old Impala. I didn't see one, but I noted there were a couple of outbuildings that could have held an automobile.

We climbed out of the Jag and made our way across the grass, then up the steps to the veranda. The dog watched us do it and twitched its tail, like its tail held hope we might play, but the rest of it had given up on people long ago.

There was a door behind a screen, but no bell, so I knocked on the frame. A moment later, the door opened, and I saw a tall woman frowning at us through the mesh. It made her look oddly like a ghost. I said, "Good morning. I hope we haven't come at an inconvenient time. Are you Ingrid Njalsen?"

Her frown deepened. "Yes . . ." She said it almost like a question.

Dehan showed her her badge. "Good morning, Mrs. Njalsen. I am Detective Carmen Dehan, this is my partner, Detective John Stone. We are here in an unofficial capacity from the New York Police Department. I wonder if you could spare us five minutes?"

She blinked a few times, then said, "Well, surely. Won't you come in?"

I pulled back the screen and she led us through a dark, spartan entrance hall to a parlor on the right. Like the hall, it was sparsely furnished with a sofa, an armchair by a fireplace, which looked about as old as the house, and a wooden rocking chair where some sewing had been laid, presumably when she came to open the door. She gestured me to the armchair and Dehan to the sofa. She sat on the rocking chair with her sewing on her lap.

"I can offer you coffee," she said, "but I usually break fast at five. I don't usually eat again until eleven . . ."

We assured her we didn't want coffee, and before Dehan could speak, I gave a small laugh and said, "This may seem like a strange question, Mrs. Njalsen . . ."

"Miss."

"I beg your pardon, Miss Njalsen, have you a car?"

She looked startled. "Why, no. I don't drive. I . . ." She faltered, smiled. It was an attractive smile, but also an uninviting one. "It *is* a strange question," she said at last. "Why does the New York Police Department want to know if *I* have a car?"

Dehan gave her the dead eye for a moment, then said, "The thing is, Miss Njalsen, we are reviewing the case of your sister's and her husband's murder, six years ago."

She paled visibly.

"And we noticed that there were several things that were not followed up in the original investigation. One of those things was that your sister and brother-in-law had a car."

"Yes."

"You knew that?"

"Yes, of course."

"You, as the next of kin, came into possession of all their things, including, presumably, the car . . ."

She paused there and waited for Ingrid to fill in the silence. Ingrid gave a small shrug and fingered the sewing in her lap. I saw it was a small child's dress.

"But when I got there, the car was missing, also all the papers and the keys."

"Did you report them missing?"

She looked directly at Dehan. "No."

"Why not, Miss Njalsen?"

Another small shrug. "I don't drive. I was very upset about

my sister's death. It was very traumatic. I have nobody to help me with things. I don't know about reporting a car stolen, insurance . . ." She gestured to the simple, clean, spartan home around her. "This is my world, Detective Dehan. New York . . . !" She shook her head. "It was very frightening."

Dehan smiled sympathetically. "I can understand that, and New York cops can be a bit intimidating, right, Stone?"

I nodded and smiled too. "They can, sometimes. That's true. However, there is something that I find a little confusing. The police must have talked to you several times when you arrived. They must have taken a statement from you about the last time you saw your sister and brother-in-law . . ."

"Yes. I spoke to them twice, first when I had just arrived, they came to the house, and then they asked me to go to the station house and make a statement."

"Didn't it occur to you on that second occasion to mention the car?"

A flash of irritation contracted her face. "No. I have already told you, I don't drive. A car would have been a nuisance for me. I was happy to let it go."

I nodded. "Yes, I see. I understand that." She studied my face a moment with no expression on her own. I asked her, "Do you know what a BOLO is, Miss Njalsen?"

She frowned. "A bolo? No . . ."

I gave a small laugh. "It's one of those endless acronyms that people like so much these days. BOLO stands for Be On the Look Out. We have issued a BOLO today, nationwide, so that all law enforcement agencies will be on the lookout for a silver Chevy Impala, 2000, fitting the description of your sister's car."

"After six years? Surely whoever has it will have changed the plates by now."

"Oh, that's okay," I said. "We are also looking into that, to see if that car has been reregistered anywhere else."

She was very still, staring at me. I held her eye. After a while, Dehan said, "Ingrid, has Amy got the Impala?"

Her eyes shifted away from me, but she didn't look at Dehan, she looked out her window at the vast flat plains of Iowa. "How could I possibly know that? I thought Amy and Charlie were presumed dead."

"Maybe. We're not sure. But I did notice, Ingrid, that you said earlier that you were traumatized by your sister's death. You didn't say anything about your niece."

She sighed. "You are trying to trip me up and trick me with words. Why don't you just tell me what you want?"

I spread my hands. "We simply want to know where Amy and Charlie are. And I have to say, I am becoming more and more curious as to why you would want to keep that a secret."

She gave her head a small shake. She was cool and unruffled. "You are the one who says I am keeping it a secret, Detective Stone. I have no idea what happened to Amy and Charlie. I have no idea of what happened to the car. If Amy and Charlie used it to escape, then I can only hope they are alive and safe somewhere. I certainly have no idea where."

Dehan frowned. "Forgive me saying so, Ingrid, but, considering that we are trying to find your niece, as far as I am aware, your only living relative, you don't seem very keen to help us." She waited. Ingrid did and said nothing. Dehan pushed a little harder. "In fact, I would say I am picking up a distinct sense of hostility."

Before she could answer, I cut in. "Miss Njalsen, I get that you are trying to protect your niece and her boyfriend. But we are not the people you need to protect them from. If they were targets in Karl's and Christen's murders, then, until we catch their killers, they will continue to be targets. We are here to help and protect Amy and Charlie, not to hurt them."

She went very still, like she was thinking. After a moment, she said, "I would like you to leave now. This has been very upsetting for me." As we stood, she drew breath and, after a short hesitation, added, "I don't know where they are. They are gone. I believe they are dead."

Dehan reached in her jacket and pulled out a card. She

handed it to Ingrid. "This is my cell. Talk to them, persuade them to talk to us."

She raised her eyes to stare at her. "I already told you, they are dead."

We stepped out into the bright morning sunlight and crossed the lawn to the car. There Dehan tossed me the keys and leaned on the roof as I walked around to the driver's side. I was surprised to see her smiling, and her eyes alight. I paused with the door half-open and made a question with my face.

"They are alive," she said. "And she knows where they are. If anybody knows what happened that night, they do."

I climbed in the car and she climbed in next to me. I fired up the big old cat and did a U-turn, back the way we'd come. As I did, I glanced at her and said, "That's a big maybe, but even if you're right, what are we going to do about it? Tailing her is not an option. We are not in the world's most inconspicuous car. And in a town with two hundred inhabitants, we can't exactly stand on the corner in trench coats reading newspapers and follow her discreetly through the crowds."

"I guess not . . ."

"But I would give a lot," I added, "to be a fly on her wall right now and see what she does next: who she phones or where she goes."

On an impulse, I turned right into Oak Street and, after a hundred yards, did a sharp left onto Hickory Street and pulled into the parking lot of the Hitching Post, out of sight of Ingrid Njalsen's house. "You didn't let me finish my breakfast," I told Dehan and climbed out of the Jag.

As we pushed through the door into the small, empty restaurant, I pointed to a table by the window. "Grab a spot with a nice view," I said. "You want coffee and pie?"

She didn't answer, but she smiled and went to sit.

There was a young girl behind the counter. She already had two cups set out and a coffeepot in her hand. She was smiling a big, sunny smile.

"I heard you say coffee," she said. "How d'you take it? Mornin'!"

"Good morning. Black will be fine. You got some pie for us?"

"Sure have! Momma makes 'em fresh every day. You missed the blueberries, but we got apple or we got raspberry. I'm Sally."

I glanced at Dehan. She mouthed *raspberry* at me. "Let's have one of each and a jug of cream."

She brought the pies out from under the counter and started cutting. "You guys are from out'a town, I guess. Come far?"

"New York..."

"Siddown. I'll bring it right over. We ain't got self-service here. You pay, we serve. That's what m'daddy says. You don't pay, we shoot you!"

She squealed with laughter. I smiled and went to sit. Dehan was watching the window and suppressing a smile. Sally followed a moment later, still chatting.

"I've never been to New York. You're passing through, I guess?"

She placed the pies in front of us, and Dehan smiled at her. "We came to visit an acquaintance. We were friends of Ingrid's sister, and her niece."

Sally's eyebrows shot up. She turned on her heel and went away to get our coffee and the jug of cream, speaking as she went. "I'd forgotten she had a niece. I knew she had a sister all right. Like you say, in New York, but I'd clean forgot she had a niece. I never met her, but they used to visit when I was small."

"They never come and visit now, then?"

She set down our drinks, frowned, and cocked a hip. "I call that sad. Family ought'a stay together. And Ingrid all alone the way she is. Must be a good few years since any of 'em come this way. I guess we *are* kind'a remote. She was pretty, bit older than me." She blinked suddenly and beamed her radiant smile at us. "Well, I'll let you have your pie in peace. I'm right here if you need me."

She withdrew on busy feet back to the counter. From where I

was sitting, I had no angle on Ingrid's house. Dehan was leaning back in her chair with her arms crossed and had barely taken her eyes off it.

"Anything?"

She shook her head, sat forward, and cut the pie with her fork. She stuck a chunk in her mouth, nodded, and with a grin she said, "Damn fine pie."

I raised an eyebrow at her. "Amy was not killed by a transdimensional being, Dehan."

She sipped her coffee, still watching the house through the window. "It's looking more and more like she wasn't killed at all. Perhaps she's shacked up with a dwarf who talks backward." Without batting an eyelid, she added, "Nahed dna Enots morf edih tsum ew."

"You're funny. You know that? Deep down funny, where it's not like funny anymore."

"Quit quoting Dashiell Hammett at me. So, partner, while we're killing time, I've been thinking, maybe it's time you met my family."

"Seriously? I didn't think you ever wanted me to meet your family."

"It was more a case of them not wanting to meet you. But they are kind of resigned to you now."

I narrowed my eyes and scowled. She glanced at me, then frowned. "What? Hey, don't take it personally. They wanted me to marry a nice Jewish boy . . ."

I ignored her. "Tell me something. How many Audi Q7s you reckon there are in this district?"

"I reckon these people have sense enough to buy a Jeep or a Dodge."

"I agree. Are you armed?"

"Of course. Let's pay up and go."

I rose and we went to the counter. Sally gave us her sunniest smile. Before she could speak, I said, "Honey, we are cops." We showed her our badges. "Some men are about to come in. They will ask you about us. We kept to ourselves and we didn't talk much. Do not mention Ingrid." While I was talking, I wrote a number on a paper napkin and slid it across to her. "They give you any trouble, you call. Understand?"

Her smile hadn't altered throughout. When I had finished, she said, "No offense, mister, but if they give me any trouble, I don't want the cops to know what I'm gonna do to them." To illustrate her intention, she pulled a pump-action shotgun from under the counter. "An' if that don't scare 'em off, I'll call my daddy and my two brothers. If we can handle a riled steer, I reckon we can handle a New Yorker or two. Like I said, no offense."

I smiled. "Damn fine pie."

"You take care now."

NINE

Outside, the Audi had pulled into the parking lot right next to my Jaguar. The doors were open and there were two men in dark suits with thin ties and black Wayfarers looking at her. They looked up as we approached. You could tell the shorter one with the gelled hair was the brains of the outfit, because he was chewing gum, and he could do that at the same time as almost anything else. The big one with the designer goatee was just there for the muscle, which he had plenty of. He also had a rueful, intelligent smile on his face, which I figured was the result of a freak accident when the wind had changed direction.

Einstein jerked his chin at the car. "Your vehicle?"

I smiled amiably. "Sure is."

"Sweet. Jag, huh?"

"Well, you've got a nice SUV there. You guys from 'round here?"

Muscle Man just raised an eyebrow. Einstein looked surprised and a little offended. His right knee jerked, and he seemed to adjust his neck in his collar. "No, man." He gave a small laugh. "No, this is Iowa, right? We ain't from Iowa."

"Right. Doing some sightseeing. Well, it's real nice around here. Hope you boys enjoy it."

I opened the door and made to climb in.

"New York, right?"

I looked up.

Einstein was smiling at Dehan. "Don't I know you from the 'hood?"

Dehan narrowed her eyes at him. "Hood? What hood is that?"

"Only one 'hood, sister, that's the barrio."

She gave a smile that would have made a polar bear shiver. "I don't think so. And I'm pretty sure if we had met, I would have forgotten."

She climbed in, slammed the door, and we reversed out of the lot. I kept my eye on them in the mirror as we accelerated down Sycamore Avenue toward the intersection. They didn't do anything, they just watched us drive away. When we had turned onto Vinton Road, Dehan said, "Those were Camacho's men."

I made a skeptical frown. "Chupacabras? In Italian suits and a Q7? They don't look like gang members."

"No, not gang members, Julio Camacho's men. It's different."

I accelerated, still keeping one eye on the mirror. "Explain."

"Julio and Feliciano were sent over many years ago from Mexico, by their father. They were in their late teens, early twenties. He wanted them to take control of the gang. Julio was a total psycho, and by the time he was twenty-two, he had established himself as the *patron* by hanging the previous *patron* from a meat hook and disemboweling him with a blunt kitchen knife. That was in Detroit."

"Nice."

"But he has ambitions. Being the *patron* of the Chupacabras in Detroit was not his idea of where he wanted to be in life. He and his daddy had bigger ideas for him and his brother. They knew—and know—that gang bosses die early, usually hanging from a meat hook in an abandoned warehouse. They also know that the big money, and the big power, lie in bringing coke and smack from south of the border and selling it to people who can pay, in cities like New York and Los Angeles.

"So they do the smart thing: they moved to the Bronx and used the gang like . . ." She searched for the word for a moment. "Like troops, foot soldiers, to distribute, to sell on street corners, to maintain order. Some of the smarter ones they use to open up new markets."

"Like Feliciano with Pamela."

"Right, but that was a bit classy, Feliciano pushing coke to the glitterati. I'm talking about heroin on the streets. As their market increased, so they started to increase their orders from Mexico, and they built good relationships with the cartel. They were selling a lot and the cartel was happy. And then it was time to start distancing themselves from the gang."

I frowned at her. "How?"

"Just the way you saw it with Feliciano. First, you select your best boys from the gang. You dress them up in nice suits. They're your private bodyguard. They're there to protect you, first and foremost, from your own gang. You treat them extra good, give them privileges, and they are extra loyal to you.

"Next, you start to whitewash your money. There are banks and high-profile accountants who specialize in that. I am talking household names here, Stone. This is an industry which is worth many billions of dollars every year—the laundering industry—it launders drug money, illegal arms money, and prostitution money. So if you have ten million bucks to launder, you will find an accountant and a bank with the will and the skill."

She paused, nodding. I watched her carefully. "In rough terms, twenty kilos of coke has a street value of two and a half million bucks, heroin is more, because it is much more addictive. Heroin you're talking about three and a half million. I'm talking rough figures. They are largely different markets in different types of neighborhoods, but if you are shifting ten or twelve shipments of coke and heroin a year, you are talking about an annual turnover of around sixty to seventy-five million. And believe me, shifting twenty K of coke or heroin in a month is not hard. It's not hard at all.

"So now we have Julio and Feliciano Camacho suddenly becoming respectable pillars of the community, living in respectable suburbs of New York and New Jersey, with no apparent connection to the old gang anymore. The gang is being run by lieutenants, and Feliciano and Julio get their laundered money through apparently legitimate interests, filtered through their 'investments.'" She pointed back toward Garrison. "Those boys were from Julio Camacho's private bodyguard."

I frowned, watching the road ahead and glancing in the mirror. "Dehan, why have you so much detailed knowledge about these people?"

She gazed out the side window for a moment. "I told you I took an interest in the case." Then she turned to frown at me. "How did they know we were here? And what was it about our investigation that made Julio follow us?"

I didn't answer for a bit. When I did, I said, "They're not following us."

She frowned. Then her frown deepened.

I repeated, "They are not following us. Right now, they are not following us. They are not behind us. And they didn't follow us. On our way here, nobody followed us. So how did they know where we were?"

"That doesn't make any sense."

"It does. You remember Feliciano asked for your cell number, so he could call if he thought of anything? He said he wanted a good relationship with the cops, yadda yadda. He's tracking the damned GPS on your phone. He isn't—his brother is."

She exploded and smacked the dash with the heel of her hand. "*Hijo de la gran puta!* He told his brother we'd been to see him, now his brother is using us to find Amy and Charlie..."

"Maybe."

"What do you mean, maybe?"

"I mean we don't know. I mean . . ." I shook my head and

turned to look at her. "We just don't know—anything!" Then I added, with a little more bitterness than I intended, "And apparently I know less than you."

She looked as though she was about to answer, but instead she reached in her pocket and pulled out her phone. I saw her go to Settings and then Location Services.

"What are you doing?"

"Disabling the GPS."

"Don't."

She stared at me a moment. "What are you thinking?"

"I'm not sure yet. But if we know they know where we are, but they don't know we know they know, that gives us a small advantage."

She crossed her eyes. ". . . Okay . . ."

We pulled into the parking lot at the hotel and went through reception into the bar. There, we had a clear view of the parking lot. We ordered a couple of draft beers and sat in the corner with them. I turned mine around on the table a few times before speaking, studying the rings it made on the dark wood. Finally, I said, "By now, they have phoned Camacho and told him they've found us."

"Agreed."

"So he has told them one of three things." I raised my thumb as number one. "Eliminate them." I raised my index finger as number two. "Find out why they are there, or three." I raised my middle finger. "Do nothing, just keep watching."

"Okay, what's your money on?"

I thought a moment, then shook my head. "He won't want to eliminate us, not yet anyway. He'll want information. He'll want to know why we were asking his brother questions about the Redferns, and he'll want to know what we are doing out in Garrison. So he needs to decide whether to interrogate us, which is a pretty drastic option, or keep following us." I thought a moment longer. "My bet is he won't want to show his hand yet. He'll wait and see what we do."

She nodded. "I agree. But, Stone, there is no way we can go back to Ingrid now."

I smiled and pulled off half my beer. "There is no way that they can *see* us with Ingrid. Not quite the same thing. I have a feeling Ingrid may be getting in touch with us before very long."

Dehan picked up her glass, then put it down again. "There is something else. Sunny Sally at the Hitching Post. She will have been over the road like a shot as soon as Laurel and Hardy were out of there. So she will be aware now that not only is the NYPD looking for Amy and Charlie, but some bad guys are too."

I grunted and nodded. "Exactly. So either she will clam up completely, or she'll seek our help."

She made a face of skepticism. "That may be a little optimistic, Stone."

"It may be, but the real question is what do *we* do now?" I jerked my head at the window, and she turned to see a dark blue Audi Q7 pulling in a few spaces from the Jag.

"About as subtle as a ring pull on a bikini."

I thought about it a moment. "Things we are more or less sure of: I think we can say that we are fairly certain Amy and Charlie came here in her parents' Chevy, and that Ingrid is keen to hide that fact for some reason. We can also say that we know Julio Camacho is interested in our investigation. So I think our next step is very clear. We need to enlist the help of the sheriff's department to see if we can locate the Impala, and squeeze out some information about Amy and Charlie, before Julio decides to take matters into his own hands."

She pulled out her phone again, made a quick search, and dialed a number.

"Good morning, Sheriff. This is Detective Carmen Dehan of the New York Police Department. I am here in Vinton with my partner, Detective John Stone, and I wonder if you could spare us a few minutes of your time . . . I appreciate that. We'll be there in about fifteen minutes."

We gave Julio's men another couple of minutes to check in

and go up to their rooms, then we walked out of the bar. In reception, Dehan handed her phone to the spotty guy with the leering eyes and told him, "Keep this safe till I get back, will you, pal?"

"Why sure, yes, of course."

"Don't put it in the safe. Just leave it there, behind the desk. Don't lose it."

"Yes, no, of course."

Outside, I asked her, "What if somebody tries to call you?"

"It'll be forwarded to your cell."

It was a short drive to the sheriff's office, up S K Avenue and then right down East 3rd Street to a vast, redbrick fortress that looked as though it might have been designed with World War Three in mind, or the advent of Skynet. We parked out front and climbed the concrete steps to the entrance. Once through the steel and glass doors, a deputy on the front desk told us to follow him. He didn't talk, or comment on the weather, he just led us through a spacious room with half a dozen empty desks to a door with a brass plaque on it that said Sheriff Rod O'Brien. He knocked, opened the door, and announced us. Then he went away.

Sheriff O'Brien took a deep breath and levered himself to his feet as we came in. He was a hard, blond man with short hair and small, pale blue eyes. His hands were like granite, and you just knew he loved being fair but firm with them.

We showed him our badges and he studied them awhile before sitting down and handing them back.

"So how can we help the NYPD?"

"You know Ingrid Njalsen?"

"Sure. Everybody knows Ingrid."

"You recall she had a sister, Christen?"

"I do. She moved to New York 'bout twenty years back, give or take a year. Hooked up with some lowlife."

Dehan gave a humorless smile. "No argument from me on that score, Sheriff. They had a daughter together . . ."

"Gimme a second and I'll recall her name. Pretty little thing.

Sweet as candy. Broke my heart to see her with them bums. Amy. Amy was her name."

"Amy Redfern. As I am sure you know, Sheriff, six years ago Christen and Karl Redfern were murdered . . ."

His eyelids drooped slightly over his eyes, and without anything in his face changing, his expression became hard.

"I did not know that."

We all stared at each other for a few seconds. Then I said, "On the same night that Amy's parents were murdered, Amy and her boyfriend disappeared. We have reason to believe that they may have been intended targets, as well as Amy's parents, but they managed to escape in Christen's silver Chevy Impala." I wrote down the registration number and slid it across the desk to him. "It may have been reregistered in this state. Sheriff, we think they may have come back to Garrison to ask Ingrid for help. We think she may know where they are."

He spent a while nodding, with his fingers laced over his belly. After a bit, the nodding became a soft rocking motion.

"What do you want from me?"

Dehan said, "We need to know if that Impala came out to Garrison. If it was ever registered with Iowa plates. If so, who owns it. Locating that Impala could help us to locate Amy and Charlie."

"Why are you so keen to locate them? From what you've told me, they haven't committed any crime."

I said, "Mainly because their lives could be at risk. Right now, we know there are men looking for them. We believe they are the same men who killed the Redferns. But also because, the bottom line is, we don't know if they are alive or dead, Sheriff. That was a very brutal murder, and we don't know if Amy was taken away and killed elsewhere, or if she managed to escape. Right now, it's even money."

"How long ago you say this happened?"

"Late September, six years ago."

"I'll make some inquiries for you. Where you stayin'?"

"The Cobblestone."

"You got a number I can reach you?"

She handed him her card. As he looked at it, I said, "There is just one more thing, Sheriff. There are two men in town, driving a dark blue Audi Q7. We have reason to believe they may be looking for Amy too, and that could lead them to Ingrid..."

"I'll keep an eye on her. I hope you're not bringing a lot of trouble to my burgh."

Dehan stood. "We appreciate your help, Sheriff. Nobody wants those kids alive and well more than we do."

He stood and shook our hands but didn't say anything.

Outside, Dehan crossed the road and sat on the trunk of the Jag with her long legs stuck out in front of her. I leaned on the lamppost, in the shade of a cedar tree opposite, and watched her a moment. I was struck, not for the first time, by how completely unaware she was of just how good she looked, and how damn lucky I was. She raised her face to return my stare.

"What was he hiding? Am I turning paranoid, or was he hiding something?"

"He was hiding something. But I wouldn't read too much into that, Dehan. Like I said yesterday, these are tight communities, they look out for each other. He'll want to talk to Ingrid before he talks to us. There is not a lot more we can do right now save wait."

She gave me a funny look. "Wait and think," she said.

I nodded. "Wait and think."

TEN

We stayed in Vinton. The afternoon was warm under a blue-white, cloudless sky. We wandered among the broad streets and the two-story buildings sited so far apart you got the feeling they'd originally planned a city, but wound up with a small town and now had too much space on their hands.

We did a lot of thinking, and occasionally we did a lot of talking, but just as we wound up walking in circles around the town, so we also ended up talking in circles, and it always came back to the same thing. I said it to Dehan as we pushed through the door of the Lotus Chinese Restaurant and sat at a table near the window.

"What has Camacho got against Amy and Charlie?"

She said, "Two spring rolls and chicken and cashew nuts, with vegetable rice."

I looked up to see the waitress standing there with two menus. "You don't want see menu?"

Dehan said, "No. Thanks. He'll have two spring rolls too, and sweet and sour pork with vegetable fried rice."

She gave a cute smile and went away. After a moment, I heard her say something in Chinese and there was a lot of laughter in back.

I frowned at Dehan. "I have just been verbally castrated in Chinese. Do you know how painful that is? You have destroyed my reputation as a man who wears the pants. Everywhere I go now, Chinese people will look at me askance and snigger. How did you know I wanted sweet and sour pork?"

"Eliminate the impossible, right?"

"It's impossible I should want chicken and cashew nuts?"

She continued to ignore me. "There is, realistically, a very narrow range of reasons why the Camachos should be after Amy and Charlie: they stole from them, they have information on them, or one of the gang wanted Amy and she said no."

I stared at the ceiling awhile and she stared at the table, trying to think of another plausible reason. Then I stared at the sunny, silent street through the plate glass window. The cute waitress came back with the spring rolls and a pink sauce, grinned, and said, "Enjoy!"

When she'd left, I said, "Sex, money, or power."

"Right. So here is what I am thinking. What did Pam tell us about Charlie? She said he was dyslexic and dyspraxic, which can mean you are awkward and socially dysfunctional, in severe cases, but it can also mean you have an above-average IQ and think in unusual and original ways." She waved her fork at me. "I have been looking into this, and I discovered that a lot of brilliant entrepreneurs are dyslexic. So let's stop thinking about Charlie as an ineffectual nerd for a moment and start thinking about him as an entrepreneur."

"Okay, I like this. He approaches Feliciano, who gives him the brush-off, so he approaches Adolfo and Mateo, and they listen to him. They take his request to Julio, and he agrees to give them a probationary deal . . ."

"Good. Now it is Karl who screws up. Maybe he uses some of the merchandise instead of selling it. Adolfo and Mateo put Karl in hospital as a warning, but Charlie, as Pamela's son—and Pamela is still valuable to them—guarantees that from now on the operation will run smoothly . . ."

"And it does . . ." I waved my fork at her. "For the six months that Karl is in hospital. In the meantime, our dyslexic, dyspraxic, original-thinking entrepreneur has opened a bank account elsewhere, with the three and a half grand he had in his account, plus whatever Amy added to that. And month by month, he starts stashing away whatever he is making from his deal with Julio Camacho . . ."

"Exactly! Now, maybe he is smart enough to know that when Karl gets out of hospital he is going to screw up again, and Julio is going to go all Sinaloa on his ass, or maybe he has bigger plans. Either way, the timing fits. Karl gets out of hospital, he and Christen get murdered, and Amy and Charlie disappear."

I ate a spring roll in silence. When I had finished, I said, "We have a very basic theory that seems to fit the basic facts, but there are questions. For example, who killed Adolfo and Mateo down by the fish market? And if they were already dead, which they were, who killed Christen and Karl . . . ?"

She was chewing a spring roll and started smiling and nodding. I was smiling and nodding back, because we had both had the same thought. She swallowed.

"Adolfo, Mateo, and Charlie had a scam running—or at least Julio thought they had. Julio had them killed, then went after Amy and Charlie. But by the time he got to Amy's place, they had taken the Impala and run. Karl and Christen didn't know where, so they paid the price."

I ate my second spring roll, thinking it through. "It's the first theory we have that actually seems to hang together, at least roughly. I have two big questions, though."

"What?"

"What was the scam they were running for six months that Julio didn't spot?"

She leaned back against the red vinyl bench and wiped her mouth on a paper napkin. "I have another question. It's related, but right now it might be more relevant."

"What's that?"

"How much could they make in six months?"

I nodded and spread my hands. "Well, that depends on what the scam was. The most likely thing would be that they were adding a percentage to the price and creaming it off for themselves. If that's the case, over six months it could run into hundreds of thousands of dollars. On the other hand, if they spent five months gaining his trust, and then on month six they screwed him out of a whole shipment, it could be a couple of millions or more, depending on the size of the shipment."

The chicken and the pork arrived.

"Chicken cashew nuts for the lady. Sweet sour pork for the man . . ."

A wink and a grin and she was off.

"Yeah." She gave a small, "that's self-evident" shrug. "That's what I thought. So they are not in Vinton and they sure as hell are not in Garrison. They were passing through. They stayed with Auntie Ingrid a few days, or long enough to change the registration on the Impala, and maybe paint it another color. Then they move on somewhere where they can change their identity and spend their money."

I chewed on the sweet and sour pork. It was good. "Not Mexico," I said.

"No, not Mexico. Too many friends and relatives of the Camachos. This is good."

I said, "Arizona, California, or Washington State." She stuffed her mouth with food and chewed, watching my face. I went on. "I would rule Arizona out for the same reason they wouldn't go to Mexico. Southern Cali, the same. So, for my money we are looking at San Francisco or Seattle."

She suddenly shook her head and flopped back in her seat. "Choomush hpekoorashum."

"I agree, too much speculation. But we have a shape, at least, Dehan, and that is good. It would be nice now to have some evidence to confirm that shape."

Right on cue, the phone rang.

"Stone."

"Sheriff O'Brien here."

"Good afternoon, Sheriff. You have some news for us?"

"Maybe so. You still in town?"

"We are at the Lotus. Damn fine Chinese."

"It surely is. We have a nice town here . . . We aim to keep it that way." He sighed, like what he was going to say would make his town less nice. "I spoke to Ingrid. She says she's willing to talk to you again—if I'm there."

"She has something to say to us, then . . ."

"Yup."

"Okay, we'll just finish up here and . . ."

"Meet me at Ingrid's place, that's where I am now."

"We're on our way."

Dehan was already wiping her mouth and sliding off her bench. She paid, and we made our way past the Benton County Courthouse, through the gardens, to where the Jag was waiting for us. I threw Dehan the keys and she grabbed them left-handed without looking. The doors slammed, the burgundy beast growled, and we were on our way.

She drove without speaking. Four minutes later, we pulled up behind the sheriff's Dodge outside Ingrid's house and crossed the lawn to her porch. All the way I had been looking for the Q7, but I'd seen no sign of it.

The sheriff opened the door for us as we climbed the steps to the porch.

"She's in the parlor."

She didn't look up as we went in. I said, "Good afternoon, Miss Njalsen. It's very kind of you to see us again." She glanced at me from the corner of her eye but didn't answer.

Dehan sat on the sofa without being invited, with her elbows on her knees and her hands clasped like she was trying to break a walnut. She smiled at Ingrid. It was a nice smile and it looked genuine.

"Hi, Ingrid. I'm really very grateful to you. I mean that. We are actually quite worried about Charlie and Amy, and we would like to know what happened to them, if they are okay. And we think that if we can find them, they might help us to find whoever killed your sister."

She didn't meet Dehan's eye. She said to the floor, "Sheriff O'Brien already explained. You don't need to tell me again."

I sat in the armchair, and O'Brien settled himself beside Dehan. "Tell them what you told me, Ingrid."

She spent a while looking down at her left hand, rubbing it with the thumb from her right. After a while, she said, "Amy never phoned me. None of them did. Christen was too far gone in sin. I don't believe she even remembered she had a sister. Karl was possessed of the devil, ain't nobody going to persuade me that wasn't so. But Amy, she used to write me."

Dehan frowned. "Letters?"

"Of course letters! What else was she going to write me? They used to come pretty regular, about once a month, just giving me the news, such as she was willing to tell it. There was things we didn't talk about, like the drugs, but she would say to me, 'Mom ain't feeling so good these days . . .' and I would know that she'd been taking drugs, or she had overdosed or some such. And I would tell her, 'Well, give her my love and wish her better. I'll say a prayer for her,' and she would say that she prayed for her every day, and we both knew that we understood each other. She was a good, God-fearing child, and God blessed us with that kind of understanding."

She paused, glanced a moment at the sheriff, then back at her hand.

"So when she called me on the telephone, I knew that something was wrong."

She didn't speak then for a while, until the sheriff said to her, "What did she say to you, Ingrid?"

She shifted around in her chair a bit. Her breathing had become shallower and now there were tears in her eyes. She blew her nose before speaking again.

"She said something bad had happened. Karl and Christen had been killed. She said she couldn't tell me how it happened, but the police were going to be in touch with me and ask me to go to New York. She said she was on her way, with Charlie, and they wanted to stay a few days. She begged me not to tell anybody. They had taken Christen's car, and they wanted to hide it in the garage out in the yard while they changed the registration and painted it."

For the first time, she looked at Dehan. "That was why I never reported the car missing in New York. I knew where it was and I didn't want to draw attention to it, or to Amy. When I got back home, I begged her to tell me what had happened. She told me she wasn't sure. She said Karl got involved with some bad people, a gang. He was selling drugs or something, and he had tried to double-cross these men, and they had punished him. Killed him and..."

There was no great display of grief, no sobbing or begging God to make it not so. She just bit her lip, kept her eyes fixed on the window, and allowed her tears to flow. Her nose turned red, as did her eyes, as though she had a bad cold. She dabbed at her eyes and blew her nose, and occasionally opened her mouth to steady her breathing. But all the confusion, all the pain and the rage against a world that had robbed her of the only family she had, the only connection she had to love, all of that stayed inside. It belonged to her, and to her god, who had his own, mysterious motives for visiting this suffering on her.

After a while, she said, "Amy and Charlie, thank the Lord, were able to get away with the car, and make it to Garrison without the gang finding them. Otherwise they might have killed her too."

Dehan asked, "How long did they stay here, Ingrid?"

"Just a couple of weeks. They never went out, and they kept the car in the garage. I know some of the neighbors saw them, but nobody minds nobody's business in Garrison 'cept his own. They're good folk."

She paused. Nobody spoke. Outside, a truck rattled by and faded, leaving eddies of silence in its wake. She took another deep breath. "Then they left. They left late at night, when no one would see them. She said they was headed south, but they wouldn't tell me where, for my own safety, they said. They told me they'd be in touch when it was all over, but I never heard from them again."

Dehan sighed. I knew how she felt. If this was it, it did little more than confirm some of our theory, but not much. Above all, it didn't tell us where they were.

"Ingrid, did they say anything at all about the gang who murdered your sister? Is there anything they said, however irrelevant it may seem, that you can tell us?"

She thought for a while. "There were names that they repeated a few times. Adolfo and Mat, I got the impression they were friends. They usually mentioned them together. And sometimes they mentioned Felix. I got the feeling he was important, a friend of Charlie's mom."

Dehan chewed her lip at me and I asked, "Did you, while they were here, form any kind of idea, or suspicion, about where they might have been headed? Did they mention any towns, locations, anything at all that might . . ."

She was shaking her head, but the sheriff spoke up.

"I think I might have an answer for you there, Mr. Stone. I really wish you had confided in me at the time, Ingrid. Things might have turned out different all 'round."

"I know . . ." She said it quietly, to the hands in her lap. "I am sorry, Sheriff."

I was frowning at him. So was Dehan. I said, "What do you mean?"

"I am not one hundred percent sure, Detective Stone, but 'round about the time we're talking about, there was an automobile accident. Car came off 18th Avenue, crashed into the Opossum Creek. I don't know what it was carrying, but it burst into flames and burned most of the night and day. By the time we was able to get to it and stop the burning, there wasn't much left." He gave his head a single shake. "Burned-out shell, and what was left, after more than eight hours of burning, of two bodies. ME said most likely a man and a woman."

Dehan looked at him like he was crazy. "It burned for more than eight hours, *in a creek*?"

He shook his head. "It crashed off the bridge, landed in the creek, but only part of the hood was in the water. Must have exploded and then burned." He gave a small shrug. "It happened at night and it was a long time before anybody got to it. It did burn an awful long time. I did wonder about that, but there was no crime committed that we could see, and what was more important, no trace of any kind of ID. Obviously no fingerprints, and in the ME's opinion, the chances of getting a reliable DNA sample were minimal. All we could do was file the report. I have what we were able to recover back at the office, if you want to come and see it."

Dehan nodded and stood. I said, "What happened to the car?"

He looked rueful. "It became part of the landscape. Nobody wanted to claim responsibility for it, nobody owned it, and nobody wanted to waste their money on it. Now it's part of the nature reserve. I'll run the registration for you, see if it's the one Amy and Charlie registered."

"Thanks. I'd like to go and see it." I glanced at Dehan. She nodded. "Then we can have a look at the possessions, if that's okay."

He shrugged his big shoulders again. "Anything we can do to help. I'll tell you where it is, you come and see me in Vinton when you're done."

ELEVEN

The crash site was ten miles south and east of Ingrid's house, as the crow flies. By road, it was closer to fifteen, driving through endless miles of flat prairie where, here and there, short lines of tall, silhouetted trees stood like lonely processions of hooded monks under a vast sky.

I wanted to ask why they would go east and then south. Logic dictated they should go west. If they were trying to leave a false scent, it was enough to tell Ingrid they were going south. They didn't need to demonstrate it. Nobody was following them. And even if they feared somebody was, why *east* and then south?

But I didn't ask, because I knew Dehan was wondering the same thing, and like me, she was aware it was just one more unanswerable question on the pile of questions that were building up with every partial answer we got.

We came eventually to 27th Avenue—because here the endless roads that crisscross the entire state, in a vast grid system, were named and numbered like streets and avenues in a city. We turned onto the avenue, and after two miles, I slowed and pulled over onto the verge as we approached a bridge. There we climbed out and stood looking down a steep slope at the rusted wreckage of a car, half-buried in mud, with its hood sunk in the lazy water of the creek.

We slipped and slithered down the bank and soon found we were squelching ankle-deep through mud, knee-high in grass and ferns. We waded up to the burnt-out shell and began to examine it. The trunk was still closed, raised a couple of feet in the air. The tires had been burned away, as had the paint. We peered through the windows. Inside, just about everything that hadn't been consumed by the flames had rotted in the rain, the flooding, and the alternating extremes of heat and cold that hit Iowa every year.

The doors were closed, but they opened with a small tug. I explored the glove compartments and the floor. There was nothing there of interest.

Dehan said, "What are you hoping to find?"

Instead of answering her, I said, "It's an Impala, isn't it?"

She nodded. I made my way back to the trunk and tried it. It was locked. Dehan leaned inside the car and after a moment shook her head. "No way. The button's burned and rusted."

"It's Schrödinger's cat, Dehan. Until we open the trunk, they are both dead and alive. After we open the trunk, they will be one or the other."

Her eyebrows shot up. "You think they are in the trunk?"

I shook my head and made my way back to the Jag. "I don't think so. But I am very curious to see if there *is* anything in the trunk."

I pulled my Colt .45 automatic from the glove compartment and made my way back to the wreck. I stopped and smiled at Dehan, who was frowning at me.

"What do you think, Dehan? Will we find twenty kilos of cooked coke? Two and a half million baked bucks?"

I shot out the lock and the rusted metal yielded easily. I heaved up the lid and found a mass of melted plastic that had bonded to the metal floor of the trunk, and nothing else. I slipped the automatic in my waistband and pointed at the hardened black plastic that lay spread all over the floor.

"Assume there had been luggage, and that the sheriff took out the luggage when the car was cool enough. It would have left deep imprints in the melted plastic, right?"

"Definitely. What is this plastic anyway?"

"Plastic gas cans. Stored for a long journey through remote country where they wanted to avoid being seen on security cameras. Perhaps they thought they might go a long time without seeing a service station. That's why the car burned so long. It was full of gallons of gas."

She nodded. "Makes sense."

I turned and looked up the track we had scrambled down. "So what made them come off the road? They swerved to avoid another vehicle . . . ?"

Dehan came up beside me. "They didn't roll, they didn't hit the side of the bridge, they just trundled down the bank. They weren't going very fast either, because they came to a stop with only the front of the hood in the water . . ."

We stared at each other, aware we were asking the same question. I put it into words. "What made the car ignite? It rolls down the bank, plops its nose in the water. It was early October, conditions much like this, only slightly cooler, perhaps wetter . . . They should have just climbed out and walked away. Instead the car ignites and burns for eight hours, and they both burn with it."

I walked back to the driver's door. I heard Dehan's voice behind me. "Oh, I see where you're going. Whatever was in the trunk besides the gas was removed before the car burned." She walked around to the passenger side and yanked open the door, scraping it through the mud. Then she set to scouring the dash and the door, saying, "And now you're looking for bullet holes."

"Mm-hm." I nodded. "But I don't see any. Goddamn it, Dehan! Everything in this case cancels everything else out! I can see," I said, "that Charlie was, as you said, an entrepreneur. I can see that he was smart enough to pull one over on Julio. I can see that he and Amy set things up so they could escape to Garrison in the Impala. I see also that they keep their phones switched on long enough to call Ingrid and then switch them off. Okay . . ." I began to pace and squelch.

Dehan said, "Julio Camacho uses the same technique on them that he used on us. He tracks the GPS on Amy's phone. Amy keeps it on long enough for Julio to get a general orientation, Midwest, maybe Iowa, but then they go dark. Julio is mad. So he has a couple of teams scouring the area. After two weeks, they switch their phones on again, thinking they are safe. Julio picks up the signal and tracks them down."

I nodded. "Okay . . ."

"His team catches up with them here and they drive them off the road. There are no bullet holes, Stone, because . . ." She was thinking as she talked. "Because A, the team don't want to attract attention, and B, they have been told to punish them. So they use knives. They take their dope, or money, or whatever it is from the trunk, and burn the car to make it look like an accident."

I stuffed my hands in my pockets and shrugged at the same time. "I guess it makes sense."

"But you don't like it."

I shook my head. "The box is still closed. What we have, over and over, is plausible explanations for the absence of evidence. So the box is still closed and the cat is still both dead and alive."

She punched me on the shoulder. "Hey, at least we found the car!"

I made a face of skepticism. "*Maybe!* We don't even know that for sure yet. Let's go see Sheriff Happy Face and see what he's got for us."

We took 66th Street west for three miles, then turned north up 24th Avenue, and after that, it was a seven-mile straight run all the way to the sheriff's office. Halfway there, Dehan said, "New York is Babylon. The grid system belongs there, but out here, overlaid on nature? It's wrong." She looked at me. "We should be wending. Why aren't we wending?"

I had no answer for her, and three minutes later, we pulled up outside the forbidding concrete and brick mass which was the sheriff's office. We climbed out into the warm afternoon sunshine and stood staring at the windowless hulk. Dehan shook her head. "I feel like we stepped into a Stephen King movie. Where are the wooden swing doors, the cowboy boots, and the 'Howdy, ma'am'?"

"Maybe they went a-wending."

We crossed the road and pushed through the steel and glass door, as we had before. The sheriff was leaning on the reception desk, talking to his deputy. He didn't greet us as we came in. He just raised his chin and said, "Follow me."

We followed him down a passage, through a door, and down some steps into a basement. There we went through double security doors into a storage area, with steel shelves crowded with boxes.

"This is the evidence room."

He led us down a long aisle, and at the end I could see a table against the far wall. On it there was a cardboard box, and next to that there was what looked like a giant Tupperware container, maybe five feet by three, and a couple of feet deep.

He laid his hand on it and said, "Here's your stuff." He leaned his hip against the table and crossed his arms. "You find the car okay?"

Dehan was opening the carton. I nodded. "Yeah. Did you open the trunk at the time?"

He shook his head. "Nope. Didn't see the point, tell you the truth. Anything that was in there was cooked."

I opened the giant Tupperware. There were two skulls and several bits of bone: thigh, tibia, a few ribs, all badly charred. I glanced at Dehan. "We need to send these to the ME's office. They might get enough DNA, check the dental records. It's unlikely they'll get anything, but it's worth a try."

I was holding one of the skulls in my hand, turning it around, examining it. A chip on the left eye socket caught my attention.

"You got a flashlight?"

The sheriff pulled a pencil light from his pocket and handed it to me. I played the light on the chip, then on the inside of the skull. Dehan had abandoned her examination of the box and was watching me. I could see a pattern of hairline fractures inside. Then I found what I was looking for.

"How thoroughly did the ME examine these bodies?"

There was something hostile in O'Brien's eyes when he said, "Not much. Why would he?"

I handed him the flashlight, then held the skull at an angle so he could see inside, near the base. "See that dark stain?" He frowned and nodded. "Two gets you twenty, Sheriff, that is lead, melted in the fire as the brain cooked away, leaving a coating on the bone."

"Son of a gun."

I examined the second skull and found the same thing.

"Suddenly we have a double homicide. They have both been shot. There are no entry wounds, except maybe this chip on the eye socket. So we can conclude they were shot through the eye. But there is no exit wound either. If you look inside, you see hair fractures along the bone, where the velocity of the bullet has caused the brain to expand, but not enough for the bullet to exit. So we're looking at either a shot from some distance, where the bullet has lost velocity, which we can rule out because it was night and the vehicle was moving, or most likely a small-caliber slug, possibly from a suppressed weapon."

I looked at Dehan and handed her the skull. "They've been run off the road. Then the killer, or killers, have come down and shot them in the eye, probably with a suppressed .22. They have removed the contents of the trunk, whatever it was they were looking for, and then they have burned the car, and the occupants. That," I said, "is the most likely explanation." I turned to the sheriff. "Are you going to dispute our jurisdiction? The way I see it, this is originally a crime that was committed in New York. It's either ours or the Feds'."

He shook his head. "I ain't got the resources or the inclination. You or the Feds take it off my hands, I ain't gonna complain."

Dehan put down the skull and pulled her cell from her jacket.

"Sir? Dehan here . . . Yeah, we're pretty sure we found the Impala and what is very likely the remains of Amy and Charlie . . . Yes, sir, in Iowa." She held my eye while she listened. "No, sir, the sheriff is happy to recognize our jurisdiction or the Feds'. What we need is to have the remains of the car towed back to the Bronx, and I am going to send the remains and personal effects to the ME." After a moment, she hung up and looked at the sheriff. "He's going to call you."

The sheriff nodded and left us with the bones, and while he and the deputy inspector sorted the red tape, Dehan called DHL to come and collect what was left of Amy and Charlie and take them back to New York.

After she hung up, we stood for a while with our asses leaning against the table, staring down the dark, steel and concrete aisles of evidence boxes, with the plastic box of charred bones behind us, and the small cardboard box of charred things that had once been important enough to take away while fleeing for her life. Now they were nothing more than tenuous bits of half-burned evidence that once upon a time had been two people called Amy and Charlie.

Dehan took a deep breath and let it go slowly but noisily. "So they didn't make it, Stone. I'd kind of hoped they had."

I nodded for a while. "There is still a lot we don't know."

She thought about that for a moment, then arched her eyebrows and gave a couple of slow nods. "Like—just about everything: who killed them, for a start, and what they did exactly to piss the Camachos off . . ."

"Where they were going and how whoever killed them knew they were going there . . ."

"The GPS . . ."

"All of that is speculation, Dehan. We need something, just

one thing, to tie Julio or Feliciano to the bodies. One thing to *prove* that the Camachos, or at least the Chupacabras, had motive, means, and opportunity to kill Amy and Charlie. So far, we have squat."

She punched my shoulder again. "Come on, don't be negative. We're making progress. However, I am exhausted, and I do not plan on driving sixteen hours tonight, so I am going to write my report, and then I suggest we go to the Ron-Da-Voo, which stays open till two. See what I did there? I made it rhyme."

"You're a poet and we didn't know it."

"We eat Mexican and we let off some steam."

"What does that mean, letting off steam?"

"Now you're doing it."

"Am I going to have to bail you out of the county jail in the morning?"

She smiled and slapped the shoulder she had punched moments before. "Don't be silly, Stone. Of course not. You'll be in the slammer with me. C'mon, stop being a sissy. I need a shower and a siesta."

We carried the stuff up to the sheriff's office and left it on his desk, telling him DHL would be there to collect it within the hour. We shook hands with him and told him we'd be out of town by sunrise, which made him almost smile. Then we stepped out, one last time, through the steel and glass doors, into the lengthening shadows of the late afternoon.

By the car, I stood a moment to look back at the bizarre fortress that housed the sheriff's office. It didn't belong in remote Iowa. It didn't belong in Vinton. It belonged in Washington—or Moscow.

Dehan opened the passenger door and paused to wait for me. I shook my head, still gazing at the ugly behemoth. "You know how many people have been murdered in Vinton in the last ten years?"

I turned to look at her. She shook her head. I looked back at the fortress.

"None."

I climbed in the car, and we drove back to the Cobblestone Hotel, there to shower, write our reports, and prepare for Dehan to let off steam.

TWELVE

The Ron-Da-Voo was more of a lounge bar than a restaurant. It had bare brick walls, and it was dark, friendly, and cozy, with country music playing softly in the background. We grabbed a table by the wall and ordered a couple of beers from a bright-eyed waitress who gave us a menu. When she came back with the drinks, Dehan ordered a Mexican potato and I ordered three pieces of broasted chicken.

We both sat and looked around for a bit. Finally, she said, "Okay, you going to say it, or am I?"

I smiled. "You're the boss, you say it."

"I'm the boss now?"

"It's your case, Dehan. You know it as well as I do."

She leaned back and stretched out her long legs under the table so that one of her boots was resting against my chair. For a moment, I wondered what it was we were supposed to be saying. She picked up her glass and took a pull, leaving herself with a Santa Claus moustache. She saw me smile again and wiped it away with the back of her hand.

"We can't close this case."

I thought of the odd bits and pieces in the box, things that had once been a part of Amy's and Charlie's lives, had somehow identified them. I thought of their bones, and their skulls, sitting in that banal, sterile plastic. I thought of their desperate dash for salvation, six years ago, how they almost made it. I felt a twist of regret and anger in my belly.

"It's too soon to say that."

She offered me a small, quiet snort, with a small smile on the left side of her face. It was an expression of amused defeatism.

"Let's say," she said, "that the lab can extract enough DNA to make a profile. What are we going to compare it to? There is nothing left of the Redferns, and the chances of Pamela having kept anything with Charlie's . . ."

I interrupted her. "We can run comparisons with Ingrid and with Pamela."

She made a face and nodded for a bit. "Okay, so in the *very* unlikely event that we can get a DNA sample from the bones, maybe we can prove that the skeletons were related to Ingrid and Pamela, and were probably Amy and Charlie . . ." She shook her head. "Where do we go from there? What is our next move after that? This is as far as we go."

"We can't know that until we get all the results back."

She leaned forward with her elbows on the table. "But we already know, Stone, what those results are going to be. They will get squat from the car. You know that. There is not enough left of the jaws to get reliable dental record IDs, and there will be no DNA left after that fire *anyway*."

I shrugged, feeling unreasonably irritated. I knew she was right, but something inside told me you don't give up just because you can't win. You don't fight just because you *can* win. I shrugged. "You're ready to give up . . . ?"

Her face contracted with anger for a second. Then she sighed. "I'm not saying that." She spread her hands, her eyebrows arched with exasperation. "But where *do* we go from here?"

I looked around, searching the dark, crowded bar for answers. "Feliciano and Julio are nervous." She made a "that's true" face. I sipped my beer. "Nervous people do stupid things. *They* don't know what we know. They know we know something, but they don't know what or how much. We still have a couple of plays left before we need to give up."

"Like what?"

"I don't know! Like maybe worrying them enough so they make that mistake."

"Right . . ." She gestured at me with her right hand open, palm up. "See? That's more like it." She made a face like a sulking kid and mimicked me: "Well, if you wanna give up . . . !"

"You're an ass, Dehan."

"I know. But I'm fun when you get to know me." She grinned with very white teeth and started to laugh. That made me laugh. She pointed at me. "You cheer me up. Most of the time I'm up, you know? But I burn a lot of energy. Did you notice?"

"Yeah."

"So sometimes I get this sudden slump, especially if I eat too many carbohydrates, and I feel everything is hopeless. You're good . . ." She pointed at me again with her finger like a gun. "You stay cool, calm, focused, and you say"—she mimicked a deep, masculine voice—"'Nervous people make mistakes, we still have a few plays, stay cool, kid . . .'" She laughed again. "I like that. It's good."

"You like that?"

"You complement me."

I shrugged. "What can I say, you look good in jeans. Maybe we should get married."

"Asshole. Complement, not compliment."

"You could compliment me sometimes."

"Yeah, you'd look swell in a tweed jacket, with a pipe and slippers and Schrödinger on your lap."

"Oh, you're the young, beautiful dynamo and I'm the wise old man?"

This time it was an English accent, like Batman's Alfred. "So, Schrödinger, my old friend, whom do we think is the perpetrator of this heinous crime?"

"As I said before, Dehan, you're an ass."

I was spared her comeback by the arrival of the bright-eyed waitress with our food.

After that, our conversation rambled. She did a lot of talking: everything from conspiracy theories to Freudian psychoanalysis, mega-politics, Budo and Buddhism, to criminology and socioeconomics. They were all connected in her mind, and she admitted freely and repeatedly: "I do not know a lot about this, it's a profound subject—and who has the time, right? Aside from a PhD student!—but you have to ask yourself . . ." And then she would launch into the question she thought you had to ask yourself. It was fun, and she was interesting to listen to.

"It's like reading books."

"What is?"

She licked her fingers and wagged one of them at me. "How things pass from being information to becoming knowledge."

I chewed and frowned. "From information to knowledge?"

"Sure, like Schrödinger's cat again. Suppose you are looking at the box where the poor damn cat is. Is it dead or is it alive? According to the theory, it is both dead *and* alive." She laughed. "To a cop that isn't so convincing, but let's say somebody tells you, 'No, that cat is dead.' That is information. Let's say somebody else tells you, 'No, I heard it meow, it's alive.' That is still information. Until you open the box and take the cat out, and hold it and have it claw you, you don't *know* the cat is alive."

"So you're saying knowledge is personal experience."

"No. Personal experience, which is *more* than just seeing something, or hearing it, you have to feel it somehow: taste it, smell it, hold it, *use* it." I drew breath, but she was off again. "You know? Somebody can explain to you how to use a screwdriver: 'You hold it with the fat bit in the heel of your hand, find the cut in the head of the screw, fit it in . . . yadda yadda.' It's just information. But pick up a screwdriver and use it, and that becomes knowledge. I think knowledge is when you experience information and it becomes *a part of you*."

I watched her while she folded the potato skin on her plate and stuffed it in her mouth. "You're very intense, Dehan."

She nodded. "Mm-hm." She swallowed and reached for her beer. "Is that a problem?"

"No. On the contrary. It's probably why I married you."

"Oh, *you* married *me*?" She didn't give me time to answer. She was off again. "Life is too short not to be intense, Stone. That's why I don't waste my time on ninety-nine out of a hundred people I meet. They are moonshine, like those glimmers of moonlight you get on the sea at night. They might be pretty, real alluring sometimes, but they wink and they are gone because they were never real."

"They were just information, not knowable."

"Right." She thought about it a moment, then said again, "Right." She raised her glass and saw it was empty. "Goddamn it. How's a girl supposed to toast?"

She hailed the bright-eyed waitress.

"Let's have two more beers, and when slow coach decides he's ready to finish eating, let's have a bottle of tequila."

"You got it!"

I set to work on the chicken, thinking about what she'd said. I had a funny twist in my belly which I couldn't identify. It might have been anger at the injustice of Amy's and Charlie's deaths, it might have been anticipation at the prospect of tackling the Camachos. When I thought about the two boys back at the hotel, I felt the adrenaline burn in my gut. But there was something else too, something I couldn't identify; something like fear.

The tequila arrived, with salt and lemon.

"You know, I am not a big tequila guy..."

"You are tonight, *amigo*." I felt her boot on my chair again and realized the feeling was fear: fear of why she was so passionate about this case—fear of losing her. She poured and smiled and said, "Another night we'll do whiskey. *Salud!*"

We walked back at two a.m., through a town that had few sidewalks but many green verges. The sky was vast, the stars beyond counting, and a cool breeze came out of the north and whispered about the impending fall.

She took my left arm with both of hers and leaned on me as we walked down the quiet path, under the vast sky. She gave my arm a small squeeze and asked, "So you're going to meet my family, Stone? You got nobody left I can meet?"

We were walking west, and I glanced back over my shoulder. A great glob of molten orange light was bulging over the tree line behind us. I shrugged and smiled. "The fall moon." I said it half to myself. Then, when she tried to read my face, I said, "Nope. Nobody left but you."

"You never talk much about them."

I was quiet, listening to the dark echo of our footsteps. "My gran, that's what I called her, grew up in London during the Blitz."

"Your grandmother was British?"

"English. My granddad was a GI. Spent the war over there. Met my gran. They fell in love and married and he brought her back here. She could never get used to how we express our emotions so openly all the time. From as far back as I can remember, she used to sit me on her knee and say"—I did a passable cockney accent, as I remembered it from my gran—"'John, you just remember, it ain't necessary for the 'ole bleedin' world to know what you're feelin'. You can always have a good ol' cry when you're on your own. But when there's people abaht, you keep a grip. Chances are,' she used to say, 'you'll have to be the strong one, and if you go to pieces, the 'ole fahkin' thing will go to pieces wiv'yah!'"

She was smiling up at me and giggling as we walked. "Fahkin'? She used to say that?"

"The Brits are a foul-mouthed lot. She used to swear like a trooper. If I fell over and cried, she'd say, 'You're not dead! Get up and stop fahkin' snivelin'!'"

"Wow, that's hard."

"Not at all. We adored each other. She was what you would

call 'knowledge.' Tough as old boot leather, and the heart of a lion. She was irreverent, atheist, no time for bullshit, and at the same time human, humane, compassionate, and loving. A hard act to follow."

"I hear you."

"She was my dad's mother. He inherited her values, but he was gentler, perhaps weaker. My mother was sweet and kind, all apple pie. I was a happy child. But somehow I guess I just never felt I was *part* of what was going on. My gran was the only person I really identified with, who really understood me. It seemed to me she had it nailed. Life is tough. You have to be tough to get through it. Where she was special was that she realized that being tough meant also having the capacity to love." I laughed. "I don't talk like this, Dehan. Stop making me drink tequila."

"Nah. It's good to let off steam sometimes. Don't worry, I'll still respect you in the morning. I promise."

We had just turned into the parking lot at the hotel. I could see the Jaguar gleaming under a lamp, and a little beyond it the ugly shape of the Audi Q7. Then, as we moved toward the main doors of the hotel, I saw a figure leaning against one of the columns on the porch. He was smoking, and I saw the red glow of his cigarette move to his mouth, burn bright, and then drop down by his side again.

Dehan released my arm. "He's waiting for us. The bar is closed by now. You armed?"

"It's in the car."

"Don't do that again. Keep it with you."

"Okay, boss."

"I'm serious."

We were close enough now to see his eyes. It was Einstein. He released a trail of smoke from his nose. "You been out on the town?"

I smiled amiably, and before Dehan could say anything, I asked, "Cigarette before bed?"

He shook his head. "We're having a drink with *el jefe*. They kept the bar open specially for him. He has that kind of pull, you know? He told me to wait for you, and bring you in for a drink."

"Tell him thank you from us, but we're on our way up. Thanks all the same."

We went to move past him. He dropped his cigarette, and his right hand went behind his back. He was still staring at the butt on the ground as he crushed it with his toe. "Detective Stone, Detective Dehan, I think you will want to talk to Mr. Camacho."

He looked up from the crushed cigarette into my face, like he was hoping I'd make an issue of it. I knew Dehan had her Glock in her hand, though he couldn't see her just behind me. I smiled at him again. "Mr. Camacho? Julio Camacho?"

"Got it in one."

"Well, gee, why didn't you say so?" I turned to Dehan. "We'd love to talk to Julio Camacho, wouldn't we, darling?"

"Nothing I'd rather do."

I saw the way she was looking at Einstein and preempted her. One thing we did not need that night was a killing. I turned back to him, still smiling amiably. "Oh, by the way, just one small thing." He jerked his chin at me. "Next time you go to pull a gun on me, be sure and shoot me. Because if you don't, I will shove it so far up your ass I'll blow your brains out with it. Now, lead the way to your *jefe*, Einstein."

He shouldered past me to try and regain some of his dignity, but I was about six inches taller and forty pounds heavier, so it didn't really work out for him. As we followed him past a scared-looking receptionist, Dehan made a face and said, "Eight out of ten. It made up in feeling for what it lacked in originality."

I said, loud enough for the jerk to hear, "When I kill him, I'll try and make it original."

She grinned. As we stepped into the short passage to the bar, she said, "I'm going to the can. Don't start without me," and ran back toward reception.

Einstein turned and shouted after her. "Hey!"

"Be patient, Einstein. She'll be back."

He scowled at me. "You guys give me a pain in the ass, you know that? And stop calling me Einstein."

"And I thought we were getting on so well."

Five minutes later, Dehan came back. We moved to the bar, and he opened the door for us. Dehan went in ahead, and as I passed him, Einstein said, "You got a big mouth, *pendejo*."

I thought that lacked both feeling and originality, but I didn't have time to tell him so. Two tables had been drawn together. Sitting at them were five men, all in suits. They had a bottle of tequila on the table, with a saucer of lemon and a saltcellar. I counted four weapons on the table: three Glock automatics and one Smith & Wesson 29 revolver.

One of the men sitting was Einstein's friend, Godzilla. I figured the Smith & Wesson was his. Besides him, there was a short, fat guy with a moustache. Even his thousand-dollar suit couldn't make him look like anything but a thug. Next to him was a guy in his late thirties with skin like damaged tree bark. He had a ponytail and a Winston cigarette hanging from his mouth. In the middle of this group there were two men whose suits had cost more than a thousand bucks and more than two. They looked groomed. They were not visibly scarred, and something about them said that occasionally they used their brains for something other than killing, screwing, and getting stoned.

The one on the right was younger and had "crown prince" written all over him. The one on the left had olive skin and blue-black hair oiled slick, but his eyes were an unsettling shade of pale blue. He gestured with both hands at the chairs opposite him.

"Detective John Stone, Detective Carmen Dehan, the Forty-Third's cold-case unit. Sit. Please don't worry. I do not intend to kill you tonight. We will just have a drink and talk things over. I am Julio Camacho."

THIRTEEN

Einstein stepped toward Dehan to frisk her. Her voice was quiet, but there was no mistaking her conviction.

"Put your hand on me . . ." He stopped, hesitated, and glanced at Camacho. She said, "Go ahead, just put your hand on me once . . ."

Camacho sighed and shook his head briefly. "*Déjelo, Gustavo, guarde la puerta, que no entre nadie.* Nestor, *vaya con el.*"

Godzilla got up, and he and Einstein, aka Nestor and Gustavo, went off to guard the door. Dehan and I sat. Camacho poured tequila and I said, "You may be interested to know that we found the car."

He let out a soft grunt as he punched the cork back in the bottle. "The car," he said, then pulled down the corners of his mouth and hunched his shoulders. "The car. You say this like it is gonna mean something to me. What car are you talkin' about, Detective Stone?"

I nodded a few times and looked at the glass of tequila in front of me. "Oh." I said it like he'd just told me something. Then I shifted my eyes to look into his. "We're going to play this game? Okay. So, what do you want, Julio? I'm tired and I have a long day tomorrow."

Again the little, impatient shake of the head. "No, we are not playing games. What I want"—he turned to look at Dehan—"is to know why the *fock* you investigatin' me and my brother. You go to my brother's house, you ask questions about what he was doin' six years ago, who he knew . . ." He shrugged, spread his hands, and narrowed his eyes, looking around the room like maybe somebody could explain all this craziness to him. "What the fock, man?"

Dehan echoed the shake of his head. "Explain to me how that is any of your goddamn business."

"How is it my business? How is it *my* business? It's my business because I busted my balls dragging my brother and me out of the fockin' sewer so we could live like respectable citizens. We left all that shit behind, you understand me? But *hijos de puta* like you ain't about to let us move on and live in peace. No! You keep hunting us down like dogs, framin' us for every fockin' deal and murder you can't solve, hanging *your* fockin' crimes on us. You got a cold case you can't solve? That's okay, hang it on the fockin' Camacho brothers! You got a dead body you can't explain, because your cops are too fockin' stupid? Don't worry, hang it on the Camacho boys. Huh?"

"Stop," I said. "You're breaking my heart. They were good boys. They never disemboweled anyone unless they really had to. Give me a break, Julio. Who the hell do you think you're talking to, Little Red Riding Hood? I've seen what happens to guys who upset you and your brother, so quit the big victim act!"

Dehan leaned back in her chair and rested her ankle on her knee. "You want to know why we were talking to Feliciano? I'll tell you. Because we connected you and your brother to the Redferns, and to the kids. You spent twenty years dodging the bullet, Julio. But it's catching up with you, and Amy and Charlie were two kills too many."

He studied her a long time with no expression on his face. Then he turned to look at me for a while, like he was reading a page of text. Finally, he drew a deep breath and looked away, up at the ceiling and the walls.

"Do you know, Carmen, what the most valuable commodity in the world is?"

"Look, Julio, if I want philosophy, I'll read the Dalai Lama, don't fucking philosophize at me."

"I am serious. It ain't philosophy. It is a commercial reality."

She spread her hands. "Oil, coke, heroin. Go ahead, amaze me."

He didn't smile. He gazed at the guns on the table. "The most valuable commodity in the world is violence. Whoever controls the violence controls everything." He pointed at her. "You got the full weight of the U.S. law behind you, so why you need that piece under your arm? And tell me something else, what is U.S. law worth, if it is not backed up by the threat of extreme violence? Law without violence is just rules, that any *chulo* can piss on. Whoever controls the violence controls everything: he has the power, he makes the law, he takes the money, he sets the price." He looked back at the guns on the table. "Who do you think controls the violence here, Carmen?"

She made a face like she was weighing up the odds. "Given that you and your boys are a bunch of *maricones*, I'd say we do. But more important than that, Julio, is that maybe you were able to hide the deaths of two unknown kids for six years out in the wilds of Iowa, but given the report I sent my chief this evening before we went out, if I don't call in tomorrow morning, you're going to have not just the NYPD crawling all over you and your boys, you'll have the bureau crawling all over your ass too, like ants at a honey fest. And believe me, Julio, the federal government controls the violence, and they would just *love* to deploy some of it on you. So I would think very carefully before you reach for that weapon."

He nodded a couple of times, like he was agreeing with some internal dialogue. He gave a small sigh through his nose and turned to me.

"All your family are dead." He gestured at Dehan with his head. "This woman is your wife. You care about her? You looked pretty close comin' into the parking lot just now." He didn't wait for me to answer. He turned to Dehan. "You? You still got family. You got uncles, aunts, cousins. Your cousin Rachel is married to that nice guy who works at the bank. They thinking of having a baby sometime soon? You know, really, family is a blessing."

I said, "Stop." He raised an eyebrow at me. It was as close as he had come to an expression since we'd come in. "We get the threats. We can't call off the investigation, you know that as well as we do. But we can do a deal. Give us a fall guy. Finger the trigger men who shot Amy and Charlie. We'll take them down and pull the investigation away from you and Feliciano."

He snorted and curled his lip. "Chickenshit. You don't set no fockin' terms here. You back off. I don't wanna hear no more about fockin' Redferns, Pamela Albright or Amy an' focking Charlie. You back away or people gonna start getting hurt." He paused a moment. "You know? Is a long time since I gutted a woman. It's nice. You wanna watch?"

"You made your point, Julio. Enough."

"You want we should do it now?"

"Stop, before this gets out of hand. The investigation goes on. If we die, somebody else will pick it up, and you will be right in the frame. So the best thing for everybody is if you give us a fall guy. Name the guy who shot Amy and Charlie. You know as well as we do that we'll find the DNA, and if he's in the system, we'll get him. If we catch him, the DA will offer him immunity. But if you hand him over to us, you can take out insurance. Be smart, Julio. Don't be an asshole."

Dehan didn't wait for an answer. She stood and leaned over the table so her face was just inches from Camacho's. I could see madness in his eyes, and the boys were eyeing the Glocks on the table. Her voice when she spoke was steady and quiet.

"You think you control the violence, Julio, but you don't. You're just more reckless and careless about how you use it. You can kill me, you can kill Stone, you can torture us and chop us into little pieces to feed to your children. The bottom line is, it won't make any difference. The State just doesn't care. It will keep coming, throwing more men, more guns, more armored vehicles, more choppers at you—there is no limit, Julio. They won't stop until they get you. And then they will crush you. Think about it. Ours is the only deal you're going to get."

I stood. She smiled at him. "You got my number, call me."

We pushed out of the bar, and Gustavo and Nestor, the Brain and the Beast, went back in. Dehan walked fast to reception. The spotty receptionist looked nervous. She reached across the counter with her right arm, grabbed him by the scruff of his neck, and pulled him to her. With her left, she shoved her badge in his face. "What room is the guy with the greasy hair in?"

He squeaked, "Two sixteen."

She ran. I ran after her. We ran up the stairs and down the corridor to our room. There she unlocked the door and we pushed through. She was already on the phone as she pulled off her jacket. I watched her switch on her laptop and sit, mouthing at me, "Get the chief!"

"What for?"

"No time! Just do it!" Then she was talking into the phone. "Bob! Did you get the chief . . . ? No, okay, never mind. Listen to me, we are going to have to bend the rules here a little. I'll take full responsibility . . . I know, Bob, but there are lives on the line here, mine included." She pulled the cell away from her ear, thumbing the screen. "These are the numbers, ready?"

She dictated a series of four cell phone numbers, then went on. "Also, the landline at room two sixteen, the Cobblestone Hotel, Vinton, Iowa. You are on the clock, pal. We have a couple of minutes. Connect me up . . ." She stared at the screen of her laptop. "Okay, I'm up. You're the best . . . Yeah, you too. Get on it!" She hung up.

I said, "Dehan, what the hell are you doing?"

She grinned at me. "When I went to the can, I collected my

cell from reception. Then I called Bob, you know, the tech from the crime scene department? I told him to contact the super and get authorization to tap these phones. He hasn't got it yet, but we are out of time, Stone."

"That's an illegal tap, Dehan!"

"Only if they find out."

"And how the hell did you get their numbers?"

"When I leaned over and gave Camacho a taste of Carmen Dehan attitude, I cloned his phone with mine."

"Sweet Jesus, Dehan..."

It was like she hadn't heard me. "So what happens next, we cannot use as evidence in court. As far as the NYPD and the court system is concerned, we do not tap their phones until we get authorization from a judge. But, I am damn curious to see what he does next, and who he talks to."

I was shaking my head. "Dehan, what has gotten into you? You're breaking the law! You're a cop, for crying out loud!"

Before she could answer, we heard a buzzing from the laptop, then ringing, and after a moment, a sleepy voice said, "*Si, quien llama?*"

"*Cesar, soy Julio. Siento llamarle tan tarde. Escúcheme, Creo que tenemos un problema.*"

Dehan said, "He says they have a problem."

"*Que problema, pues?*"

"*Dos detectives del departamento de Nueva York estan metiendo las narices donde no deben, vamos a tener que eliminarles.*"

"*Como quiere hacerlo?*"

"*Mejor me manda vos el Sicario. Que sea de fiar, y eficaz.*"

"*Lo mando llamar a Méjico, pues?*"

"*Si, mejor.*"

"*Que instrucciones le doy?*"

"*Ya se los doy yo. Que venga con la entrega el Jueves, con el vuelo a Beyerville. Yo estaré en el Rancho Beyer.*"

"*Okay, jefe. Ya lo llamo ahora. Chao.*"

"*Chao.*"

The line went dead. She remained frozen, staring at the screen. I waited. Finally, I sat on the bed and said, "You want to tell me what they said?"

She looked up at me, searching my face.

"They're making a drop on Thursday. Some kind of shipment, I'd have to guess coke or heroin. A plane is coming in over the border to Beyerville. I think that's Arizona, on the border, right?"

I nodded.

She went on. "They have a ranch down there. So this Cesar is bringing *el sicario* over from Mexico in the same delivery."

"*El sicario?*"

"It means the assassin. Julio is going to meet him there to give him his instructions."

"What instructions?"

"To kill us, you and me."

I went cold inside.

Then she gave a strained laugh. "Looking on the bright side, at least we're safe till Thursday, right?"

I gave a small, humorless laugh. "Dehan, we call in backup. This is a major, federal operation now. It's not just Amy and Charlie and trying to prove they're connected to Feliciano Camacho. This is a major drug delivery, and an international assassin targeting U.S. law enforcement. You proved your point and you made the connection."

She stood and crossed the room, looking out at the small, scattered lights of Vinton. I said, "What the hell has gotten into you, Dehan? We have to call in backup!"

"It's not that simple, Stone."

"What do you mean, not that simple? How much simpler can it be?"

She turned to face me but avoided my eye. "Well, for a start, Bob's job is on the line."

I sighed noisily. She went on:

"And so is mine, for that matter."

"What got into you?"

She flared suddenly. "If I hadn't done it, Stone, neither of us would know that there was an assassin on his way to eliminate us! Would that be a preferable situation? Huh?"

"No, of course not, but we have a responsibility, Dehan! We are officers of the law!"

"Great! We'll die, but we won't have broken the rules!"

"Stop it!"

"Fine! But you stop it too! I've seen you break the rules when you thought it was right—more than once!—so stop lecturing me! I know these scumbags and I know what they are capable of, and I *knew* that we needed to hear what Julio was going to do next. You don't want any part of it, that's fine! Go back to New York!"

I went and took hold of her shoulders. "Dehan, stop . . . Nobody is going anywhere. It's done now. We'll have to deal with it. But stop going off at the deep end, will you?"

She nodded. "Okay."

"What is it with this case, Dehan?"

"Nothing! What do you mean? Nothing . . . Why would you ask that?"

"Dehan, I am not blind. You knew the Camachos' life story like you'd memorized it. You are too emotionally invested in this case. This, what you've done tonight . . ." I shook my head. "It was wrong, Dehan!"

She rubbed her face with her hands, then placed them on my chest. "You're right. Of course you're right. But not now, Stone. We need to get some rest. We'll talk in the morning, okay?"

I held her a moment, looking into her eyes. "Okay, but we talk in the morning. This has got out of hand."

"Okay!" She nodded, then repeated more softly, "Okay . . ."

FOURTEEN

I was awoken by Dehan sitting up. Dim gray light was filtering through the window. She had her back half turned to me, reached out with her left hand, and patted my face and my arm, like she was groping in the dark.

"Morning, dear," she said in a groggy voice. "Race you to the shower."

After that, she walked unsteadily to the bathroom. The loud hiss of water followed, accompanied by some loud groaning, which might have been relief, then a loud squeal, then a sigh of pleasure. After five minutes, the noises stopped. Two minutes after that, she stepped out, wrapped in a big white towel, with her wet hair hanging loose down her back. She was grinning.

"Was I noisy?"

"Yes."

"Hot, cold, hot, cold. Really wakes you up."

"So I heard."

"Why are you sleeping in the bed, dressed?"

"Perhaps you don't remember, the Camachos are borrowing an assassin from the Sinaloa Cartel to eliminate us. I thought it might be smart to stay alert as you had passed out."

"You were protecting me? That's sweet."

She was still smiling. I reached under the pillow and pulled out her Glock to show her. "Just as well. You were out for the count."

"Go shower, Galahad. We have a busy day."

When I came out ten minutes later, drying my hair, she was dressed and on the phone, sitting on the chair with her boots crossed on the table beside her laptop. Her voice sounded dead.

". . . Yeah, I'm sorry about that, sir. I thought you'd be up by this time of the morning . . . Seven thirty. I've been up for over an hour, I guess I kind of lost track . . . Yes, sir. I'll try not to, sir."

I groaned silently and started to dress, listening to her as she went on with that ill-repressed insolence in her voice.

"Sir? May I explain? Only, perhaps we'll finish sooner . . . Yes, sir. I will certainly try to be aware of my tone. Thank you, sir. We got back to the hotel last night and Julio Camacho was here . . . Yes, sir. Julio Camacho was at the hotel. With five of his men. He asked us to join him and they had three automatic weapons and a revolver set out on the table in front of us. He told us that we should desist from our investigation or they would kill me and my family."

I pulled on my pants, and as I was buttoning my shirt, she stood, paced the floor a moment, leaned her ass on the table with the phone to her ear, and rolled her eyes.

"Yes, sir, I realize that is very serious, especially for me and my family. So, sir? We overheard some conversation . . ."

She went very still and very quiet. I watched her as I laced up my boots. She winced silently a couple of times.

"He told you, did he, sir? Sir, that wasn't his fault. I should take responsibility for that . . . That is very big of you. Yes, sir."

She walked away to the window. I heard her say, "Yes, sir, thank you, sir," a couple of times in a small voice and hang up.

I said, "Bob ratted on you?"

"Son of a bitch!"

"He did the right thing and you know it."

She turned to face me. "*Son of a bitch!*"

"He probably saved your life, Dehan, my life, and your family's lives too."

"Shut up."

"So what's the deal?"

"He's letting us off with a caution this time because of the value of the information we got. Bob was listening in and went straight to him with it. Woke him up."

"He did the right thing."

"I know. Stop saying that. The chief said next time, he'll throw the book at us."

"There won't be a next time, Dehan!"

She sighed. "I know."

"So what about Camacho?"

"The superintendent is going to talk to the Phoenix FBI field office and get back to us. He figures this should be a fed case now. That means it will be their baby and *if* we get to go along, we probably go along for the ride."

I shrugged. "For the bust, but we still get to interrogate them about Charlie and Amy, right? And that is our interest, after all. And you still get credit for busting the thing open." She curled her lip, but before she could say anything, I added, "Plus, we get to go home alive, which in my book is a good thing."

She sighed again, then smiled. "Your problem, Stone, is that you always focus on the small details."

We went downstairs and Dehan went to the reception desk. The spotty kid was off duty and there was a blond girl with freckles and a ponytail.

"You had some guests arrive last night. Four men in suits. Room two sixteen." She showed the girl her badge and the girl smiled brightly at it. Dehan said, "They look like gangsters and they are. Are they still here?"

She gave her answer the intonation of a question. "They left real early?"

"What about the other two?"

The girl hesitated.

Dehan sighed. "Yeah, the little one with gelled hair and the big gorilla. Suits, shades, hard-asses."

"They haven't checked out yet. They're having breakfast."

We stepped out into the warm morning sunshine and started strolling toward the Jag. Dehan slipped on her aviators.

"I don't want to tell you what to do, Stone. But you need to be armed, as of now."

I nodded.

She went on. "And we need to get rid of these two jackasses. We can't go to Phoenix with them on our tail."

"Assuming we go."

She frowned at me like she didn't really understand what I'd said. "It's going to be a twenty-four-hour drive. I guess we could fly from Iowa City, but by the time we get there, book the flight, wait for the damn plane . . ."

"You want to drive to Arizona from Iowa. That has to be at least one and a half thousand miles, Dehan."

"I know, Stone. I just told you, it's twenty-four hours. But we don't leave a trail. I don't want to sit around in the airport like a couple of luminous dildos waiting to be spotted by Camacho's goons. And believe me, they are going to keep tabs on us every damn step of the way, so they can tell *el sicario* where we are when he arrives."

We arrived at the car and she rested her ass on the trunk.

We stared at each other for a moment. Finally, I nodded. "Okay. We need to shake these two and disappear. They have no idea we know about the shipment, so they have no reason to suspect we're headed for Phoenix. So we pack up our stuff, stick it in the trunk, do a couple of figure eights around the Iowa grid system, and take off west. They can eat our dust. We could even drop the Jag in Albuquerque and rent a nondescript car for the rest of the drive to Phoenix."

She stared at me for a long moment, chewing her bottom lip. Finally, she said, "Do me a favor, will you? Put your damned gun in your holster."

"What the hell is that supposed to mean?"

"Just do it, please."

I felt a stab of irritation, yanked open the passenger door, pulled open the glove compartment, and took out my Colt. I slipped it in my waistband, underneath my jacket, and slammed the door again. I glared at her over the roof. She was staring past me at the hotel. She spoke absently. "Don't be sensitive. We haven't time for that. Let's go pack our bags."

She started walking across the parking lot, taking long, fast strides, doing something with her phone as she went. I followed after her. I saw her put the phone to her ear as she reached the entrance porch and went back through the door into the reception hall. As I pushed in after her, she started talking like she was mad.

"*The Vince Wolowitz case?* What the hell for?"

I stopped, watching her. She started to pace, listening. She rolled her eyes, looked at me, gestured at the phone, and shrugged, then mouthed, *Start packing. Gimme five.*

As I climbed the stairs, she started to shout again. "You gotta be kidding me, sir! What possible reason . . . But *why*? *Why Wolowitz?*"

I went to our rooms thinking about the Vince Wolowitz case. It was a cold case, and one that I had suggested to Dehan when she had suggested the Redfern case. I figured the deputy inspector had informed Dehan he wanted us off the Redfern case and on the Wolowitz one. Maybe he thought, as I did, that she had some personal investment in the case, she was becoming a loose cannon, and he wanted to keep her out of harm's way. I knew how he felt: her behavior so far had been increasingly unpredictable.

I piled all her stuff in her bag, and then started packing my own. I put on my holster, slipped my weapon into it, and felt strangely uncomfortable.

Two minutes later, she appeared in the doorway.

"I paid the bill. You ready?"

"Sure. What's happening with the Wolowitz case?"

"Nah, nothing."

"I heard you . . ."

"Don't worry about it. C'mon! Let's go."

I followed her down the stairs and across the lobby.

"Dehan."

"Yes, Stone?"

She pushed through the glass door out into the parking lot and held the door for me as I went through. I said, "Slow down. What's going on?"

"I do that sometimes. I get all speedy. May I drive?" She held out her hand and gave a grin which she knew was disarming. I handed her the keys and she continued talking as she strode toward the car. "My uncle says I have ADHD. Personally, I think he is wrong. You know why I think he is wrong, Stone? C'mon! Keep up!"

This last was shouted as she ran the last thirty feet to the Jag. I was aware she had steered the conversation away from Wolowitz and I was wondering why. She opened the trunk and threw in her bag, then stood bouncing slowly on her knees and grinning at me while she waited for me to catch up.

I started to say, "Why . . ." but she cut in.

"Because I think people say other people have ADHD . . ." I dropped in my bag and she slammed the trunk closed. "When they just can't keep up." She climbed in behind the wheel and I got in the other side. She fired up the big, old bruiser, gunned the engine, and made the tires complain as we screamed out of the parking lot. "Me," she said over the roar of the engine, "I like to do things speedy."

As we pulled out of the lot, I saw Gustavo and Nestor, aka Einstein and Godzilla, loping across the lot toward their Audi. We cruised down West 8th Street and she had her eye on the mirror all the way.

I said, "Dehan, cut the crap and tell me about Wolowitz."

"Crap?" she said absently. "What crap? My uncle really does think I have ADHD." She turned left onto 1st Avenue and started moving north, past the Ron-Da-Voo, where we had spent the night before, toward the sheriff's office. "But you must have noticed by now, Stone," she said, still with her eye on the mirror, "that I have in fact exceptional powers of concentration."

"Yeah, and that's why I am wondering what the hell you're playing at."

I turned and looked out the back window. The Audi was following us, but keeping its distance.

"What's going on, Dehan?"

We passed the sheriff's office and she accelerated onto the bridge that spanned the Cedar River, surging from 25 MPH to 70 in a couple of seconds. Then it was a drag race. Almost two miles of straight road across the river basin, with lakes and dense, marshy woodland on either side.

After a mile and three quarters, she began to slow. I looked out the back window and saw the Q7 at least a mile back. She dropped to third and made the tires complain again as she turned down a dusty track that wound in among the woods. Now it was impossible to see if they were following us because of the vast cloud of dust we were kicking up behind us. I snapped, "If you're trying to lose them, you just advertised where we are to the whole damn county!"

"Try," she said, and she said it not unpleasantly, "not to talk or think, for just ten minutes, and let me do my stuff, please."

We came to a fork in the track. Here she slowed right down and eased her way across a wooden bridge that spanned the river onto a narrow spit of land which protruded from the far bank. She rolled along the spit and then backed along a rough track in among the trees. There she killed the engine and got out.

I got out after her. I was beginning to get mad. "Okay, I haven't spoken or thought for three minutes. That's as good as it gets. Now tell me what the hell is going on and what you are doing."

She was standing a few yards from the car, watching the gap

in the trees where you could just make out the spit of land and the river. She glanced at me and shook her head.

"It's because I am a woman, isn't it?"

"*What?*"

"No, no, deny it," she went on absently. "If I were Holmes, you would be all full of admiration and talking about my intellectual vanity without doubting for a moment..."

"*Dehan!*"

"What?" She frowned at me irritably. "First, they see the dust and realize we took the track. They think we are trying to shake them. They follow us. Then, once the dust has drifted away, they see the little bridge in among the trees. They figure we crossed the bridge and they think they have us trapped..."

"And they haven't?"

"Shut up."

She walked back to the Jag and sat on the hood, still watching the gap in the trees. A moment later, the Audi nosed through, rolled forward a few feet, and came to a halt. The doors opened, and Nestor and Gustavo climbed out, looking like the mice who just found the cheese but have a feeling something is wrong with it. They were about fifty feet from us. Dehan said, "Why are you following us?"

Gustavo, the smart one, did a little knee dance. "What? You own the roads now. We can't drive where we like?"

"One more time, asshole. It's an offense to stalk an officer of the law. Did you know that? Start talking before I cuff you. Why are you following us?"

He did more knee dancing and shrugged his shoulders. "We were just takin' a drive, Popo, right, Nestor?"

"Down here? Seriously? In an Audi Q7?" She stood. "C'mon, hands on your head and get down on your face."

Nestor had started frowning. Gustavo was momentarily paralyzed. Dehan reached behind her back for her cuffs, and I reached for my piece. My mind was racing, trying to anticipate what Dehan thought she was doing.

Then there was no time to think. Dehan had taken two steps and was saying loudly, "On your face! On the ground! Both of you!" But Gustavo was not getting on the ground. He was not raising his hands to his head. Instead, he was reaching behind his back. He seemed to move in slow motion. Nestor was watching him. I saw him blink. And now he too was reaching behind his back. I swore profusely, shouting at them to freeze, but unable to decide in that fraction of a second which one to line up. Both had their weapons in their hands; both were swinging them around on Dehan.

Then there was a strange noise, like snapping branches, and Gustavo seemed to hesitate and frown. Then he looked down at his chest. It was less than a second. Then two more cracks. Gustavo fell backward and hit the grass with a soft thump. Nestor sighed, got down on his knees, grunted softly, said, "Ay . . ." and lay down.

I stared, struggling to comprehend what I had just seen. She checked the bodies, then inspected the grass behind them. Finally, she walked over to me, examining my face with a frown as she approached. She said, "Through and through and landed in the water. You need to talk about what just happened?"

I stared at her for a long time before answering. "You murdered them, Dehan."

She shook her head. "No. I gave them a choice."

"But you *knew* they wouldn't take it. You knew they'd go for their guns."

Her eyes narrowed. "I knew no such damned thing, Stone. I knew there was a risk, because when you investigate the likes of the Camachos, there is always a risk. And the risk was no higher today than it was last night or yesterday. The difference was today, I confronted them and demanded they obey the goddamn law. Which is what we are supposed to do, Stone. And they chose to try and kill me, so I defended myself."

I shook my head. "But you provoked this situation, Dehan. You didn't need to do this!"

Her face flushed and she scowled. "Come on, Stone! Do you know how many lives the Camachos destroy every year? Do you know how many young girls they kidnap, rape, and force into prostitution?" She stepped toward me, pointing past my head toward Arizona. "We have a chance to take that asshole down. I have no time to pussyfoot around with legal niceties. They had a choice, the county jail or try to kill me. They made the wrong choice. Now if you want to sit here and mourn their civil liberties, be my guest. While you're at it, you might mourn all the lives they destroyed while they were enjoying those civil liberties. Meantime, I need to get to Arizona. So now *you* have a choice: reconnect your balls and come with me, or drive me somewhere where I can get a goddamn car!"

I held out my hand. "Give me the keys."

FIFTEEN

As she handed them over, her phone rang.

"Dehan!"

She glanced at me and put it on speaker.

"... spoken to the Phoenix field office. So, they have control of the operation. They have agreed to have you and Stone on the team, but strictly as observers. They run the show. You understand that, Carmen?"

"Yes, sir."

"You get to Phoenix, you report to Detective Brad Tucker. Be there by tomorrow. He will debrief you and give you your instructions. I have informed him that you need to interrogate Camacho and his men regarding the Redfern murders, so you will have full access to them."

"Thank you, sir. Sir?"

"Yes, Carmen?"

"There was an incident. Two of Camacho's men followed us. We confronted them and attempted to arrest them. They drew their weapons, and we were forced to defend ourselves. The two men are dead."

We heard the sound of a loud sigh. "This really complicates matters. Where did this happen? Are you with the bodies?"

"I'm sending you the coordinates."

"You must contact the local sheriff's office immediately. There will have to be an inquiry. I want a written report from you and Stone as soon as you get to Phoenix."

"Sir, can I suggest that you contact the Feds again, whoever you spoke to before, explain the development, and get them to contact the sheriff of Benton County and explain to him that we are cooperating in a federal investigation . . . ?"

The inspector's voice came sharp over the phone. "Detective Dehan! The New York Police Department and the Federal Bureau of Investigation are not here for your convenience! You will follow procedure and . . ."

"Sir, forgive me, but it is imperative that we get to the Phoenix office immediately. The success of this operation hinges on our being able to talk to the team there. If the sheriff decides to hold us, it could be disastrous. It could cost lives . . ."

Another loud sigh. "Very well, Carmen. But I am not happy about this!"

"No, sir, neither am I."

She hung up and we stood a long while, looking at each other. Finally I said, "That easy."

"Get off your high horse, Stone. They were tailing us on behalf of a drug cartel who intend to assassinate us. I went to arrest them, which was the proper thing to do. They resisted arrest and tried to kill me. I defended myself."

"But you deliberately lured them here, Dehan!"

"What? I should try to arrest two dangerous killers at the hotel? Or in the middle of Vinton, where they can grab hostages and get innocent people killed? I'm sick of having this conversation with you, Stone. Are you in or out?"

I thought about it for a moment. "Okay, Dehan, but you and me are going to have a conversation about exactly what this case means to you. Because it is blurring lines in your mind that were never blurred before."

Her cheeks flushed. "Yeah? Maybe you just see lines where there are none. Are we done?"

We waited in silence for the sheriff to show. When he did, he didn't look happy, but he'd been told the Feds had jurisdiction and he must do no more than preserve the crime scene. We told him we'd send him copies of our reports and we left, headed southwest toward Vinton and Des Moines. We drove in silence for a good half hour. But as we turned onto the IA-330, she started to talk.

"Look, Stone, leave aside that I am your wife and I am crazy about you. What's important right now is I like you and I respect you. I always have, even before we met. I like your integrity, and I like the fact that you stand by what you believe. That's why I asked to be partnered with you in the first place."

"*What?*"

"Never mind that now," she said, as though she was talking to an invisible person riding beside us. "I get that the issue is not *who* I shot. They were bad people—maybe you don't know just *how* bad—but that is not the issue. The issue is that we stand for the Rule of Law. And if the Rule of Law is to mean anything, then it has to apply to Nestor and Gustavo as much as to Mr. and Mrs. Brown, who have never knowingly broken a law in their lives."

I looked at her and raised an eyebrow. "You *asked* to be partnered with me?"

She ignored me. She still spoke to the invisible guy outside the window. "Believe me, I do get that, and I believe in it." Finally, she turned to look at me. "But you know what the problem is? Shall I tell you what it is? That crime syndicates are becoming as rich as countries. And while good guys like you are busy observing the letter and the spirit of the law, people like the Camachos are becoming *billionaires* and retiring to Englewood with private armies of assassins; and they use you and your honorable legal system to do it. Because while you are busy giving them the full protection of the law, they are busy buying and murdering officials, officers, cops, and judges from Vancouver to Mexico City.

"And in the end, Stone, you, and good men and women like you, can sit and watch that long procession of murdered corpses—fathers, mothers, children, young girls, two hundred and fifty thousand minimum in Mexico alone, not counting the tens of thousands outside Mexico—you can watch the long processions of young girls addicted to heroin and forced into prostitution, you can watch the *millions* of lives destroyed by the drugs; and as you watch them all shuffle by, you can watch the likes of Julio Camacho grow fat and rich and powerful on all that suffering, and you can console yourself that you gave those *bastards* the same protection that you gave Mr. and Mrs. Brown, who actually deserved it."

I didn't say anything. I didn't know how to answer her. But she didn't give me a chance anyway. She plowed right on. "And the thing is, Stone, I agree with you. But what do you do when a system you created to protect justice starts enabling *injustice*? Is the principle of the matter more important than the people whose lives are being destroyed?"

"Dehan, stop! Where do we end up if everybody starts thinking like you?"

"I don't know, Stone! And that is the point! Because I am not concerned with the principles of the matter. I am not concerned with the philosophical niceties. I am worried about Maria Ibañez, aged fifteen, who was abducted from her home in Ciudad Juárez and is right now, in this moment, while we are discussing philosophy, being forced into prostitution. She is a *child*! I am worried about the kids, the individual children, Tommy, Pete, Jane, who will be seduced into taking the crack and heroin that the Camachos are bringing in, whose teeth will fall out by the time they are twenty-one, who will die of overdoses before they ever get a chance to enjoy the Rule of Law which *you* protect so vigorously for the Camachos!" By now she was almost shouting. "I don't *know*," she half yelled, "what the answer is to your philosophical problem! But I *do* know that the system we are sworn to defend *does not work when it is under this kind of attack*!" She was quiet for a moment, breathing hard, then added, "And I am more concerned about protecting the people than the principles!"

I looked out through the windshield at the vast, flat expanse of land, under the vast sky, where a few clouds were beginning to gather. What trees there were were turning copper in the morning sun, lost amid the endless golden fields. The fall was closing in.

Eventually, I said, "I am not a philosopher, Dehan, and I don't hide behind theories so that I can ignore individuals. I have seen my share of suffering people. But if we don't respect the system we have created to protect those individuals, what do we have?" I shook my head. "We have vigilantes taking the law into their own hands. We have cops shooting people on the streets because they don't like the way they dress or walk. Before long, we have lynchings and mob justice."

She seemed not to hear, keeping her eyes on the passing, glaring landscape. After a while, when I had almost forgotten that I had spoken, she turned and said suddenly, "I agree. I agree with you. We agree. But now answer me this: What do we do when that system collapses? And don't give me theoretical bullshit, Stone. This is not a rhetorical question. I am asking you . . ." She pointed an angry finger at me. "You, who are passing judgment on what I did back at the river, you tell me what we do when the system breaks down and starts protecting the guilty instead of the innocent."

I sighed. "Well, we don't take the law into our own hands . . ."

"Bromides and clichés. Don't tell me what we don't do, that's no damn use to anybody. Tell me what we *do* do."

Again I had no answer.

I took the I-35 out of Des Moines toward Kansas, and the landscape began to change and the hills began to roll among patches of woodland and tall evergreens. Dehan opened her window and the air whipped her hair across her face. She fingered it away from her sunglasses, then pushed her shades up on her head and squinted at me, raising her voice above the air battering at the window.

"Last night, you slept next to me and took my gun so that you could defend me if those two guys broke in. Those same two guys. What would you have done if Nestor and Gustavo had come in and tried to rape and kill me?"

"That is hypothetical, Dehan . . ."

"Bullshit! Would you have killed them if necessary?"

"Of course I would!"

"Well, here's a news flash, Stone, you don't get to cherry-pick! This killing is okay because I was defending my partner. That killing was not okay because my partner led them into the woods . . ."

"You cannot compare a personal threat with . . ."

"They are *always* a personal threat to *somebody*, Stone! And that is what you do not get! Just because it is not personal to *you*, does not mean it is not personal!"

After that, we fell silent.

We eventually stopped for a late lunch at a gas station in Kearney, outside Kansas. We hadn't spoken for about an hour, maybe more. As I chewed on my plastic burger, I watched her face. She was aware I was watching, and I could see some of the anger had drained away.

"What has made this so personal for you, Dehan?"

She shook her head and gave a small sigh. "Before I met you, before I decided to be a cop even, I had one overriding passion in my life. There was just one thing I wanted to do. Avenge my mother and my father. My family, my neighborhood, my whole world was terrorized and controlled by Mick Harragan, and the people who gave Mick power. There were several, but chief among them were the Chupacabras and the Camacho brothers."[1]

I sat back in my chair and sighed. "Your parents . . ."

She shook her head. "You know what happened to them. But this had nothing to do with Mick, and it didn't affect me directly. This was a neighbor of mine, lived a few doors down, I didn't

---

1. See *And Ace and a Pair*.

even like her much. But she was raped and her boyfriend was stabbed. He lived, but he was broken, and they broke up afterwards. She ended up getting sucked into that world and became a hooker. The guys who did it were probably Chupacabras, but it was never proved. All the witnesses were too scared to testify, as was she, so the case got shelved."

I frowned. "And that made you so passionate about this case . . .?"

She shook her head. "No, Stone, it's what I keep trying to explain to you. When Maria got raped and I saw how everybody was too terrified to testify, it was like an echo of what happened to my dad and my mum. It made me realize that our system favors the most violent members of society. Julio Camacho was right in what he said, violence is the most valuable commodity there is. And I swore to myself that I would wage war on these people, one way or another . . ." She hesitated. "When I joined the cops, my intention was to use the system to hunt down these bastards and kill them. I asked Captain Peralta to team me up with you because you were the best, and when she told me you'd be doing cold cases, that suited me to the ground."

I was frowning at her. "You *planned* to be a vigilante?"

She nodded. "Yes, Stone, and it was because of you that I never did. You gave me something else to live for."

"And this case . . ."

"This was one of the cases I had an interest in. Because I was sure the Camachos were involved, I was sure there was a tie in with the cartel . . ."

"Why didn't you tell me?"

She gave a small, dry laugh. "Asked the man who never talks about his early life or his family."

I puffed out my cheeks and blew. She gave a sad smile and shook her head. "In any case, that is not important. What is important is that there were no reasons that were personal *to me*! That was what I learned. Moral justice is *always* personal.

Murder, rape, the destruction of a person's life—they are not worse because they happen to somebody *you* happen to love."

She leaned across the table and pointed at me. "Listen to me. I knew we had to get rid of them so we could get to Arizona. I knew we had to do that fast. We didn't have time to piss around, so I took a calculated risk. I drew them into a situation where they would have to make a choice: allow themselves to be arrested or try to kill us. They made the wrong choice, and I took them out. I will not mourn their deaths, because the world is a better place without them. But I will mourn you if you turn around in Phoenix and go home."

She leaned back in her chair and took a pull on her coffee, then held out her right hand, palm up. I frowned at it. "My turn to drive. You do the night driving this time."

It was a long, tedious drive. At first, we tried taking it in turns to sleep while the other drove. But the long, straight, dark roads through Oklahoma and New Mexico were hypnotic, and we found we needed to keep each other awake by talking. Finally, at three in the morning, we pulled into the Sky City Travel Center Casino and Hotel, slept four hours, and at seven o'clock the next morning set out with a thermos of strong black coffee and a couple of donuts.

We were about three hundred and seventy miles from the FBI field office, so I hit the gas and kept it between eighty and a hundred and ten most of the way. So we entered the Deer Valley area of north Phoenix at about eleven that morning. As we approached down the Black Canyon Freeway and turned into Happy Valley Road, Dehan called the field office and was transferred to our designated contact on the team. He told us his name was D.C. and he would alert the gate and meet us in the parking lot.

The field office is a large complex which sits on the intersection of East Deer Valley Road and North Seventh Street. Technically it's inside the city of Phoenix, but sitting at the intersection, at close to a hundred degrees under the glaring sun, all I could see in any direction, besides the five-story box of concrete and glass, was desert: hot dust and scrub as far as the eye could reach.

The lights turned green; we crossed the intersection and turned into the gates. We were buzzed through and saw a man waiting for us. He didn't look like an FBI agent. He looked like a university professor approaching retirement. He was bald on top, with a band of unkempt, sandy hair across the back of his head, and an easy, amiable smile. He was wearing Timberland boots, blue jeans, and a University of Arizona sweatshirt.

We shook hands through the window and he waved at Dehan, then pointed ahead. "Sharp left will take you into the parking garage. I'll catch you up there."

Inside the cavernous darkness, I found a spot near the elevator and killed the engine. As we climbed out, I saw him, a small, black silhouette warping in through the entrance against the fierce glare of the sun outside. He raised a hand and his voice echoed.

"Welcome to Phoenix! Hell of a drive you did there. You must be exhausted." As he approached, he turned steadily from a black silhouette to a slightly out-of-breath man. "D.C., I'm your point of contact on the team." He slapped me on the shoulder. "Let me take you upstairs and introduce you to Brad and the guys."

The elevator took us to the second floor, and we stepped out into a broad, busy area with a lot of desks and cubicles. Over on the left, there was a series of doors into conference rooms and offices. He pointed at one of them, and we crossed the open space.

He pushed through the door, and we found ourselves in a functional briefing room. There was a big, athletic man with very short hair and deep-set blue eyes sitting on a desk against the far right wall. He was wearing cowboy boots, a white shirt, and a shoulder holster. Sitting on a chair with her back to the window was a girl who looked Chinese or Korean. She smiled as we came in. Opposite her, by the door, was a young guy in his midtwenties with sandy hair and a sandy moustache. He also smiled. D.C. closed the door behind us and said, "Guys, meet Detectives Carmen Dehan and John Stone. John, Carmen, please meet

Angel, she is in charge of logistics. This is Randy, nobody knows what he does, but he does it with computers and he tells us he's good at it. And sitting on the desk over there is Brad. He's the team leader and supervising agent."

We all said hello to each other and Dehan and I were invited to sit. D.C. was dispatched to get coffee, and Brad examined us a moment with narrowed eyes.

"You must be real tired, and I bet you'd give just about anything for a rest right about now. Thing is . . ."

He didn't get any further. Dehan cut him short.

"Brad, excuse me interrupting, but it may save us time in the long run. We're here to work, not rest. I am sure D.C. is a really nice guy, but we don't want to be fobbed off. We've been busting our asses on this investigation, and we do not want to be sidelined. So my request is, debrief us and let's get to work."

He grinned at the floor, then lifted his grin and showed it to Dehan. "Okay, I appreciate your directness, Carmen. Here's the deal. It's the only deal there is. I am in charge of this operation, and I am taking with me the people I know and trust. Why? Because this has not been short notice, it has been *no* notice. It is a very dangerous operation, and there is a very high probability that people will get injured—or killed. Now, my number one priority is that those people are not *my* people.

"Carmen, if I had a month to train with you and work with you, I would be very happy to put you on my team, *if* I thought you were good. I haven't got that luxury. Today is Wednesday and we hit the ranch tomorrow. So, like I said, I am taking the team I know and trust."

She raised an eyebrow at him. "Is this your team?"

"No. And you will not meet my team. I will debrief you. I will be *very* grateful for all the information and advice you can give us regarding Julio Camacho and what is going down tomorrow. *We* will carry out the operation, D.C. will take care of you, and then you will be given full access to everyone and anyone we arrest, so that *you* can interrogate them. That's how it is and that is final."

She sat nodding at the floor. Then she looked at the walls and the ceiling. Finally she gave him a smile that was devoid of anything resembling friendliness. He was a nice guy, a responsible leader, and a good agent, and she wanted to string him up and gut him right there, in the briefing room.

SIXTEEN

There followed a very stressful hour during which Dehan didn't so much brief Brad and his two agents as lecture them on Julio Camacho, the Chupacabras, and how dangerous the Sinaloa Cartel was. At least three times, Brad stopped her. The last time, he said, "Detective Dehan, we live with the Sinaloa on our doorstep. We know better than anybody what they are like. We don't need a lecture on how dangerous they are. Please confine yourself to the facts."

By the time we had finished, the facts proved to be precious few. Brad looked at Angel, Randy, and D.C. in turn and said, "So in fact, we know little more than when the New York field office contacted us yesterday. We know the location, we know it's a shipment, and we know that it will arrive by air with a *sicario*. We *don't* know how many men we are up against, we don't know what the shipment is or how big it is, we don't know what time it's arriving or if the aircraft will touch down at the ranch."

I saw Dehan's cheeks color. "That intel was the product of last-minute improvising in a high-risk situation while we were investigating a murder. I'm sorry if it doesn't meet your usual standards..."

"Detective Dehan!"

She stopped.

"Nobody is criticizing the intelligence, or the gathering of it. We all believe you did exceptional work. We are just assessing the risks." He turned to Angel. "We don't know how many men we are up against, so we will need maximum firepower. We must also have backup available, and air cover if necessary. Get onto that. We are on the clock. Randy, we need intel on aircraft coming into that area. We have taps on phones courtesy of Detective Dehan and Detective Stone, but let's see what else we can get at the ranch." Angel and Randy left.

Dehan drew breath, but I spoke before she could dig herself any deeper.

"Brad, we are both exhausted from driving, not just from Iowa, but a couple of days before that from New York to Vinton too. We would appreciate a few hours' rest. Meantime I, personally, would be really very grateful to you if you would consider a request?"

He knew what I was doing and smiled. "What's your request, John?"

"Detective Dehan and I both have experience with Julio and Feliciano Camacho going back many years. We have a . . ." I spread my hands. "A *feel* for them. Would you consider allowing us to come along as observers? In the event of something unexpected, we might be able to anticipate Julio's behavior better than most people, just because we know him so well."

He thought about it a moment, then smiled at Dehan, who didn't smile back. "You could learn something from your partner, Detective Dehan." He sighed. "Let me give it some thought. I'll let you know. But I need to make this point. We are tight, and we have good rapport. There is no room for ego-tripping in this team."

He said it to Dehan, who looked away and muttered, "Yeah, thanks."

"D.C. will look after you."

We followed D.C. out of the office and back across the big, busy room toward the elevators. "You'll be staying at my place. Kids have flown the nest so there's plenty of room, and Penny, that's my wife, she'll take good care of you while I'm not there."

We stepped into the elevator. He looked at Dehan's face as the door slid closed and laughed. "I can understand why you feel sore. I'm pretty sure I'd feel the same. In fact, I know I would have, back in the day. But look . . ." He gestured at me with his open hand. "Your suggestion seemed very reasonable to me. I'll do my best to persuade him when I get back. But if I know Brad, he's a real reasonable guy, and what you said made sense to him. I think he'll let you ride along, just so long as you don't try and go in with the guys."

The elevator came to a halt and we stepped out into the parking garage. It was dark, and our voices and our footsteps took on a strange, cavernous echo. I asked him: "You're not on the team?"

"No, I got injured pretty bad a few years back. Lucky to be alive, truth be told. So I push a pen these days. Your car is pretty recognizable. If they have a contract on you, I think it would make sense to leave it here. What do you say?"

I said it made sense, and a big Buick sedan flashed and bleeped from the darkness in the corner. We grabbed our stuff from the trunk of the Jag and transferred it to the Buick. After that, it was a twenty-minute drive through glaring desert from the field office to the suburb of Fountain Hills, to the east of Phoenix.

In New York, his house would have been palatial. It was a two-story Spanish villa shaded by tall palms and what looked to me like a jacaranda tree. Out front, there was a double garage and a desert garden with cacti and yucca. He parked the car by the sidewalk and led us around back, where there was a large pool and a paved terrace in the shade of the trees.

"Penny is usually out here by the pool in the afternoon," he said. But she wasn't. She was in the kitchen, making lemonade, and opened the back door to welcome us.

She was a woman who, in her late forties, was still attractive and had a good figure. She had blond hair tied up on her head; she wore a green bikini and a light, transparent floral housecoat. She and D.C. kissed affectionately and he introduced us. She kissed Dehan on the cheek without affection and shook my hand.

Then D.C. was slapping my shoulder and saying, "Okay, I'm leaving y'all in capable hands. I'll see you for dinner in a few hours."

He kissed his wife again and was gone.

"You guys must be pooped!"

She pushed the kitchen door open and held it for us while we went in. The kitchen was large and modern, with a terra-cotta floor and a dining table in the middle. She led us through to a broad hallway with a parquet floor and wooden stairs leading to the upper story. She spoke over her shoulder as she walked ahead of us. "I'll show you around once you've showered and rested. I have no idea where you've come from, but I know you've been driving all night, and I *know* Brad and Daryl have not shown you any mercy since you got here."

The landing divided into two passages that led to the right and left from the top of the stairs. She paused there and pointed to the right. "That's me and Daryl down there, and you two have this room here on the left. This pretty pink one . . ." She opened a door onto a very girly room with a spindly four-poster bed. ". . . used to be Alice's room. She's at college, so now it's yours! Make yourselves comfy. You have an en suite, she insisted on it! Come down when you're rested and I'll fix you some food."

We told her she was too generous. We closed the door, fell on the bed, and within thirty seconds, we were unconscious.

Something woke me up. I didn't sit up. I lay with my eyes closed, listening to the buzz of cicadas outside the window and the desultory slosh of water in the pool, where I figured somebody was swimming. After a while, I opened my eyes, half expecting Dehan to be sitting on the end of the bed, watching me. But she wasn't. I was alone.

I stood and went to the window. I could see the cool turquoise of the pool almost directly beneath me. The water warped and rippled as a body moved beneath it and exploded to the surface. It was Dehan. I searched for Penny, but she wasn't there.

I had a shower and went downstairs in jeans and bare feet. When I stepped outside, the terraced area around the pool was in the shade of the trees, but the glare and the heat from the sun were intense. There was a slosh of water, and Dehan's head emerged sodden from the brilliant turquoise, blowing spray and pushing her hair back from her face. She laid her arms on the salmon-pink slabs and almost smiled at me.

"You rested?"

I nodded. "I wish I had a bathing suit."

She shrugged. "I tore the legs off a pair of jeans. You could do the same."

"That's my Dehan. Where is Penny?"

"She went to the store."

She pulled herself out of the pool and stood gushing water from her cutoff jeans and an AC/DC T-shirt while she squeezed more out of her long hair. She looked somewhere between a street urchin and a Californian throwback to the '60s. There was a round garden table in the shade of a small cluster of palms. I sat in a canvas director's chair and watched her finish drying off. I realized I was smiling and wondered why. I was supposed to be mad at her.

She came and sat with me, across the table. "We should move to Arizona," she said. I didn't answer, and after a moment she looked at me. "You made up your mind?"

I looked her in the eye and was struck for the millionth time by how beautiful she was. And yet somehow, in that moment, I knew I could not be a party to an operation that deemed it acceptable to murder suspects. However much I loved her as a person, I could not be a party to law enforcement that decrees itself judge, jury, and executioner. I couldn't deny that I understood her arguments. She was passionate and articulate about them. And she was right. The system, as it stood, too often failed the victim and favored the ruthless, but that didn't mean that her answer was the right answer.

I nodded slowly. She must have read the answer in my face, because her cheeks colored and she looked away at the pool. "What are you going to do?"

I drummed my fingers on the table for a moment and looked where she was looking at the glare on the pool. I heard my voice as though it was somebody else's and wondered if I had lost my mind. I said, "You have to promise me, Dehan, no more vigilante bullshit."

She looked away, so I wouldn't see her smile. I said, "I am serious. For all your justifications, and I admit some of them make sense, I do not approve of what you did in Vinton. That is not the law we swore to uphold."

"Hey!" She turned to look at me. "The case will be closed within the week and the Camachos will be behind bars. Even if I wanted to shoot the son of a bitch, I probably wouldn't get the chance. Stop bleeding from your liberal heart. The issue won't even arise."

"Dehan? This is a deal . . ."

"Okay! Okay! I promise. Even if I get the chance, I promise not to shoot him in a form or manner not approved by the U.S.A. Bleeding Hearts Association." She raised an eyebrow at me. "Satisfied?"

"Not really, but for now it will have to do." I hesitated, feeling vaguely sick, feeling that something shapeless and nameless was coming between us. "Dehan, please don't trivialize this. I am serious. The day law enforcement starts executing people without trial is the day the Camachos of this world have won. So don't go down that path."

She gave me the dead eye for fifteen seconds, which is a long time to get the dead eye, and finally gave a single nod. "I hear you."

We sat in silence for a bit, listening to the pool and the buzz of the cicadas. Then she asked, "You think Brad the Man Tucker will let us go along for the ride? Thanks for that, by the way."

"Probably. I don't think he wants to be obstructive. He's just looking out for his team. You'd do the same . . ."

"That heart of yours ever going to stop gushing, Mahatma?"

"Cut it out, Dehan, you're being a pain in the ass. And if you think you ever stood an ice cube's chance in a supernova of getting on that team, you are out of your mind."

"I know. Sorry."

"He took one look at you and thought, 'I ain't lettin' that there gun-totin', trigger-happy cowgirl anywhere near my boys, 'else she'll fair shoot 'em all dead for me!'"

She considered me a moment while I chuckled. "What is he now, from China? He was Chinese? I didn't notice. 'Cause that accent was from China, right?"

"Sure was, Annie. Git yer gun, Annie. Who you gonna shoot t'day, Annie? You gonna shoot them Chinese Commies?"

"That's not funny."

While I laughed, she went and jumped in the pool again. I sat and watched her long, sleek form go beneath the water and thought about going into the kitchen for a pair of scissors, but before I could make up my mind, I heard a car pull up, the engine die, and the single slam of a door. A moment later, D.C. came around the side of the house.

"You ain't swimmin' there, boy!" He laughed. "The lady's got more sense. You want a beer?"

"Sure do."

The lady erupted from the depths, saw D.C., shook the water

from her face, and said, "News?" Then she grinned. "Hi, also. Hello, D.C."

He laughed. "Yeah, news. Drag yourself out of the pool and join us here at the table, Carmen, while I get some beers."

She got out, and he went to the kitchen. He returned a minute later with three cold bottles, which he set on the table while Dehan sat down.

"Here's the thing." He opened them, sat, and took a long pull from his bottle. "Brad called your deputy inspector at the Forty-Third, they had a long talk, then he consulted with Angel and Randy and me..."

Dehan scowled. "He is aware that between us, we have half a century of experience...?"

D.C. raised both hands. "I'm on your side, but to be fair, he is playing with people's lives here. Everyone who goes on that operation has a family waiting for them to come home on Friday. So every decision that varies even a little from the norm has to be very carefully thought through."

He considered her a moment, then sighed. "Carmen, Brad is one of the best team leaders we have. You can imagine that, situated where we are, on the border, we do a lot of this kind of operation. Brad has never lost an agent, because his preparation is so meticulous. His guys all love him, because we all feel safe in his hands.

"Now, with this operation, he is facing last-minute action where he has had very little time to prepare, a lot of unknown variables—not least how many men he is up against—so a new team member that he knows practically nothing about is something he does not need."

She nodded and forced a smile. "Okay, I know. I get it."

"His go-to response is, 'no.' It's an unnecessary risk."

"It's okay, D.C. I get it. It's his operation and he is doing the right thing. It makes sense."

"However, he has agreed to have you come along as observers. I've been instructed to make it very clear that you will not participate in the operation in any way, shape, or form. You will stay back with the vehicles and simply, strictly, observe." He frowned at her. "I need your word that you will do that."

She smiled. "You have my word that I will behave appropriately. How much can you tell us about the operation?"

"I don't want your promise that you'll behave appropriately, Detective Dehan." Suddenly the amiable face was gone and in its place there was the hard face of a federal agent who had spent almost forty years working the Arizona-Mexico border. "I *assume* that as a federal agent, you will behave appropriately. I was very specific that I want your word that you will not participate in the operation in any way, shape, or form. This operation will be clockwork, and you will stay out of it. If I have the slightest inkling that you are going to interfere, you don't go. It's that simple."

I smiled at Dehan. "He's saying, stop trying to be a wiseass and make an unambiguous promise, Dehan. Let them do their job."

"Okay!" She held up her hands. "I promise. I will not interfere in any way, shape, or goddamn form. What the hell did the chief say about me?"

D.C. laughed, and the amiable host was back. "He said you were a brilliant detective with a hot head. I've been there, I've done it, and I have the wet T-shirt. We all have. In my case, it got me badly mangled and I was lucky to make it out alive. But you know why I count myself really lucky? Because what I did didn't cost *anybody else* their life. Your own scars you can live with, but another person's life? That I could not live with. Especially a partner, a colleague, somebody you've worked with for years..."

He shook his head. Dehan nodded. "I get it, D.C. Sold. You don't need to sell it anymore."

"Good." He studied her face a moment and smiled. Then he shifted his gaze to the long shadows of the palms that were now reaching across the pool. "We'll leave here at two thirty a.m. sharp. I'll drive you to the field office, where you will join the team. You won't be part of the briefing. That is strictly need to know. You will then be driven down to Nogales, where a field base will be set up near the Beyer Ranch. ETA is five fifteen a.m. That is pretty much all I can tell you."

"Good enough." She looked at me. "What do you say, Stone?"

"No less than I asked for. Thanks, D.C., we appreciate it."

At that point, Penny turned up with her arms full of shopping bags, and we started discussing an early dinner.

SEVENTEEN

WE HADN'T SLEPT. D.C. HAD MADE A BARBEQUE AS DUSK turned to evening, and Penny and Dehan had swum in the pool while he grilled burgers and sweet corn. Overhead, the desert sky had turned from a scorched blue-white to an infinite dark translucence, where the stars were like shards of ice, unimaginably far away.

"When you see the moon rise," he'd said, "that's something else. I've never lived anywhere else, so I can't compare. But people who have tell me that at night, this is the most beautiful place on Earth." He laughed. "I ain't hankering to move, I'll tell you that."

He turned then to his wife, who was sloshing water with her hands and talking quietly to Dehan. "Hey, sweetheart, how does this compare with back home?"

"Mexico? Oh, Mexico is very beautiful, Daryl, but Arizona has something special. For me, it is the most beautiful place in the world. There was one place which was similar, you remember, babe, in the south of Spain? The Sierra de Cádiz, like Arizona with the sea! Beautiful! But not *as* beautiful!"

He nodded. "Yeah, Andalucia was something. That was special." She smiled and turned back to Dehan. I said:

"Mexico? I would never have guessed."

"Oh, yeah. Came over years ago, she was like four or five. She completely assimilated. We met at high school and been married now thirty-five years. Never regretted it a day in my life."

"Kudos."

He shrugged. "It's not for everybody, but it was definitely for me."

Later, we sat and talked while we ate. D.C. had the slightly didactic manner of a schoolteacher, and I wondered if he taught classes at the bureau.

"For me," he said at one point, "it's all about loyalty. But there is a lot of political confusion in this country. Republicans and Democrats work so hard at polarizing us that things become, instead of good ideas or bad ideas, liberal ideas or conservative ideas. So if you're a Democrat, you are required to believe a whole load of stuff, a lot of which is plain stupid, whether you agree with it or not. But if you're a Republican, you have to believe a whole load of different stuff, much of which is also plain stupid, whether you agree or not. And suddenly your loyalties have been sequestered."

He sat back and spread his hands, as a gesture that what he was about to say was self-evident.

"I think, as normal people, our first loyalty is to our family, wife, husband, kids, even close friends. After that to our state. That's where our home is, and those are our people. And after that to the United States, the Federation. And I speak as a federal agent. Beyond that, well, the parties should be loyal to me, not the other way around. But whichever way you look at it, the bottom line is, loyalty."

Something in what he said had taken my mind back to Amy and Charlie. Perhaps it had been the stark contrast between D.C.'s vision of life and family and the Redferns'. I couldn't help wondering, futilely, how different Amy's life might have been if she had had somebody like D.C. as a father; and Charlie, whose mother had invited Feliciano Camacho as an honored guest into their house. Would they have found happiness and fulfillment?

Instead, their bones lay in a Tupperware box, waiting for a machine to give them a name and make them somebody again.

Now, hours later, we lay huddled against the cold in the predawn dark, peering down out of the hills north of the Santa Cruz River at a complex of buildings surrounding a large swimming pool, which occasionally glinted in the floodlights that illuminated the area. The largest of these was a palatial Spanish affair built around two central patios. Located around the driveway, there were what appeared to be a garage for at least six cars, stables, a tennis court, and various other, smaller outbuildings. This was the Rancho Beyer.

A hundred and fifty yards, maybe two hundred, east of the main complex, there was a landing strip running about two thousand feet diagonally across flats at the foot of the hills, not far from the river. It was fringed by trees, along the southeastern side and at the north end. This was barely visible in the dark, but it had been detected the day before by high-flying drones with high-resolution cameras, and when we had arrived, in two jeeps and two personnel carriers, Brad had sent a scout team to confirm its location and guide in the two assault teams. Later, they would also guide in two choppers that were circling five miles to the north, ready to swoop in and provide air cover.

He had then dispatched the two six-man assault teams, dressed in full battle gear, through the sparse woodland and undergrowth to take up positions on either side of the runway. They were armed with assault rifles, grenades, and two heavy machine guns. So the runway was covered from the northwest and southeast sides, as well as the northern end. After the teams had been dispatched, Brad and three more men had taken the jeeps back down the canyon to the River Road, ready to storm the runway from the southern end. The airstrip was covered on four sides.

We were left with the personnel carriers and the binoculars, listening to the sporadic chatter on the radio in our earpieces. Brad had told us all at the final briefing, "Normally, on this kind of operation, as you know, we observe radio silence until the order to move in. That's something we can't do this time because we've had practically no preparation time. So, keep it to an absolute essential minimum. I'll spot the plane's approach from my position on the road. When I see it, I'll give the order to stand by. When it has landed and the shipment is exchanging hands, I'll give the order to go."

There had been no questions, and the two teams had disappeared into the predawn, melting into the darkness, surprisingly silent for their bulk and size.

Brad had then pointed at us and said, "Say nothing, do nothing, just observe and wait for us to return."

He had climbed into the lead jeep and they had rolled down the canyon track.

Now we lay in the long grass, looking down into the valley below, and we watched and waited. After twenty minutes, there was a series of short bursts of radio crackle, each one less than a second, confirming the teams' arrivals at their positions. Then more silence.

Eventually, the sky over the Patagonia Mountains began to turn a pale, soot gray. Five minutes after that, it was tinged here and there with red, though the sky above us was still dark and speckled with stars. I nudged Dehan's arm and pointed south and slightly east, because there was a very bright star there that was moving.

She spoke softly. "That's our boy."

The light became brighter, and soon we could make out the red-and-blue lights to port and starboard, and then the soft drone of the engine on the air.

We waited for Brad's signal.

Dehan chewed her lip. Our earpieces remained silent. The plane, now just about visible as a Cessna 172, was descending over the Patagonia Highway, clearly headed for the ranch. The teams below must by now be aware of it. Dehan grabbed my arm and pointed. Two vehicles were emerging from the ranch and making for the airfield.

A voice crackled in my ear. "This is Alpha Team, Team Leader, what is your status? Are we on standby? Target is landing."

Silence.

The plane was coming in low over the trees. The radio crackled again. "This is Bravo Team. Team Leader, please confirm your status. Are we standby or abort? Repeat, stand by or abort?"

The plane touched down in a cloud of dust and a squeal of tortured rubber. The engine pitch dropped and groaned. The radio crackled. But this time the voice did not identify itself. It just screamed, "*Abort! Abort! Abort!*" Then the woods lit up with what looked eerily like sheet lightning under the canopy. It flickered red and blue under the trees, northwest and southeast of the runway, and at the northern extreme. Dimly, over the dying drone of the aircraft, we heard the sharp stutter, like firecrackers, of automatic rifles. There were a couple of explosions from the woods, probably grenades. Then more gunfire, growing sporadic.

We watched through binoculars as the Cessna and the cars approached each other. They seemed oblivious to the slaughter that was being carried out just a couple of hundred yards away. The plane came to a halt. The airscrew thudded to a halt and a handful of men spilled from the side door. Two of them were dressed sharp. One was small, the other had a ponytail. The cars drew up, and I counted six men who climbed out. One of them, dressed in a suit, seemed to move with authority. I figured he was Cesar, but I couldn't be sure. The two groups met, and there was a lot of handshaking and backslapping. Meanwhile, in the woods, a short distance away, there were a few last, sporadic bursts of gunfire. Then silence.

The group divided now. Three of the men moved back toward the cars. One was the man I'd pinned as Cesar. The others were the big guy with the ponytail and his small friend. The rest of the group had moved to the plane and started unloading packages into the trunk of a dark Audi. I looked at Dehan. She was filming what she could on her cell phone.

I said, "Dehan, they knew we were coming."

"I can see that."

"Snap out of it! They knew where the teams were going to be positioned, all three of them. They knew where Brad was going to be."

She scowled at me and snapped. "I know, Stone! I can see that!"

I grabbed her wrist and made her face me. "*For Christ's sake, Dehan! So they know we are here too!*"

Her face went pale in the early light. She stared at me a second, then looked down at the car that was driving off with Cesar and the other two. It wasn't headed back to the ranch, it was headed to the road.

"*Shit!*" She moved for the personnel carriers.

I grabbed her and pulled her back, speaking savagely to her. "*Think, Dehan!* There will be men climbing the hill toward us now, from the woods. The car will be heading for us up the canyon path. We can't take the personnel carrier. We'll be ambushed on all sides . . ."

"Then what . . . ?"

"We head into the hills and the canyons. We call the field office and report what happened. Find a hiding place and wait for them to come for us. But right now, we *run*!"

She nodded, and then we were scrambling down into the canyon that lay at our backs, running, jumping, falling, and sliding. Branches and twigs tore at our skin and our clothes. Rocks and stones stabbed into our hands as we fell and scrambled to our feet.

Then we were at the bottom of the canyon, sprinting for the far side. The whine of engines carried on the dawn air. Now, instead of falling and tumbling, it was an agonizing, slow climb, slipping on the loose, dry earth, scrabbling over the loose stones, clawing at shrubs, taking three slow steps up, and sliding down two, pulling ourselves up with branches and bushes. All the while, the whine of climbing engines grew louder behind us. Then, as we were approaching the top, the tone of the engines changed, slowed, and grew deeper. I rasped, "*Lie flat! Don't move!*"

The vehicles, whatever they were, had reached the path that climbed out of the canyon to where Brad had set our camp. Now we could hear the engines in low gear, grinding their way up that path. I whispered, "*Crawl to the top. Stay under cover!*"

We were maybe seven or eight feet from the crest of the hill. Staying flat, we pulled ourselves, arm over arm, a foot at a time, through the tall, yellow grass, toward the cover of a couple of gnarled oaks. We wriggled the last couple of feet and lay behind the short, thick trunks, peering back toward the other side of the canyon. There was nothing to see but oaks, mesquite, yucca, and tall yellow grass.

I hissed, "*We have to go!*" Dehan was on her phone. I tugged at her. "*Come on! We have seconds!*"

We began to half stumble, half run down the slope into the denser vegetation below in the ravine. Dehan spoke as she slipped and scrambled ahead of me, keeping her voice low.

"This is Detective Carmen Dehan, badge number . . ." She slipped and fell. I pulled her up as she recited her number into the phone and we continued stumbling down, crouching now under the broad canopy of branches and leaves that lay in a tangled mesh across the bottom of the valley. Dehan was hissing, "I need to talk to the SAC about Agent Brad Tucker's operation at . . . No, listen to me! *I know Agent Tucker isn't there! I was on operation with him!*"

She sat at the foot of a mesquite, squeezing her eyes tight and clenching her fist. I said, "We haven't got time for this. We need to move . . ."

She rasped, "*Listen to me. Stop talking. Listen. I was on the operation with Agent Tucker . . . as an observer! Will you shut up and listen to me! I need to talk to the special agent in charge!*"

I took the phone from her hand and hung up. She glared into

my eyes. I said, "If you don't stop, we'll be dead inside five minutes. Let's go."

We followed the course of the bottom of the valley. Progress was slow and difficult. The undergrowth was impenetrable in some parts and we had to fight our way through a morass of twigs, branches, and tangled weeds and grasses. At times the undergrowth was so dense we had to climb up the side of the ravine to get around it, taking it in turns to keep watch on the horizon for Cesar's men. There was no question in my mind that they were following us, led by the *sicario*; the only questions were, how close was he, and was he closing on us?

After half an hour, we heard the first chopper. We followed the sound with our eyes, though we did not see it. We were in a kind of cave formed by a narrow gully, two large oaks, several mesquite, and a cluster of desert ironwood trees. Dehan had stopped and was leaning her back against a large rock. Her breathing was shallow.

"We are screwed six ways from Sunday, Stone. We've put some distance between ourselves and Cesar's men, now we need to take a couple of minutes to think and make some kind of plan."

"Agreed." I pulled out my phone and looked at the screen. "No signal."

She frowned and shook her head in rapid jerks. "How can they expect to get away with this? They just murdered eighteen federal agents! They will have the bureau and the National Guard all over them before lunch!"

I glanced up at the sky. "I only hear one chopper at the moment."

"Come on! The girl I spoke to wasn't exactly a genius, but even she, once you had helpfully hung up for me, would have to go to her supervisor and report the call. They haven't heard from Brad—the two choppers on standby never heard from Brad. They have to put two and two together; they're not just going to shrug and say, 'Oh, well, I guess he'll call!' They have eighteen agents who just went AWOL! There must be alarm bells going off all over the bureau."

"Dehan, keep your voice down and stop ranting. You're right. But it is not that simple."

"Not? How is it complicated?"

"Shut up. Please. Just for a bit. Our *first* priority is not getting disemboweled this morning. Agreed? So this is what we do. We go, predictable, predictable, unpredictable; predictable, unpredictable, predictable; unpredictable, predictable, predictable."

"We do what now?"

"We follow the easy, predictable path, as we have been doing for the last half hour or so, to a particular point. In this case the end of this canyon. The closest town is Rio Rico. So we are going to head northwest toward it. That's predictable, so that would be two predictable things we've done. So then we do something unpredictable."

"Like what?"

"Like instead of turning west and north at the end of this canyon, we continue east into the next one instead, follow that for a while, and then climb to the top to see if we can get a signal."

"So for every two predictable, logical decisions we make, we make one that is totally illogical, but in a random order."

"Yes."

"I like it. Okay. Let's keep going."

We set off and started picking our way through the dense undergrowth again. Above us, to the left, the top of the steep incline was gradually sloping down as we reached the end of the gully, where three canyons met. I pointed ahead. "Here they would expect us to turn either north or west. We keep going east."

"Got it. So explain to me why you think the combined force of the bureau and the National Guard are not coming down in force on that ranch."

I was quiet for a bit, picking my way carefully over loose rocks and shrubs.

"The first thing is that by the time they realize something is wrong, the bodies have either been incinerated at the ranch or flown back to Mexico. They had a lot of manpower there, and it would not have been that difficult to remove any trace of their presence."

She drew level with me and opened her mouth to object. I said, "Wait. The shipment of coke, or whatever it was, is already off the ranch and on its way, presumably, to New York. So there is no trace on the property itself of anything that brought the Feds there in the first place, or of their having been there."

"But there *is* a judge who saw the evidence and signed off on an order to raid the ranch. There is in existence an order to that effect *and* the evidence that gave rise to that order. There is also an SAC who ordered the raid and two personnel carriers sitting outside the ranch. And now, on the morning that order was executed, we have eighteen missing federal agents and two NYPD detectives."

She gave me a look that said I must be crazy not to see that. I nodded.

"Sure. That's true. But it is also true that before anybody goes storming in after Brad Tucker, they will need a warrant, and they will be very unlikely to get one, because any judge asked to sign off on it will know that they are not going to find anything on the ranch. That chopper we heard was probably the Feds looking for Brad. There is probably a drone up there looking too. But you know as well as I do, Dehan, before a single shot was fired, Cesar and Camacho had already briefed their lawyers. And before the day is out, those lawyers will bombard the state with complaints, injunctions, and possibly even legal actions."

I looked at her, waiting for my meaning to register on her face. It didn't take long. "Yeah, I know," she said. "Because he already knew we were coming. They were waiting in the woods for the teams to take up their positions. So they slaughtered them and cleaned away the evidence and now the ranch is pristine."

"And that begs the question: Did he know we were listening

at the hotel, and plant this information? Or is there a leak at the field office? Did somebody tell him we were coming?"

The bed of the intersection where the three canyons met was dense with undergrowth and trees. We crossed it with difficulty, but unseen, and when we had reached the far side, we began to climb the slope toward the top of the canyon, in the hope of getting a signal there. Halfway up, we came to a rocky outcrop where we could rest and hide. There we sat, gratefully, and checked our watches. It was half past nine, and we were both becoming hungry and thirsty.

I stared out west, toward the ribbon of the Santa Cruz River and the road that followed its course. After a moment, I became aware that Dehan was staring at me and I turned to meet her gaze.

"It makes no sense," she said, "that Camacho would plant this information at the hotel and set this up. It doesn't benefit him in any way." She shook her head. "No, he and Cesar were alerted. Somebody told them we were coming."

I nodded. "I agree."

She held my eye a moment longer. "There was gunfire from the airfield, and grenades. There was none from the ranch or the road where Brad should have been. And Brad had all the information about the operation. He was the one man who had the authority to stop the choppers coming in, *and* to preempt a response after Camacho's men had started their attack. He never gave the alert that the plane was approaching."

"A man who was at such pains to protect his team?"

"A man who was so keen to keep us off it. I'm telling you, Stone, there was more than corpses on that plane back to Mexico."

I looked at my phone and saw I had a signal.

EIGHTEEN

There was no sign of Camacho's men, or the *sicario*, but a couple of miles south and west, there was a helicopter that seemed to be circling over the ranch.

"Who did you talk to?"

She shook her head, watching the chopper. "I don't know, some dame."

I smiled. "Some dame?"

"She kept telling me I wasn't part of Agent Tucker's team and she had no authority to talk to me about it." She sighed. "You got a signal?" She pulled her phone and looked at the screen.

I said, "You know what? Don't call the field office."

She glanced at me.

"We don't know anything right now, do we? The fewer people we communicate with . . ."

"What do you suggest?"

I pointed west and slightly north. "We have Rio Rico about four or five miles over there. We take any of these canyons in front of us, it will lead us to the river. Then we follow the river for an hour and it will take us to the town. We call D.C. and tell him what happened."

She gave a couple of nods, like she was agreeing with only bits of what I was saying. "What makes you think D.C. isn't our leak?"

"Nothing. It could be anyone. But we give him a location, like the travel center on the I-19, intersection with Ruby Road . . ."

"The Pilot Travel Center."

"Right, but we are not there when he arrives."

"What do you mean? Where are we?"

"We tell him to park outside the fast food burger joint. That's right by the river and there are lots of trees along there. We stay in the cover of the trees and we watch, see if he comes alone, if he comes with other Feds, or if he comes with Cesar's men. Then we decide what to do and whom to contact."

She made a face. "Makes sense. What's going to stop Cesar from killing us along the river?"

I shook my head. "Remember, his plan was even more improvised than Brad's. He had maybe twenty-four hours to set it up. When we ran, he missed his chance. He won't keep searching. That's what he brought his *sicario* over for. The Feds may not be storming the ranch, but they are taking a good, hard look at it, so he has to pull his men back. And the *sicario* will not be wasting his time scouring almost two million square acres of the Coronado Forest to find us. He knows we have to surface sooner or later, and he knows roughly where. That's where he'll look for us."

She thought about that for a moment, looking down at her battered, dusty boots. "Where?"

"The field office, D.C.'s house, the Bronx, and all along the route connecting those three."

"Nice."

"The sooner we get to the field office and get debriefed, the sooner we get the leak identified and plugged, and the sooner we can go on the offensive."

She sighed and stood. "That I like."

As it turned out, we covered the mile and a half to the river in a little under two hours. At first, the going was difficult and slow, struggling over loose rocks and through shrubs and woodland.

But when we reached the far canyon, we found a narrow, beaten path and were able to follow that all the way to the Santa Cruz. From there it was easier.

We picked up the South River Road and followed it at a brisk pace for three and a half miles. Just over an hour after that, we'd finally crossed the railroad and the river on the Ruby Road Bridge and were resting our asses outside the Pilot Travel Center. I looked at my watch; it was closing on ten to one.

"I'm starving. You want to grab a couple of burgers and some coffee while I phone D.C.?"

She nodded and we pushed inside. I grabbed a table by the window, where I could keep an eye on the lot, while she went up to order at the counter. I found D.C.'s number and called. He answered after the first ring.

"John, is that you?"

"Yeah."

"Are you okay?"

"Yeah, we're okay."

"What about Dehan? Where are you? What the hell happened?"

"She's okay too. I don't want to talk too much on the phone, D.C. Can you come and get us?"

"Where?"

"We're at Wendy's, the Pilot Travel Center, just south of Rio Rico on the I-19."

"I know it."

"D.C.? Just for now, till we get back to the field office, keep this to yourself, okay?"

He was quiet for a long moment, then said, "I hear you."

"Good."

"I'm at the Resident Agency in Tucson right now. It's going to take me forty-five minutes to get to you. I'll try and get there sooner."

"Okay, park outside Wendy's where we can see you."

"You got it."

Dehan sat down with a plastic tray bearing two coffees and two burgers with fries.

"Forty-five minutes. Maybe a little less."

"How did he sound?"

I bit into the burger and chewed for a bit, then swallowed and shrugged. "Worried, anxious. He asked all the right questions."

"What does your gut say?"

I shrugged again, this time with my eyebrows. "My gut says I am starving, and I don't know who is whom or what is what."

She grunted, bit, and spoke with her mouth full. "Nothing is what it seems, and nobody is who they appear to be."

"Thanks."

She waved her burger at me, still chewing hungrily. "If nothing is real, everything is possible. You know who said that?" Before I could answer, she added, "It's eleventh-century Persian and can also be translated as, 'If nothing is real, everything is permissible.'"

"Hassan-e Sabbah, the Old Man of the Mountain, founder of the Hashshashin, from which word we derive both the words assassin and hashish."

"Huh, and there was me thinking I was going to teach you something." She swallowed, then took another bite and asked with narrowed eyes, "Isn't that what Schrödinger's cat is all about?"

I made a "maybe" face. "Hash and murder? More Sinaloa than Schrödinger."

"Not Schrödinger, Schrödinger's cat. In the box. He is both alive and dead till you open the box. If nothing is real, everything is possible."

I stuffed the last bit of burger in my mouth and scanned the lot while I chewed. When I had swallowed, I said, "You really do think about things like that at times like this, don't you? I'm not sure, Dehan. Are you insane?"

"Hey! It is when they are most relevant, right? When I die, I don't want to be thinking, 'The son of a bitch shot me!' or, 'Jeez, my pancreas hurts!' I want to be thinking, 'Huh! Now I get why the cat was alive *and* dead!'"

I burst out laughing.

She laughed back and asked, "Am I right?"

"Yes. Yes, you are right." I put my hand on her wrist. "By the way, Schrödinger thought the whole thing was a crock. He invented the whole cat story to show that Heisenberg and Niels Bohr were out of their minds."

"Heisenberg, now?"

"Him and his uncertainty principle."

"Great."

"But they turned out to be right."

"And his cat?"

"Both alive and dead. A bit like us. Let's go. We'll sit down by the river till he gets here."

We went out into the midday glare, crossed the small service road, and stepped over the low barrier into the wasteland that sloped down from the gas station to the river below. There we found a fallen tree in the shade of some acacias. I sat on one of them to finish my coffee while we waited for D.C. to arrive, and Dehan leaned against the trunk of one of the acacias, sipping and watching me.

"So what did Heisenberg say that Schrödinger thought was so stupid?"

I smiled. "Seriously?"

"Seriously. What are you going to do instead, keep turning over questions you already know you can't answer?"

I sighed. "I'm not a physicist. I don't really understand this stuff. I just read about it sometimes."

"Tell me."

"It wasn't just Schrödinger. It was Einstein too. There were a whole bunch of them arguing about this in the twenties."

"What did Heisenberg say?"

"He said it was impossible ever to know precisely where something was and how fast it was moving. The more you knew about where it was, the less you knew about how it was moving. But if you focused on how it was moving..."

I trailed off, thinking suddenly about my own words and what they meant, and Dehan filled in what I had left out. "The less you knew about where it was."

"Exactly..."

"You're going to have to explain that to me properly sometime. I think that's D.C. pulling in there."

She was right. D.C.'s big, dark Buick was turning in to the gas station. We watched it pull up outside Wendy's. The engine died and he climbed out. He stood a moment looking around, then pushed into the restaurant. I looked at Dehan. She shrugged. We scanned the lot and the road in both directions. There didn't seem to be anybody watching, nobody had pulled in directly ahead of him or after him. A moment later, he stepped out again and stood staring around the lot. He pulled out his phone, thumbed the screen, and a second later, my cell rang. He stared in our direction, frowning. We stepped out from among the trees.

"What the hell are you doing?"

I told him, "We needed to make sure you were alone."

He scowled. "Jesus... What the hell's going on?"

"Not here."

"Get in the car." He pointed to the Buick. "We need to get you to the field office and debriefed."

We climbed in, and he pulled away onto the I-19, headed north toward Tucson. He had trouble keeping his eyes on the road and kept glancing at me with worried eyes.

"Where is Brad, John? Where are the guys?"

I watched his face carefully. "They were expecting us."

The car swerved. He stared at me like I had slapped his face. I snapped, "Keep your eyes on the road!"

"That's not possible! Nobody knew...!" But even as he was saying it, he was thinking. "Who? Who knew? Apart from...?"

I said, "He deployed the teams according to the plan. Then he took up his position on the road, near the entrance to the ranch. He was supposed to give the order to stand by as the plane came in. Dehan and I saw it approach from the southeast, but the order never came. Next thing, the teams asked for the order to go. There was no reply. The plane touched down and then all hell broke loose. They were waiting for them in the woods, and they knew where they were going to be. They knew we were there too. They knew everything."

He had gone pale and there were tears in his eyes. He said, "No . . ." He turned to me like he was asking me to tell him something different. "So . . . they're dead?"

"It looks that way. They came after us too. We had to run. You want to pull over? You want me to drive?"

He shook his head. "Brad?"

"We didn't see anybody shot. But we saw a lot of gunfire. We saw the assassin arrive and what looked like a big shipment of coke. The gunfire was going on all around them, and grenades, but they ignored it."

He was frowning, like he had a headache. "It doesn't make any sense . . ." He frowned at me. "Where was Brad?"

"He went with three other guys down to the main entrance to the ranch, exactly according to the plan. He was going to storm in from the north."

He went to speak, but hesitated, then said, "I guess they must have ambushed him there."

Dehan's voice came from the back of the car. It sounded neutral, almost dead. "Brad married?"

D.C. glanced in the mirror to see her. "No. He lives . . . lived with his girlfriend. Why?"

"Kids?"

"No." He shook his head, frowning like he was trying to focus. "No, she's with the bureau too. She's an analyst. They don't have time for a . . . what has this to do with anything?"

I growled, "Stop kidding yourself, D.C. You know damned well what she's driving at."

"No . . ." He was shaking his head and sounded crazy. "No, no, no! No, you don't. Not Brad."

"Who then?"

He closed his eyes. I snapped again, "Keep your damned eyes on the road, D.C.! Pull over and let me drive!"

"I'm okay. Just give me a minute. I need to think."

Dehan wasn't about to give him that time. "Cesar knew exactly where each team was going to be. They also knew that we were not included in the operation, and where we were going to be observing from. Who had that kind of information prior to our deployment?"

"Brad, he was in charge of the operation. Pat O'Leary, he's the field office SAC, me. I'm not sure how much he told Angel and Randy, but I doubt he gave them everything."

He glanced in the mirror as she replied, "So that narrows the field down some, huh?"

"You mean I am a prime suspect."

I said, "You have to be, D.C. You're not a prime suspect. You have to be *the* prime suspect. It's either you, Brad, or the detective in charge of the field office."

Dehan's voice came from the shadows at the back again. "Or Brad's girlfriend."

"Jesus Christ . . ." He was biting his lip and he had tears running down his face. "How did this happen?"

We were entering Tucson, and as we approached Valencia Road, he turned off at the intersection and started heading west. I asked him, "Where are you going?"

He shook his head again. "I need to think."

We drove in silence for a couple of miles, then he turned off Valencia into a shopping mall. There he pulled up in front of Sam's Famous Sports Bar. He killed the engine and sat staring through the windshield at the sign in front of us. It said, *Fun Food & Spirits*.

"Just give me five minutes," he said, "to think this through. Somehow it has to make sense."

"Give Dehan the keys."

He sighed. "Sure." He handed them back and she took them.

I smiled back at her. "You're driving. I plan to have a drink."

"Great."

Inside, it was dark and cool. The TV was playing reruns of old games, but the bar was empty save for the big guy behind the counter. D.C. ordered a bourbon on the rocks and I had an Irish straight up. Dehan had pineapple juice. We found a table at the back in the shadows and we sat. I sipped and felt the warmth start to ease away the aches, bruises, and scratches.

D.C. sat holding his glass with both hands and staring down at the rocks of ice.

"This is a lot to assimilate in a very short time," he said. "To you it's pretty straightforward, but to me there is a lot involved. I've known Brad for fifteen years. Now I have to accept that either he is a traitor to his country, or he's dead. Which is the better option? I've known Pat, the SAC, I am not sure how long. Years. He is a good, decent man. It is impossible that he is bent. So I am looking also at the very real possibility of spending the rest of my life in jail, humiliated before my family, labeled as a traitor. When I *know* that I am not guilty."

We didn't say anything. We waited. He sat and turned the glass in circles. Finally, he said, "Or it may be Brad's girlfriend, Susanne. So there is only one way to deal with this."

"How?"

"We don't go to the SAC." He looked at us in turn. "We go straight to Washington. We put it in their hands. This office—this whole office—is compromised. So we have Washington take over the investigation."

I looked at Dehan. She made a face that said she couldn't see anything wrong with what he was suggesting.

I frowned at him. "What exactly are you proposing?"

"I don't know." He took his first pull on his drink and set the tumbler down carefully on the ring it had left on the table. "I think I'm in shock." He looked at Dehan and blinked a few times. "Is my wife at risk?"

"I don't know. Why would she be?"

"I don't know," he echoed her. "Who else have you spoken to?"

I said, "We called the field office and spoke to a girl . . ."

He pulled his phone from his pocket. His hand was trembling. He dialed. He waited with the phone to his ear, then smiled suddenly. "Hey, sweetheart. Listen, baby, things are going to get pretty hectic around here for a few days. So listen, I was thinking, why don't you go and stay with your mom for a few days, in Florida." He listened for a moment, then nodded. "Yes, baby. That's a good idea. I'll call you when things settle. Maybe I'll even come and join you . . . I love you too, baby."

He hung up and we sat in silence for a moment. Finally, I asked him, "So, what's next, D.C., how do you want to do this?"

He glanced at me. Dehan was watching him like a cat watching a goldfish. He said, "Everyone I know and everything I touch is tainted from now on, you know that. You have to consider that I am your prisoner. You've taken me in and you need to contact Washington and appraise them of the situation."

Dehan nodded. "Okay. Let's find a motel. We'll call from there."

I asked, "Did you tell anybody you were coming to meet us?"

He shook his head. "No."

He was about to stand, but I asked, "Why not?"

He sighed. "You asked me not to, remember? Besides . . ." He sagged. "I didn't want to admit it to myself, but I already suspected what had happened."

I still didn't get up. "What's going on at the field office? What steps are they taking?"

"The SAC is shitting bricks, basically. He doesn't know what the hell's hit him. He's had almost two dozen agents disappear into thin air. All he can do at the moment is search the area and have emergency conferences with the legal team and the judge."

"Okay." I drained my glass. "Let's go find that motel."

NINETEEN

"If you know where it is, you can't know where it's going. And if you know where it's going, you can't know where it is." I was leaning on the roof of the car, staring at the door of our motel room, talking half to myself. D.C. was unlocking the door, and Dehan was standing by the hood, looking back at me.

She said, "What?"

I sighed. "The uncertainty principle."

"Seriously, Stone? At a time like this?" She turned to go.

I said, "I need to buy some stuff. Keep him entertained. I won't be long."

She took a couple of steps back toward me, holding out the key. "If you're buying toothpaste . . ."

I took the key and opened the car door. "I know what flavor toothpaste you like, Dehan. I also know what size panties and bra you use. And believe me, it's time you changed all three."

I heard the muffled "Asshole!" as I slammed the door and chuckled. She knocked on the window, nodding her head that she needed to tell me something. I pressed the button and the glass slid down. She smiled. "Asshole. Just in case you didn't hear me."

I reversed, shrugging and gesturing at my ear that I couldn't hear.

We were at the Saguaro Garden, a motel five minutes north of Tucson, just outside the little town of Rillito, on the I-10. Instead of turning right and south, back toward Tucson, I followed the frontage road and crossed under the interstate, then turned left and north toward Phoenix.

I drove as fast as I dared. I didn't know how long I had, but at the same time I didn't want to draw the attention of the cops. What I needed to do needed to be done fast and quiet.

It was a ninety-mile drive, and sixty minutes after I joined the freeway, I was pulling into the Phoenix International Airport parking lot at Terminal 4. From there I ran. I tried to convince my brain I was twenty-two again. My brain didn't believe me, but by the time I'd decided to give up and walk fast instead, I was in the main hall of the airport, scanning the lines moving through passport control into international departures. I didn't see anything there that interested me, so I began a methodical search of all the coffee shops, bars, and restaurants. All the while, I was aware that I might have the wrong terminal, and even the wrong mode of travel. I didn't know for sure where she was, or where she was headed. All I had was an educated guess bolstered by a hunch.

As it turned out, the guess was a good one, and so was the hunch. I finally spotted her at the Cheuvront Wine Bar sitting in front of a vodka martini, looking pale and worried. She didn't notice me until I pulled out the chair opposite and sat. Then she stared at me for a moment in astonishment and said, "Oh, my goodness..."

I smiled. "Don't worry, Penny. He's safe with Detective Dehan."

"Did he tell you where I would be? I can't believe..."

I shook my head. "I figured staying with your mom in Florida for a few days was code for 'get the hell out of here,' the Sierra de Cádiz was a safe bet for where you were going." I shrugged. "For that you'd need Terminal Four."

"Oh . . . Are you going to stop me from leaving?"

"I don't know yet. I don't know what D.C. has done. Somewhere in the region of fourteen to seventeen agents were killed this morning, by Cesar and his men. They knew exactly where the agents were. They were sitting ducks. There are not many ways they could have got hold of that information, Penny."

Her eyes went to her drink. The ice was melting, but she hadn't sipped it yet. She spoke suddenly.

"He arrested me." She flicked her eyes at my face and smiled. "He tells everyone I came over with my parents when I was four. It isn't true. I was nineteen or twenty. I don't remember. He was such an easy target, so full of honor and goodness and decency. He really believed in all that Christian stuff. His mom and dad were Quakers. Did you know that? And he *really* believed in it. He still does."

She sighed and sagged back in her chair. "El Patron, the boss who controlled the area where I lived . . ." She stopped again. Her eyes roved my face like she was wondering if I could understand what she was talking about. "I was born in Altar. It's the southernmost tip of the triangle, between Nogales, Sonoyta, and Altar. There is no law there." She shrugged. "It's the law of the *patron*. I was fourteen, I was pretty. They could get good money for me. So they took me. They worked me in a club in Nogales for a year, then brought me over, first to Socorro, then some clubs in El Paso, finally to the Club Gasolina, just south of Tucson. It's closed now. By then, I guess I was nineteen."

She smiled at me for a while, then shook her head. "It is such a long time ago now, it seems like another life. I was a nice girl before they took me, a good Catholic, decent, kind . . . Can you believe that when the Feds raided the Gasolina, I hated them? 'My people' were the bastards who were beating me, prostituting me, raping me on a nightly basis. They were *'los mios'!* My people. This is the loyalty that Daryl talks about so much. I would have killed those agents that night if I'd had the chance. I was nineteen and I believed that my place in the world was as a whore for the Sinaloa Cartel."

She laughed suddenly. It was a nice, happy sound. She leaned forward and put her hand on my wrist. "The minute I saw Daryl, and he looked at me, I knew I had him. He was mine! *I owned him!*" She laughed again. "I began to work him straight away. He was going to get me released. For sure."

The joy and pleasure drained from her face and her gaze drifted back to her vodka martini. I waited a moment, then asked, "What happened?"

"He wasn't as easy as I thought. I could see he was in love with me, crazy, head over heels for me. But he had so much *integrity*. I had never seen anything like it. And the stupid thing was that, because of that, *I* began to fall in love with *him*." She raised her eyes to meet mine. "They say, don't they, that we are shaped in the first five years of our lives. My father was like Daryl; not so smart, not educated. He was a very simple man. But he had that kind of religious, moral integrity. Kindness, humanity. You must never tell D.C., but I am a total atheist. I lost my faith when I was a kid. It's something that Daryl doesn't need to know. But he reminded me of my father."

"What did they do to him, Penny?"

She asked, "My father?" but she knew that wasn't what I meant.

I shook my head. "D.C. Cesar caught him, didn't he?"

She shook her head. "Not Cesar, Camacho. It was . . . eight? Eight or nine years ago now. He was already too old for the job! I told him, 'Get a desk job!'" A spasm of irritation flashed across her face, then passed. "So much time had passed. We had both forgotten my past. Can you understand that? It was like I had died and been reborn. I am an American now. We had forgotten. It was that simple."

"Then the Camachos arrived?"

She nodded. "The Camacho brothers are not based in Arizona."

"I know, they are from New York."

She wagged her finger at me in a gesture that was totally Spanish. "No. They are not *from* New York. They are *based* in New York now, but the Camacho family is from Hermosillo, and they did *a lot* of money laundering in Puerto Peñasco, Rocky Point. They used to spend the summers there. It's not far from Altar. So we all knew about the Camachos.

"The gang who took me when I was a kid were controlled by the Camachos, and the *patron* paid his percentage every month to them, he bought his merchandise from them." She gave a small snort and nodded. "So you can imagine how I felt when I heard from Daryl that Camacho's boys were moving in along the border and taking control of the supply line from Nogales to the northeast."

"Did he realize there was a connection between you and the Camachos?"

She gave her head a single shake. "No, and I was sure, so much time had passed, I was just a nineteen-year-old whore when I was arrested. They would have forgotten about me. I was nothing to them." She took a deep breath and sighed. "But the older brother, Julio, he is very sick. I never met him and he never met me. But he heard a story, gossip—I don't know—that ten or twelve years before, there had been a raid and one of the whores had married an agent."

I gave my head a little sideways twist. "That kind of thing can be very valuable to them. I know Julio Camacho. It's exactly the kind of thing he would play on. They came for you?"

"Never. They never came close to me. But they took Daryl. They beat him and tortured him for a week. Then they dropped him outside our front door. I called the office, and they came with the ambulance. He was a month in the hospital and six months without working, receiving medication and counseling. They told him that what they had done to him, they could do to me anytime they wanted. If we tried to run or hide, they could find us. The only way to be safe was to provide them with information about drug operations."

I frowned. "Nobody ever noticed?"

She wagged her finger again. "No, no. They are very smart. He is more useful to them if they can play him for ten, twenty years. So let the Feds have a small success here, a small success there. A hundred thousand dollars here, two hundred and fifty there. To them, it is nothing. Because what is getting through is worth millions. If they get advance information about surveillance operations, raids, busts, patrols . . . they can plan everything so that Daryl's position is never compromised. I know these people very well. I spent five, six years living with them, eating with them, sleeping with them. I know how they think." She held my eye for a long moment, then added, "But I am not one of them."

"I believe you."

"And if Daryl told them about the operation, he did not expect them to kill those agents. They have never done anything similar. I can promise you that he expected them to abort the delivery, nothing more. He would not have sacrificed those men. He loved Brad like a brother."

It made sense. It made sense of D.C.'s reaction when I spoke to him in the car. You can fake surprise, but you can't fake turning pale.

She said, "What are you going to do?"

"I don't know. What time is your flight?"

"Ten thirty tonight."

I frowned at her. "How long have you had this escape plan in place?"

"Ten years . . ."

"I have to tell you, it's not a great plan when you have to spend seven hours in a public place where just about everybody can see you."

She shrugged. "I know. We used to stay on top of it, modify it—even talk about escaping and faking our own deaths. But the crisis never came, nobody ever got hurt, eventually we just kind of settled and grew complacent."

"Where is your baggage?"

"In left luggage. It's a long time to be carrying . . ."

She trailed off and I got to my feet. "Okay, Penny, let's go."

There was fear in her eyes. "Where are we going?"

"To see Daryl. Then we'll decide what to do. Where is your car?"

"In a parking garage in town. I took a cab."

"Good."

I left the Buick for the cops to find in the parking lot. I was pretty sure that if there wasn't a BOLO out for it already, there would be before very long. I hired a car from Hertz instead and drove back south toward the Saguaro Garden. By now, the heat was fierce and there was a dead, dusty stillness to the desert as it slid past outside the windows.

As we passed Red Rock, she spoke, looking out at the rusty flats, scattered with gnarled, exhausted bushes. "Is Brad dead, then?"

"I don't know. Probably."

"He has a girlfriend, Susanne . . ."

"I know."

"I read once, nothing ever happens in isolation. Whatever you do, if you touch one person, really you are touching five, or ten. You cannot isolate yourself, ever." I glanced at her. She was talking in a monotone, almost droning, looking at nothing. "She told me they were thinking about having kids. Now they never will. So they killed Brad, and they also killed his unborn children."

Five minutes later, I told her, "We're here."

I pulled off the road at the intersection, turned back up the frontage road, and finally came to a halt outside the room at the motel. When I opened the door and Penny stepped in, D.C. went pale and stood up, shaking his head, saying, "No! No, no, no! *You can't do this!*"

Penny went to him and put her arms around him. They clung

to each other. His eyes were squeezed tight. Dehan was watching like I had just pulled a white bunny from my holster. I made a "whatcha gonna do?" face and put my ass on the windowsill. After a moment, D.C. opened his eyes and stared at me. "They'll kill her. She has to go. She has nothing to do with this. You don't understand."

"Her flight is at ten thirty tonight, D.C. Unless I learn something completely unexpected before then, she'll be on it. But the worst place in the world for her right now is the airport. This right here is about as safe as it gets." I gave that a moment to sink in, then I went on. "Now, you need to listen to me, Daryl. Because we have no idea where this is going to go, or how it's going to play out. So you need to focus. You need to stop trying to be smart, and you need to tell me *exactly* what happened."

He drew breath and I interrupted him. "I told you, don't try to be smart. Penny already told me about the beating and Camacho's threats. The only way out of this for you is to come clean with me and Dehan."

He stared at Penny for a moment. She held his face in her hands and said, "He had already guessed it, Daryl. We have to face this now. We should have done it before."

He sagged. All the air seemed to hiss out of him, and he sat on the bed. Penny sat next to him and held him. Dehan was in a chair by the door, frowning and sucking her teeth.

He spread his hands a moment, then let them drop on his knees. He wouldn't look at me. He spoke to the floor. "I've been giving Camacho information for about ten years. Not him personally, but his organization down here, based at the ranch, mainly Cesar. In exchange, they agreed to stay away from my wife. If I didn't cooperate, they would do to her what they did to me."

His face crumpled like a small child's. His bottom lip curled in. His eyes puffed up and tears spilled down his face. Dehan got up and went to the bathroom. She returned with a roll of paper and gave it to Penny. She pulled off a handful and gave it to him. He took it in his hands and buried his face in it, leaning against his wife, sobbing convulsively, like ten years of pain and toxic fear were all spilling out in a torrent in that moment.

Eventually, the convulsions stopped and his breathing, though still tremulous, became steadier. Finally he stood and went into the bathroom, where he blew his nose noisily and splashed his face with water. When he came back out, he stood awhile, holding the doorjamb and looking at me.

"I have never told anyone what they did to me, not even . . . *especially* not Penny. But if you know anything about the Camachos, I don't need to tell you. There was no way—there *is* no way—that I am going to allow that to happen to her. I don't care who I have to betray, or who I have to kill."

"You don't need to kill or betray anybody, D.C. Let's not make this any more complicated than it already is. Just answer me a question. Until today, has anybody ever been hurt as a result of the information you have given—and remember, this can and will be verified."

"No. Never. I was useful to them. As long as nobody got killed or injured, they could use me indefinitely. They knew that as soon as anybody got hurt, my days would be numbered."

I sighed and rubbed my face. The weariness was getting to me. I looked at Dehan and she nodded. I said, "How good is your information on them?"

"It's pretty good." He nodded a few times to himself. "Over the years, they've grown to trust me. They pay me." He looked up at me like he was ashamed. "You have to accept or they get offended. It's like you think you're too good to accept their money. In the end, they were paying me a lot. I put it all in an account in Belize. My idea was, we could use it if we ever had to escape. It's still there. I never touched it . . ." He dithered a moment. "My point is, they've grown to trust me. We've become kind of . . . *friends* . . ." He said it like the word made him nauseous. "I drive down at least once a month. We talk. They tell me what's going down, and I tell them whatever they need to know that's relevant to their operations."

"So they keep you in the loop so you can select what information they need to know."

"Yeah. It wasn't like that in the beginning, obviously. But like I say, it's been ten years. More."

"So you can provide names, dates . . ."

"I have enough information to sink the whole operation, take down the Camacho brothers and maybe a dozen or more of their lieutenants."

"Then you know as well as I do what you have to do. Do it right and it might actually pay off for you. You make a deal with the bureau. Like you said, we talk to Washington. You offer them the Camachos, Cesar—everything from Mexico all the way to the East Coast. You give them Julio and Feliciano, and all their head honchos . . ."

"Eighteen agents died because of the information I gave, Stone."

"And they are not going to forgive you for that. But there *are* mitigating circumstances, and the bottom line is, you did not expect the Camachos to take the action they did. When you found out what they had done, in retaliation, you were prepared to give the Feds the whole operation. Their choice is, punish you or take down the operation. It's obvious, they will cut you a deal."

He nodded a few times, then looked up at me, and across at Dehan. "But Penny boards that plane tonight."

I jerked my head in a question at Dehan. She shrugged. "Makes sense to me."

I narrowed my eyes at him and added, "But there is one more thing I need from you."

TWENTY

Outside the window, the desert was turning gold. The sky in the north was turning a darker shade of blue, and there was one huge saguaro whose shadow was stretching long across the dust. I was trying to estimate the height of the cactus, and the length of the shadow. I figured it was at least fifteen feet high and the shadow had to stretch for at least thirty or thirty-five feet.

I zoned back in and realized that Special Agent in Charge Pat O'Leary had been talking to me. I narrowed my eyes and tried to look like I'd been thinking about D.C., then lost interest and said, "What?"

He raised an eyebrow at me. I wasn't sure if it was irritated or skeptical. It may have been both.

"I asked you, Detective Stone, if you had anything to add to what Detective Dehan has told me."

That would have been an easier question to answer if I had been listening to Detective Dehan.

"Not really, Special Agent O'Leary. In fact, given that we were both almost killed because of intelligence that was leaked from this field office, you will understand that I, we both . . ." I trailed off, having made spaghetti of my grammar. ". . . We are both reluctant to say too much. No doubt Washington will be contacting you in due course."

He sat and jerked his eyes around my face for a bit, then shook his head like a man who is having trouble understanding something. "This attack, that you allege, occurred at shortly before seven o'clock this morning." He spread his hands. "Where have you been all day?" He gestured out the window at the lengthening shadows that had been distracting me moments before. "That was about twelve hours ago."

Dehan smiled, and it was actually a nice smile, which made what she said next all the more jarring. "Well, Special Agent, there were the few hours that we were escaping through the desert attempting not to get disemboweled. After that, we were continuing the investigation which brought us here in the first place. And, as Detective Stone pointed out a moment ago, given that a leak from this field office led to the deaths of some eighteen agents, and almost cost us our lives, we were somewhat cautious about coming in, so we contacted Washington instead."

He sighed and closed his eyes. After a moment, he opened them again and asked us both, "Has either of you any idea of where Agent Daryl Collins or his wife are?"

"As Detective Dehan has already explained to you, first we called the field office and were given the runaround, then we called Daryl. We met him at Wendy's, at the Pilot Travel Center at Rio Rico. He then drove us back toward Tucson. After that, Detective Dehan and I continued to conduct our own investigation. Where Agent Collins is now is impossible to say."

He drummed his fingers on his desk, eyeing Dehan. "You were here as observers. You have no jurisdiction in Arizona. So what is the nature of your investigation?"

"We were making unofficial inquiries."

He studied her for a long moment, then asked, "Are you being deliberately obstructive, Detective Dehan?"

She thought about the answer for a moment, then nodded. "Yes, and I hope you understand why. There is a leak in your office, and right now we don't know who it is, though the pool . . ." She made a circle with her hands, indicating a pool. "The pool of possible suspects is very small. So I am afraid that with all the due respect, we are not going to be very cooperative with this office. We will cooperate fully with Washington and New York."

He gave another big, deep sigh. "I guess that makes perfect sense."

After that, we rose and left his office. We collected my Jag from the parking garage and headed south, out of Phoenix, toward Tucson on the I-10, with the windows open and the desert air battering our faces. I kept it to a steady seventy, and Dehan stretched out in her seat with her shades up on her head and her eyes closed.

"Man," she said, "I am tired."

"It's been a long two days, and a long week."

She nodded, then asked, "Are we okay, Stone?" She half opened her eyes to look at me. "What happened, does it change . . . *us*?"

I didn't answer straightaway, glanced at her, and saw that she looked a little sick, worried. I said, "I thought about that. I almost went back to New York. What you did goes against everything I believe in, Dehan. You have to know that. But no, it doesn't change us. I can't imagine life without you."

She grinned, made a "tss!" sound, and looked away. "You're such a sissy."

"But don't do it again, Dehan, not while you're working with me. You understand that?"

She nodded. "Yeah."

"You're a cop, not a vigilante. You can't use the NYPD as a means to exact your personal vengeance."

"I get it, Sensei! No more vengeance. I'll behave."

She closed her eyes again, and afternoon moved to evening. We passed through Tucson and took the I-19 out, moving south toward Rio Rico and Nogales. The sky was turning dark overhead, and the first stars were beginning to poke through the translucent, dark turquoise dome. Headlamps were coming on, and I was beginning to feel the first stirrings of hunger.

"I have to say," I said, and she opened her eyes and turned her head to look at me. "I do like the arrangement we've made for tonight. Do you know they've been making wine in Arizona since the sixteenth century? That's Henry the Eighth, Sir Francis Drake, Sir Walter Raleigh, five or six hundred years."

She grunted and closed her eyes again. "I don't know much about wine, but Arizona? Really?" She did a passable generic cowboy accent. "Ah sure do like the boo-kay from that thayah Cabernay, Slim. Think I'll git me some a' that they'er wine, give it to mah dogies."

"Ha! Do I detect an East Coast snob in my car? I'll have you know..."

She opened one eye. "You'll have me know?"

"I will. I'll have you know Arizona is producing some of the best wines in America."

"Yeehaw."

"Well, I'm looking forward to it. The food sounds good too."

"Okay. Just let me sleep for an hour or two and I'll probably sound as much like Frasier as you do. Or Niles. Which was the gay one?"

"Funny."

"By the way, did you buy me panties and a bra in the end?"

"Mm-hm, they are black lace with strategically placed strawberries on them. I thought you'd like them."

I glanced at her, but she was smiling and snoring softly.

Just outside Nogales, we took the exit for Grand Avenue and followed it as far as Kino Park. There I took the exit for the West Patagonia Highway and pretty soon we were past Beyerville and climbing into the Patagonia Mountains. Meanwhile, behind us, the sky caught fire across the horizon, and ahead, the darkness closed in.

We arrived in Sonoita a little after eight. There wasn't a lot to see. The last of the sunlight had drained out of the west, and, aside from the light cast by a few scattered buildings, there was no illumination in the town. I say town, but I use the word in the loosest sense. Sonoita is a crossroads with a gas station, a hotel, and two excellent restaurants. There is little else besides a handful of houses and a couple of wineries that make wine from the vineyards to the west of the town. One of those wineries, the Dos Cabezas, Daryl had told me was highly respected in oenological circles, competing with the best that California had to offer.

The other, Bodegas del Diablo, was a relatively new enterprise, barely five years old, but it was starting to produce some wines that people who said things like, "shy but with a cheeky hint of vanilla and *bags* of fruit" were beginning to talk about. The Bodegas del Diablo had bought up a number of local vineyards and had also converted an old ranch, north of the town, into a bodega in the Spanish tradition. They also had a big warehouse for distribution, right on the main street. From what Daryl had told me, they were distributing wine to Los Angeles, San Francisco, Chicago, and New York, which was pretty impressive for a wine producer that had not, as yet, been written up in any of the major wine industry magazines. Given that the Camachos had invested heavily in it, that made us both wonder whether they were distributing more than just wine.

We had booked ourselves into the Sonoita Inn, and after that we had booked a table at Hank's Diner. Hank's Diner, just a short walk from the hotel, was a fashionable eatery, frequented by people who talked about wine as though it was a lovably impertinent fruit salad. They would fly and drive from California, New Mexico, Texas, and the East Coast to experience the genius with which Hank combined fine Arizona wines with exquisitely crafted food. As though that were not enough to bring on a gourmet orgasm, while you were eating and drinking his perfect combinations, he would explain them to you in a culinary variation of talking dirty. Hank's Diner was also frequented, so D.C. told us, by Cesar and, when they were in town, the Camachos.

We parked at the inn, in the farthest, darkest corner of the parking lot, behind a couple of trees, and then I checked in at the reception desk while Dehan yawned a lot and stared around at the unusual décor. After that, we walked a hundred yards down the road, under an infinity of stars, for what was billed on the website as an "Unforgettable Gourmet Experience."

As we approached the diner, she slipped her arm through mine and leaned her head on my shoulder. "If you ever tell anyone I said this, I will castrate you with a blunt razor, but being happy with you is more important to me than seeking revenge..."

I kissed the top of her head. "I know how much that means. Thank you."

She turned her head and pointed behind us. "You know the other place? The Steak Out? The place we *didn't* reserve a table at? They specialize in mesquite chargrilled, home-cut steak. And they don't talk to you while you're eating."

"We discussed this already, Dehan..."

"No, we didn't. *You* talked and I slept. Home cut. Chargrilled. Steak. And also margaritas."

"You'll enjoy it, darling."

"So weird."

"Besides which, our boys will not *be* at the Steak Out, alluring as it sounds..."

"Why are you talking like that?"

"I don't know. It's since you compared me to Frasier."

We crossed the dusty forecourt onto the decked terrace and pushed through the door. A boy in jeans and a red T-shirt met us at the entrance, smiled, and asked Dehan if we had booked. He had a face that said it would have been sexist to ask me. Dehan looked up at me and said, "I don't know, darling. Did we book?"

I smiled at the stud in the boy's upper lip. "Yeah, Stone. Table for two."

"Oh yes, Mr. Stone. We have you by the window. We hope the view will enhance your dining experience."

The place was not swanky, but it was attractive in a plain kind of way. The floors were plain wood, as were the tables and chairs and the wine racks that dotted the redbrick walls. The bar was an irregular slab of wood polished to a high sheen. The décor was simple and unaffected. There were no wagon wheels.

There were not many customers either: a man and a woman at the bar having a cocktail, a table of four women, and two tables occupied by two couples in shorts, tennis shoes, and unwashed T-shirts. The waiter, who said his name was Clive, or James, or something that wasn't "waiter," led us to our window table and offered us a couple of menus.

"Can I get you a drink while you decide?"

I nodded. "My wife needs a margarita, and I'll have an Irish whiskey, in a cognac balloon, with no ice."

He cocked a hip. "In a . . ." He made the shape of a cognac balloon. "With no . . ." He made the gesture of putting ice in the glass. "Got it."

He went away, and we scanned the room the way first-time tourists would. Dehan shook her head. "I don't see them."

"How would we know for sure?"

She gave me a dead look that said I should engage my brain. "Well, for a start, they wouldn't look like anybody in here right now. And they wouldn't be driving any of the cars we saw outside."

I sat back and sighed. "Yes, dear. As usual, you are right."

Her eyes narrowed into a sly smile. "I think you get off on this whole suburban, retired-married thing. I think you have a secret desire to be one of those cardigan, pipe and slippers guys who potters around his garden while his wife makes blueberry pies."

"You could be right. I may have been kidding myself all these years. Perhaps it's time to come out."

Zack appeared with our drinks and told us what they were as he set them down in front of us, in case we'd forgotten what we'd ordered. Dehan smiled at the margarita, sipped it, and sighed, then offered her smile to Zack.

"We'll have the antipasto to start, then my husband will have the chef's signature burger, and so will I. You choose the wine, but in the meantime, you'd better be fixing me another one of these."

He narrowed his eyes, smiled with his mouth, and gave a small giggle, then he hurried away.

I asked her, "Do you think you should have another, dear? You know how you get. It'll be up and down all night, emptying your incontinence pants."

"Ass. That's them."

The door had opened. I forced myself to stare at her face and laugh instead of turning, like she'd said something adorable.

"How can you be sure, you silly monkey?"

She took my hand and smiled into my eyes. "It's something about the Italian suits and the scar down the side of his face."

"You say such lovely things."

"I'm serious." She leaned a little closer. "Remind me why we have to lay this on so thick."

"According to you, so that I can fulfill my cardigan fantasy. Also, because if we don't, we come across as a couple of hard-boiled New York cops from the Bronx."

She batted her eyelashes. "I'm going to the can. Pretend to watch my ass as I walk past them. You'll see what I mean."

She got up and crossed the dining room. It was a very easy ass to watch, and I realized as she passed their table that I was not the only man in the room watching it. The two men who had sat at the table near the bar were also watching. They were both in expensive black suits that had that Armani look which says you make up in money for what you lack in taste. The younger of the two had a burgundy shirt with a bootlace tie. He had hair gelled into spikes and a diamond in his left ear. The guy sitting next to him looked less Latino and more Indian. He had long black hair in a ponytail, an aquiline nose, and black eyes. He wore a black shirt and a thin gold chain around his neck. I was pretty sure he was the guy I'd seen getting out of the Cessna. A deep scar ran from the corner of his right eye to the corner of his mouth.

If D.C. was right, and I had no doubt he was, these were

Cesar, who ran the Beyer Ranch, and the *sicario*. It wasn't hard to guess which was which. Two minutes later, while they were giving a pretty waitress with scruffy jeans and a red T-shirt their order, Dehan came back and sat.

"What do you think?"

I nodded. "I had never noticed before, but you're right. You have a very nice backside."

"Not funny."

"Also, I think you are certainly correct. These are our boys. I think the scar is the *sicario* and the guy with the gel is Cesar."

"So if the information D.C. gave us is right, the merchandise is at the Bodegas del Diablo warehouse."

I took her hand and looked at her dreamily. "You know? You talk just like a cop." I laughed and leaned toward her. "If I were in this room with somebody else, say a coke dealer, I'd point you out to them and say, 'Look, that beautiful young woman over there is a cop.'"

"You would?"

I nodded. "I sure would, darling."

"Not a murdering, fascistic vigilante?" She sighed and sipped her drink. "It's hard."

I shook my head and smiled. "You are an attractive, intelligent, interesting woman who has a lot to offer *besides* the ability to bring down a two-hundred-and-twenty-pound man with a flying side kick while simultaneously cleaning and loading a fifty-cal Smith and Wesson 500 revolver." I sat back. "Look, we know what we have to do, and we don't have to do it till after dinner. So in the meantime, let's chill, enjoy the food and the wine."

She smiled, and for the first time in a long while, there was no sarcasm in her face. "And the company?"

I nodded. "Above all the company."

TWENTY-ONE

We drank a lot less than we appeared to and spent the evening apparently engrossed in each other. We took photographs of our food and of each other and WhatsApped them to imagined children and parents, and laughed at how jealous they would be. In at least four of them, Cesar and the *sicario* were clearly visible and recognizable.

I sent one to D.C. with the message, *Can you identify the ingredients?*

His reply was less coy: *Burgundy shirt is Cesar. Other guy could be Sicario, I never met him tho.*

By ten o'clock, they were eating roasted prime rib and we were sipping coffee. I signaled the waiter. He approached with a thin veneer of a smile on his face. "What can I do to make your dining experience more fulfilling?" he asked.

"Two things," I told him with no kind of smile on mine. "You can stop calling it a dining experience, and you can bring me the check."

His smile became a rictus and he said quietly, "Heavens . . ." before going away to get the check.

Dehan was frowning at me. It was an expression of intelligent inquiry. "Why *is* everything referred to now as an experience? You don't travel, you have a travel experience. You don't go for the groceries, you have a shopping experience. You don't go to the can, you..."

"Yeah, I got it. It's part of Mankind's eternal quest to be ever greater assholes, Dehan. Or perhaps there is an evil genius manipulating society and attempting to persuade us that everything is just an experience, nothing is real..."

She nodded. "And therefore everything is permitted. You're probably right."

Zack returned with the check. I paid cash and left a generous tip. As we stood, he smiled at me with spiteful eyes and said, "I hope you enjoy your Arizona experience. Do come back soon."

Outside, the desert air was cold. A moon like a fat orange was sitting over the mountain peaks in the east and casting a strange, translucent blue light on the sand. It made inky shadows out of the scattered cars in the parking lot, the fence posts across the blacktop, and the solitary, scattered trees in the fields beyond. One of the cars in the lot was a dark Audi RS 7.

Overhead, the sky was vast and the stars crystal clear. I shuddered and felt suddenly exposed. I put my arm around Dehan and we started to walk with loud footsteps across the gravel, toward the road.

The road was long and very straight, and it was a good ten-minute walk back to the hotel. A little over halfway, on the right, there was a cluster of stores, houses, and small businesses. And right there among them was the Bodegas del Diablo warehouse. It was a big, whitewashed building, faintly luminous in the moonlight, with large, green gates leading onto a courtyard which I figured was a loading bay. As we approached, I slowed and glanced around. The whole town was silent and still—aside from our footsteps, which were loud and seemed somehow to echo in the emptiness.

"How'd you want to play this, Stone? The coke is in there, two and a half million bucks' worth. We are ninety-nine percent sure of that. They are in the diner..."

"The secret to a successful operation is careful planning," I muttered. "But how the hell do you make a careful plan when all you've got is ifs, maybes, and probablys?"

"According to D.C., the usual routine for a New York shipment is to bring it up here and conceal it in a wine delivery to be shipped out next morning. If he's relaxing over dinner at his favorite restaurant, two gets you twenty he already unloaded it from his trunk."

"If the merchandise came by car, it won't have been his. It will be another vehicle on the other side of those doors."

We had stopped and were standing on the road, looking at the warehouse. It was dark and silent, like the town. The air was cold enough for our breath to make clouds of condensation. She said, "We can't stand here staring at the warehouse. Somebody is going to spot us."

Behind us, maybe three or four hundred yards away, voices rose on the night air. We looked back, and two figures were stepping out of the diner, moving across the lot toward where I knew the Audi was. I heard Dehan breathe, "*Come on!*" and next thing, she was running across the dirt to the general store twenty feet from the western wall of the warehouse.

I rasped, "*Dehan!*" I could see what she was thinking, and I didn't like it. The general store had a large porch with a dense vine growing up its facade and over the roof. Concealed behind it, on the decking, peering through the leaves, she would have a clear view of the big green doors that gave access to the Bodegas del Diablo warehouse.

I went after her, but she was almost twenty years younger than I was and a hundred pounds lighter. She vaulted over the railing and hissed at me, "*C'mon! Hurry up!*"

I ducked under and we crouched down in the shadows, peering through the vine. She pulled her Glock and cocked it. I sighed and did the same with my Colt. Away at the diner, I could see the Audi backing up. For a second, its headlamps glared directly at us and I had the irrational feeling we had been seen.

Then they turned, pulled slowly onto the road, and cruised in our direction. The moon, now turning silver, laid bright reflections across the roof of the car.

They came level with us, and for a moment I thought they were going to continue on past, but they didn't. They slowed and turned, then rolled, crunching gravel, up to the big green doors. They didn't get out. They waited, with their lamps making big, luminous circles against the green wood and the walls. After a moment, there was a noise of heavy iron on wood, and the massive doors swung slowly inward. From where I was crouched, I could see one guy. He looked Latino, though it was hard to tell in the poor light. The Audi rolled in out of sight and then the engine died. Doors slammed like two gunshots. Then there were voices. I counted four. One of them said, "*No, dejen la puerta. Si nos vamos ya.*"

Dehan breathed in my ear, "*He says to leave the doors, they're leaving in a minute.*" She had her phone in her hand and took a picture of the open doors. "*I can't get the car, without the registration it's not worth jack!*"

Then she was on her feet, vaulting silently over the rail onto the gravel. Fear and nausea lurched in my belly. I bit my tongue. To shout to her would be a death sentence. I got to my feet. She had holstered her Glock and was holding her phone with both hands, filming, stepping sideways, trying to capture the trunk of the car. I swore silently and profanely in my head and came off the veranda, covering the door with my Colt.

She stopped filming, stepped over to me, and breathed on my other ear. "*They've gone inside.*"

Before I could answer, she was running down into the space between the general store and the warehouse. I went after her, reaching out to grab her arm. But she was away, flattened against the wall, inching toward the open green doors. I followed, keeping her covered as best I could. She paused, inches from the opening, and I closed in behind her. We waited. There was silence. She squatted down, went on one knee, and leaned forward. She smiled, filmed the trunk of the car, with the registration plate, then panned slowly around to show where it was. Still filming, she stood and took in the sign over the door, *Bodegas del Diablo*.

She stopped and stared at me, chewing her lip, then shook her head. She was telling me it was not enough. I shook my head back, telling her the risk was too high. She nodded like she'd understood, put her phone away, and pulled her weapon. I scowled. She ignored me and stepped around the door, scanning the area. I followed. The car was eighteen or twenty feet away, in the center of a large, dirt courtyard, maybe forty or fifty feet square. At the far end, there was a kind of raised platform from where the trucks were loaded, with steps leading up to it over on the far right. It was about eight or ten feet deep, with a huge steel roller blind and, at the top of the steps, a green wooden door. The door was open, dim light was spilling out, and there were quiet voices inside.

To the left of the Audi, there was an old TerraStar backed up against the platform. There was nobody in the cab. I touched her arm and pointed at the truck. Then I pointed at the trunk of the Audi and back at the truck. She thought about it and nodded. Then I pointed at us and gestured behind the truck. We were in the middle of the yard and needed to take cover. She looked skeptical, but as the voices began suddenly to grow louder, she sighed and jerked her head toward the shadows.

We slipped behind the TerraStar and she dropped silently to her belly. The Glock was on the ground by her side and she had her phone out again. I dropped beside her, keeping the Audi covered.

There was the scuff of feet. Bodies came down the steps and boots came into view around the car. The car bleeped, and the boots, at least four pairs of them, moved to the back of the car. We heard the trunk open. Almost simultaneously, with startling suddenness, the roller blind in the back of the truck was wrenched up, no more than ten feet behind us. Dehan half rose, stared at me wide-eyed, and mouthed, "*They are loading the stuff!*"

I scowled and mouthed back, "*No!*"

"*Yes!*"

I held up four fingers and mouthed, "*Minimum!*"

What she did next took a matter of less than a second. She clenched her lips into a tight line, narrowed her eyes, and flopped down on her belly, pulling the Glock into both hands. In that moment, everything went into impossibly slow motion. I could see three pairs of legs. I noted two pairs were in dark, woolen pants. The third was in faded jeans. My brain calculated absently that the fourth pair of legs was above and behind us on the loading platform, or in the truck. In the hundredth of a second it took me to note that, Dehan had taken aim at the back of one of the legs in jeans and pulled the trigger. There was a loud crack, like a firecracker. Blood erupted from the far side of the leg. There was a scream and Dehan was rolling. Her face, a mere inch from mine, gloated for a second and she said, "Three, not four."

Then she was on her feet and I was scrambling after her. She stepped around the cab of the truck with the pistol held out in front of her and snarled, "Okay, *pendejos*, police! Freeze!"

I came around after her in time to see the guy on the ground pull his piece from his belt. She didn't flinch. She didn't take her eyes off Cesar and the *sicario*. She just moved her hands to the left and shot him where he lay, right between the eyes. He sagged back, his eyes wide and startled, a neat, red hole in the middle of his forehead.

Before he'd lain back down, she was covering the other two again and speaking. "You want to have a go, huh, Cesar? How about you? You look like a pro, *Sicario*. You fancy your chances?"

They had their hands up and they were watching her without expression. The trunk of the car was open. I glanced in. It was full of blue plastic packages sealed up with duct tape. I moved behind the two men toward the steps and Dehan kept talking.

"Tell your boy to stand down, Cesar. If he does anything heroic, I drop you first and my partner will take out the *sicario* here."

I climbed the steps, and a boy of about eighteen or twenty

stepped out of the truck with a pump-action shotgun in his hands. His eyes said he was scared, but they also said he'd rather die than let down his boss. Dehan didn't even look at him. She just took careful aim at Cesar's head. Her voice was cold and steady. "Take out the *sicario* first, Stone." Then she grinned. "Guess this is what they call a Mexican standoff, huh, Cesar?"

Cesar looked at the kid and said, "*Mátela.*"

Kill her.

Then all hell broke loose. I didn't hesitate. I double-tapped and shot the kid twice through the heart. His shotgun went off and shattered the windshield of the Audi. Dehan fired. Cesar went down and simultaneously the *sicario* screamed and spun into a flying roundhouse kick. All that happened in less than two seconds.

Next thing, Dehan was sprawled in the dirt, but before I could run to her, the door by the steps erupted less than six feet away and three guys piled out on me, screaming. For a split second, all I saw was a fat guy in a vest with wild hair and sweat all over his face. In his hand, he had a machete. I emptied two rounds into his gut when he was just inches from me. His face screwed up in a wince and I jumped from the steps. I heard his body fall behind me. I ran two steps and turned, raising the Colt. I heard a scream and wasn't sure if it was a man or a woman.

On the steps, there were two men, backlit by the door. They were both training automatics on me. I thought, *I'm going to die now*. I shot the one on my right through the chest and saw the other gun jump. I heard a pop, and my face burned as I turned to aim. My stomach was panicking. I fought to control my movements, not to overswing. It felt like agonizing minutes, but it was probably a tenth of a second. I heard his bullet hit the Audi, saw him adjust. His next shot would kill me. I squeezed the trigger, twice. I saw his head jerk and a dark plume of spray behind him.

But I was already turning. The scream I'd heard was ringing through my brain. I ran two more strides to the trunk of the car. Dehan was on her back. Her Glock was in the dirt three or four feet from her head. The *sicario* was sitting astride her, leaning down. He had a long switchblade in his hands, putting all his weight on it, driving it down toward her throat. I felt a hot rage well up in my belly that fogged my mind. I rushed him, bellowing. I grabbed him by his ponytail with my left hand and dragged him to his feet, pounding his kidneys with my right fist, roaring something at him.

He spun and slashed at my face. I blocked him with my left and drove my fist into his face. He staggered back, and I went after him, swinging. I drove my left fist into his ribs, then pounded his face, right, left, right, and he went down. I stepped up and kicked the knife away from his hand, then turned. Dehan was on her feet, moving toward me.

"Are you okay?" My voice sounded odd, thick.

"Yeah. Are you?" I nodded. She pointed. "Look at your arm."

I looked at my left arm. It was slick with blood from a deep cut.

She said, "Take off your shirt."

"What, now?" I smiled idiotically and the world started to seesaw.

"You're going into shock and you're losing a lot of blood. Sit down."

I sat in the dust. She tore off my sleeve and made a rough, improvised tourniquet-cum-bandage. I was shaking with cold, and she put my jacket and hers around my shoulders. Then she had her phone in her hand and she was dialing as she walked over to the *sicario*. She knelt down beside him and felt his neck.

"This is Detective Carmen Dehan . . . We have a bit of a situation in Sonoita, and I was wondering if we could count on your cooperation. It's a complex situation, and we are going to need the sheriff. We have five dead and one seriously injured. We also have an injured police detective. This comes under the direct jurisdiction of the Washington HQ, and they will be contacting you shortly. Right now, we need some deputies to secure the scene, a couple of meat wagons, and some paramedics. It's pretty urgent."

Then she hung up and called Washington. The conversation was brief, and when she'd finished, she came over and hunkered down beside me.

"Stone?"

"Yeah. I am very cold."

"Hang in there. I'll get you over to the hotel right away. Just tell me something while you remember. Why did you throw down your gun instead of shooting him?"

I pulled the jackets close around me and lied. "I might have hit you."

She stared at me with narrowed eyes, like she knew I was lying. She said, "You broke his neck. That's a hell of a right hook you have there."

I nodded. "I guess it is."

TWENTY-TWO

As it happened, the sheriff and his deputies arrived at the same time as the FBI chopper from the San Diego field office, about an hour and a half after Dehan had called. In that time, Dehan had managed to enlist the help of the hotel management: a calm, dependable husband and wife team who had brought blankets and hot drinks, and roused the Sonoita pharmacist, who was the closest thing they had to a doctor. She had stabilized Cesar's condition and fixed my arm, at least temporarily, telling me I was lucky he had missed the artery and vein, but I had lost a lot of blood and was sure as hell going to need stitches.

With all the activity, a curious, mildly sympathetic crowd had gathered, and Dehan had moved me, the pharmacist, and the hotel owners outside the warehouse gates, to preserve the crime scene.

Now I was sitting in the cold dust with my back against the wall, watching the caravan of sheriff's department vehicles stream off the road and form a cordon around the building. Pretty soon, the deputies were telling people to move on and back off, and the crowd was steadily dispersing. The sheriff had a "what the hell is going on" face, which he had brought with him all the way from

Nogales just for Dehan, and he was marching it over to show it to her now. As he approached the big green doors, Dehan was waiting for him with her badge.

"Sheriff."

"Miss, do you mind telling me what the *hell* is going on here?"

She stuck the badge in his face and said, "Detective. Detective Dehan. What the hell is going on here, Sheriff, is that the FBI have jurisdiction over this crime scene. There is a forensic team on its way now, and I would be grateful to you, Sheriff, if you would assist me in securing the area."

He scowled at her badge and then scowled at her even harder. "First, that is an NYPD badge, not an FBI badge, second, if there are people getting shot up in my goddamn county on my goddamn watch, I want to know who the hell they are and what the *hell* is going on!"

"Keep running your mouth, Sheriff, and I won't tell you a goddamn thing. This is my investigation, I am collaborating with the bureau, and you have no jurisdiction here. You want to play nice, we'll talk. You want to sling your dick around, you lost my interest. Take it down a notch, Sheriff. Now, where is your medical examiner?"

He was saved from having to answer by the sound of an approaching chopper. As it came in to land, it kicked up huge clouds of dust and sent clusters of people, hunched, covering their faces with their arms, scattering. The turbines whined, and the rotors thudded slowly to a halt. A team of three men in jeans and sweatshirts climbed out and started hawking equipment out of the helicopter. A tall, red-haired woman in her late thirties, dressed in a blue pantsuit, came striding over. The sheriff watched her approach with a face that was eloquent of what he thought of women in pantsuits.

The redhead pointed at Dehan. "Are you the detective who called this in?"

"Dehan."

"Murphy."

They shook, and she introduced the sheriff, who opened and closed his mouth a few times and stuck his thumbs in his belt. I saw the three guys from the chopper, now dressed like aliens in white plastic suits, carrying large amounts of equipment across the dirt toward the warehouse. Ice-cold air touched my face, and I closed my eyes. Somebody said something about the deceased, and I wondered if I had died. I tried to hold on to Dehan's voice, but it kept drifting away, which made me think that maybe I was.

I could see her, a long way down beneath me, small, talking to the sheriff and Agent Murphy. There was a Chinese woman too, and somehow I knew she was the ME. Red-and-blue lights kept pulsing over the dust. There was a gurney being wheeled toward an ambulance. The *sicario* was on it, with his broken neck. I looked up. I was closer to the moon now, where it sat over the desert hills. It had changed from orange to silver, and now it was silver tinted with turquoise. It had a bright halo that bathed the vast expanse of dust and shrubs and mesquite trees, creating a world of half shadows and misleading light, where it was easy to get lost and drawn down into the dark. This was the fall moon, and the fall moon was for killing.

I opened my eyes. There were fewer vehicles, and most of those that remained were pulling away, heading west. Agent Murphy was talking to a couple of men in white plastic. Dehan's face was very close to mine, peering at me.

"Come on, tough guy. The doc wants to look at you."

I realized I was freezing. She pulled me to my feet and we walked a long distance across cold dust toward the back of an ambulance. I saw a Chinese woman frowning at my belly. Somebody said, "Jesus Christ!"

I wondered why, because I was feeling very peaceful.

I OPENED MY EYES. There was bright sunshine lying across the foot of my bed in big, warped squares. It was a very comfortable bed, and I felt very tired. Slowly, it occurred to me that I did not know the room. I lay and breathed peacefully for a while and slowly, recollections started to seep back. I shifted my eyes and saw Dehan sitting in an armchair by the window, reading a book. Her hair was tied in a knot behind her neck. I liked that and smiled.

I said, "Good morning." It came out very quiet, and I had to say it again.

She looked up from her book and returned my smile. "Hey, big guy. How you feeling?"

"Tired. More than I ought. Why?"

"Why?"

"Why do I feel worse than I ought? What happened?"

"You gave us a scare."

I looked down at my inside elbow, saw a bruise and a sticking plaster, and realized I'd had a drip. "I lost a lot of blood?"

She nodded and came over to sit on the bed. "He didn't just cut your arm, Stone, though that was bad enough. He stabbed you in the gut too. I don't understand how you didn't notice. I guess the heat of the moment, his blade was probably razor sharp . . ."

She shook her head. My left arm was bandaged, and when I peered under the covers, I saw my waist was bandaged too.

"How bad is it?"

"They were going to airlift you to hospital. Doc said a couple of inches to the left and you'd have been fighting for your life. It's a miracle he missed any major organs. As it is, your biggest problem is anemia, you lost a lot of blood. We need to get you to a hospital pretty soon for a thorough examination, and meantime, you keep an eye on the can to make sure you don't crap or pee red. You're a lucky man."

"How long have I been asleep?"

"Fifteen hours."

"Jesus. What's happened?"

"You up to it?"

I nodded.

"Agent Murphy is still here. Special Agent in Charge Pat

O'Leary, D.C.'s boss, is also here. D.C. is here, and so is Agent Mike Turner from Washington. As soon as you feel up to it, we all need to have a powwow."

I smiled. "A powwow? Okay, well, you get me some coffee and something to eat, and I'll be ready for your powwow."

She stared at me for a while. I gave her a "what?" face, and she got up and called room service for a pot of coffee and some bacon and eggs. When she'd hung up, she took a deep breath and leaned on the foot of the bed as she let it out in a long hiss.

I said, "What's on your mind, Dehan?"

"How well do you remember the events of last night?"

I shrugged. "Up till I sat down by the big gates, perfectly."

"Then you need to explain something to me, before we have our debriefing." She came around and sat on the bed again. "You're an experienced detective. You aren't stationed in some sleepy village in New England. You're working the Bronx. You have been in violent situations many times before."

I nodded. "Sure. What's your point?"

She stared at me for a long moment. "I get that you used his ponytail to drag him off. What I don't get is why you threw your gun down. Stick it in his neck, his back, the back of his head . . ." She shrugged, spread her hands. "But you threw it down in the dirt and started pounding him. Stone, you lost it. You went crazy. You were screaming at him like a madman."

"What was I screaming?"

"No."

"No?"

She nodded. "Just no. But there's more, Stone. Not only did you not notice you had been stabbed, you hit him so hard you *broke his neck*. And he wasn't a ninety-pound weed. He was a tough guy." She shook her head. "What the hell got into you?"

I held her eye, going over the events minutely in my mind. I remembered it perfectly, and in vivid detail, though I didn't remember screaming. Finally, I said, "I dropped the gun by accident. I was going to take the shot, realized the risk to you, and, in that moment, the reflex made my hand open and I dropped the gun." I shook my head. "I honestly don't remember screaming. Perhaps when I realized I was unarmed and he was trying to stab you . . ." I shrugged again. "As to breaking his neck. I guess I am stronger than I thought, or he was unlucky in the position of his head."

She didn't answer for a moment, flicking her eyes over my face. "I don't buy that and neither do you. I'll let it pass for now. In the debriefing, be vague about your recollections of the fight. Put it down to an unfortunate fall . . ."

I shrugged. "You're the boss."

She didn't smile. "No, I'm not. We're partners. And Stone?"

"What?"

"Thank you. You saved my life."

I smiled. "Did I? I didn't realize."

She smiled back. "You're such an asshole."

Then there was a knock at the door and my breakfast arrived.

AFTER EATING, I was feeling strong enough to get up and dress and go very gently down to reception, where management had granted us the area around the fireplace to have our meeting and debriefing. There was a sofa and there were two armchairs and a long coffee table. Two extra chairs had been provided.

By the time we'd got down the steps, all the others had assembled in a horseshoe around the cold fireplace. A large armchair had been reserved for me at the right-hand extreme of the horseshoe, beside the fireplace, and I lowered myself carefully into it with Dehan's help.

I had Dehan on my right, sitting on the stone hearth, and Daryl on my left. He watched me anxiously, and once I was sitting, I gave him a weary smile and shook his hand.

Next to him was Agent Murphy, watching me carefully. Beside her, with a face that could have turned fresh milk sour, was the special agent in charge of the Phoenix field office, Pat O'Leary.

Next to him, almost opposite me and at the far extreme of the horseshoe, was a man I didn't know, but I guessed was Mike Turner.

My first impression was that he was too young, barely thirty-five, too well groomed, and too willing to smile like he knew everything already. But maybe that's just the way it is in DC. Dehan gestured at him and said, "Special Agent Mike Turner, this is Detective John Stone, who was injured last night."

He raised a hand and offered an amused smile. "Good to know you, John. Time to start thinking about a desk job, huh?" With that, he glanced at Dehan and winked. Then he looked around the room and said, "Before we get started, guys, can I just ask, who is liaising with the sheriff's department?"

Murphy raised her hand. "For the moment I am, but I think we are about to hand over to SAC O'Leary. It makes more sense for Phoenix to take charge of that."

I saw O'Leary's cheeks flush, and Turner turned narrowed eyes on him, then looked at Dehan and at me with the same eyes. "Yeah. I am not clear on this. I am not sure why you didn't contact Phoenix last night, Carmen. In fact, I am not exactly clear why Phoenix haven't had control of this whole operation from the get-go. You feel like enlightening me?" She drew breath to answer him, and his eyes drifted to D.C. "And while you're at it, perhaps you can explain to me why this man is not in prison."

If he thought he was going to intimidate Dehan, that was probably because he had never met her before, and because he was taken in by her looks. She gave him the dead eye until he stopped looking at D.C. and turned to face her, making an enquiry with his eyebrows. Then she said:

"Yeah, I feel like enlightening you, Mike. You're asking me three questions, and if you'll allow me, I'll answer them one at a time. First, why didn't I contact Phoenix last night? That is pretty simple. We were aware that the Camacho gang, and probably the Sinaloa Cartel across the border, were receiving information from the Phoenix field office. We knew that Agent Daryl Collins was involved, but we did not know the full extent of the leak, or its ramifications. So the first thing we did was to secure Agent Collins so that he was no longer a threat, and inform Washington.

"Last night, continuing our ongoing investigation, using information provided by Agent Collins, we managed to stop a shipment of twenty-five kilos of cocaine on its way to New York. Given that Phoenix was compromised, it would not have been just negligent, it would have been plain stupid, to put that operation in their hands. Not only was it my investigation, but we had no idea who in the Phoenix office was working with the Camachos. So I believe that answers your first two questions."

She paused to study Turner's face. It looked amused. She went on.

"Which leaves the question of why Agent Collins is not in prison. The answer to that is as simple as the other two answers I have given you. It would not just be negligent, it would be stupid to put him there. I spoke to Assistant Director Henderson yesterday on the telephone and outlined the situation for him, so *I* am not sure why *you* are not sure, Mike, why this man is not in prison."

He drew breath but she went on.

"This man was tortured to within an inch of his life, and then told that his wife would suffer the same and worse if he did not cooperate. I am guessing that Agent Collins is not the only person in this room with a wife or a husband, or a family, but he is probably the only person in this room who has been tortured. So he is probably the only person in this room qualified to talk about how easy it is to defy a group as powerful as the Sinaloa Cartel, and put your family at risk of being tortured, raped, and murdered—especially when you don't know who else in your office has been compromised.

"I do not condone what he did, and I would like to think that I would have taken a different approach and sought help from headquarters, but more important than that—much more important than that—is that Daryl Collins can offer us a deal that will break the Camacho gang forever and bring down the whole network from Nogales to New York. And however you feel about what he did, the opportunity we have for bringing down this gang, and possibly causing serious damage to Sinaloa across the border, outweighs any personal feelings any of us might have. That, Mike, is why he is not in prison. I would have explained earlier, only I assumed Assistant Director Henderson had already explained it before dispatching you here."

He kept his cocksure smile on his face throughout. When she stopped, he said, "Have you finished, Carmen?"

"I think I have answered your three questions, Mike."

"Thank you." He turned to Murphy. "Agent Murphy, what can you tell us about Cesar and this *sicario*, and the other men who were killed last night?"

She nodded briefly, like she was agreeing it was her turn to talk. "All the deceased were known to us as minor operators involved with the Beyer Ranch, except the one Detective Dehan refers to as the *sicario*. *Sicario* is a common term used by Mexican gangs to mean assassin, and we are aware of various men using that title, but we have never come across this particular man before. He is unknown to us." She glanced at O'Leary and added, "I think SAC O'Leary will confirm that.

"As to Cesar Hernandez, he was very well known to us in San Diego and in L.A. He is now in a secure hospital wing in Los Angeles. My latest information is that he is stable and will be available for interrogation in a few days.

"We knew he was based here in Nogales and ran the ranch for the Camacho brothers, but . . ." She turned to O'Leary. "As you know, sir, we had the same problems you guys had in making anything stick against him." She shifted back to Turner. "We liaised constantly with Tucson, Phoenix, and L.A. We knew that L.A. was a major recipient of merchandise coming in through Nogales via Cesar's ranch. But every operation we set up came to nothing. He always seemed to be two steps ahead of us." She looked at D.C., who was staring down at his hands in his lap. "I'm guessing that was you, right?"

"I'm afraid so." He looked up at Turner. "Logically, any operation San Diego wanted to mount against the Beyer Ranch had to go through Phoenix. I got to hear about it and alerted them."

"How could you?" Everybody turned to look. It was SAC Pat O'Leary. His face was twisted with contempt. "How could you put your comrades at risk? Seventeen agents died because of your *cowardice!*"

"I am not sure I am the only one, Pat. I am not sure how far the rot has spread. I would have come to you ten years ago, when it first happened. I wanted to. But believe me, they are everywhere, and their power and their influence spreads everywhere."

"*Excuses!*"

Turner held up his hand. "Okay, enough. We'll find out in good time whether it's excuses or not." He looked at Dehan and raised an eyebrow. "I know for damn sure the next person to get caught spilling intelligence to the enemy is not going to get a deal."

He kept looking at her and smiling, even though he was talking to O'Leary. I glanced at her, saw she was holding his eye, and for some reason I felt a hot needle of anger in my gut. Turner said:

"SAC O'Leary, two agents under my supervision will have arrived at the Phoenix office by now and will begin a thorough investigation of all your operations over the last ten years in which the Beyer Ranch or the Camacho brothers were involved." He finally turned away from Dehan and looked at the man he was speaking to. "You will afford them full cooperation, and I gather" —he looked at D.C.—"that you will assist us in this investigation."

"Once I have spoken to AD Henderson in Washington and the deal is agreed, yes."

The disgust was patent on Turner's face. "Naturally."

I sighed noisily and made a face that suggested that everybody was being a little stupid. They all looked at me.

"It seems to me that perhaps our perspective is getting a bit skewed here. Two things stand out as important to me: the first is that Detective Dehan and I have an ongoing investigation, and Daryl is vital to that investigation, as is Cesar Hernandez. So we are going to need access to both of these witnesses." I paused and took a deep breath. "The second point, which you are all missing, is that *everybody* in this room is vulnerable to what happened to Daryl Collins. If you have a family, if you have a wife, a husband, a child . . . *anybody* you care about, you are vulnerable." I waved my hand at them. "You can sit there looking holier than thou and damning this man to hell as a traitor. But tomorrow Camacho could be knocking on your door asking *you*, '*Plata o plomo?*,' with a gun held to your daughter's head, or your wife or husband's head." I shook my own head. "It's not so easy to be a hero with somebody else's life."

I glanced up at Dehan. "Last night, I watched as the *sicario* straddled my wife and tried to push a knife into her throat. I don't remember much, but I do remember it was intolerable to watch. I can't begin to imagine what it's like to watch something like that when torture is involved and you are powerless to help. So, I suggest you all get off your high moral horses, lest ye be judged, and start addressing the issue of how you *protect* good, loyal agents like D.C. from this kind of thing, rather than how you punish them for it."

Everybody stared hard at the floor. Turner muttered something about, "Thank you for that . . . Detective . . ." and shortly afterward the meeting broke up.

Murphy, O'Leary, and Turner stepped out into the parking lot together. D.C. stayed sitting. He stared at me a moment, then at Dehan. He said, "Thanks. Now what?"

It wasn't an easy question to answer.

TWENTY-THREE

Next had been another day of convalescence, during which I did a lot of sleeping and eating—and checking for signs of internal bleeding. I didn't find any. Dehan had a Skype conference with AD Henderson in Washington and Deputy Inspector John Newman, our chief at the 43rd in New York. Apparently they had thrashed out some kind of plan, which I had been too tired and too hungry to take in, but which involved having the Jag sent back to New York and me and Dehan flying to Washington, DC. There I would receive a proper medical examination and we would all discuss the future of the Redfern case, the Camachos, and the Chupacabras. It hadn't made a lot of sense at the time, but like I say, I had been too hungry and too tired to care much.

D.C., it seemed, was already on his way there, with Agent Turner, where he would remain under the protection of a couple of U.S. Marshals.

I guess Dehan was the bureau's blue-eyed girl right then, because they laid on an air taxi to fly us the two thousand miles to DC from Phoenix. It was a four-hour flight, and we were the only passengers, but we didn't talk much on the way. Probably because

I did a lot of sleeping, but it was also true we somehow seemed to have run out of things to say to each other.

At one point, I opened my eyes and saw her staring out the window, like she wasn't staring at the clouds but at some image inside her own mind. She noticed me looking, blinked, and smiled. I said, "I guess you got everything you wanted, huh?"

She looked down at the high-polish table between us and slowly ran her hand over it. "I don't know, did I?"

I gave my head a small, sideways twist. "You wanted to tie the Redferns to the Camachos, and the Camachos to Arizona and the Mexican cartels. You did that. You wanted to find out what happened to Amy and Charlie. You did that. Plus, you are the bureau's darling now. You even get a private jet."

She didn't answer straightaway. The only sound in the empty cabin was the muted sigh of the engines. She gave a sudden snort and said, "Who gives a damn about the bureau? Besides, we're not done yet! We need to debrief Daryl, we need to interrogate Cesar, then we need to round up and start pulling in the Camachos and their boys. And there's the DNA to come in yet . . ."

I nodded. "You realize they're going to headhunt you."

"Don't be stupid." She gave me an oddly hesitant smile. "The way I upset people?"

"I wouldn't worry too much about that. You didn't upset Turner. He likes you."

She made a skeptical face. "You feverish, Stone? The guy's a tool."

I dozed off again shortly afterward, feeling strangely sour, and when I next awoke, we were in Washington. We were met by a driver and taken across the Potomac into DC, and then by way of 17th Street and Virginia Avenue, through the heart of the city to a cute little redbrick with a red door and red wooden shutters, opposite a small park on 32nd Street, NW.

As the driver let us into the house, he said, "There will be somebody out front twenty-four seven. Any problem, just give a shout. Special Agent Turner will be in touch."

We thanked him, he gave us the key, and we went inside.

I dumped my bag and lowered myself carefully onto the sofa. The place was unimaginatively comfortable: open-plan kitchen–living room, a melamine coffee table in front of a flat-screen TV. Two vinyl armchairs and a sofa to match. There was a sideboard, and there were pictures on the wall of horses galloping.

Dehan sat in one of the chairs. She looked awkward and uncomfortable. She examined the wall and the TV while clicking her teeth, then examined the ceiling. Finally, she looked at me and said, "You okay? I mean . . ." She shrugged and pointed at my belly. "Apart from the obvious thing that you got stabbed and cut up. I mean, you know, in yourself, are you okay?"

I nodded. "Sure. You?"

"Yeah. I'm great."

I sighed. "Look, Dehan . . ."

"I know what you're going to say."

"Of course you do, but let me say it anyway."

"Okay."

I frowned at her. She looked oddly like a naughty child who was about to get told off. She didn't look like Dehan at all, and I wondered if my anemia was playing tricks on me. I spread my hands and shook my head. "I think you've got this. You managed to pull in the big guns, I don't really know what I'm doing here."

She stared at me for a long time and finally said, "Oh."

"That's not what you were expecting me to say?"

"No. But, never mind. Sure. I mean, whatever you want. We're a team. This is a cold case. I thought you'd want to be part of the debriefing and the interrogation."

I gave a small laugh and realized I was exhausted. "Yeah . . . Yes, I would, but this isn't a cold case anymore. This is a federal investigation. I'm not sure what I can contribute. You've got Turner, the Washington Bureau . . ."

She narrowed her eyes. "Stone . . . ? What the hell is going on?"

Before I could answer, her cell rang, and she picked it up and answered it.

"Dehan . . . Yeah, we just arrived five minutes ago. Sure, tomorrow is great . . . What? When, tonight?" She made a face as she listened. "Okay, sure . . . seven thirty." She listened again, frowning. "But nothing too fancy." She listened, laughed. "You got it."

She hung up and stared at the phone a moment.

I said, "Turner?"

"Uh-huh."

"Taking you out to dinner?"

She gave me a quick look. "Us, Stone. To discuss plans for tomorrow and how we proceed. We're still partners, and he knows we're married. What the hell has got into you?"

I shook my head. "Nothing. I'm just tired. I'm not up to going out. You go."

She hesitated. Smacked the arm of her chair a couple of times with her palm. "Look, Stone, about what happened back at the warehouse . . ."

"Yeah, I'm sorry about that."

"No, that's what I want to say. You don't need to apologize. Hell, you took out five guys *and* saved my life!"

I laughed. "I hadn't thought of it like that. Badass Stone."

"I . . . Maybe I didn't . . ."

"What are you trying to say, Dehan?"

She took a deep breath, puffed out her cheeks, and blew noisily. "Maybe I didn't express my gratitude properly. You know, questioning you and everything. Maybe I came across . . ."

"Don't worry about it. This case means a lot to you. I understand that. You handled it well, and it can really open doors for you."

She narrowed her eyes. "What?"

"Just tell me something. How long have you been in touch with the Feds about this case?"

"*What?*"

"I got the impression they weren't surprised to hear from you, also you seemed to know exactly who to go to. That's why you were so keen to prove it was a federal case, right?"

She stood. "I'm going to let that pass because you're not yourself right now."

She went to the kitchen and started opening and slamming cupboards. I stood and walked to the breakfast bar. I wasn't sure what I was going to say, but a wave of weariness tinged with bitterness washed over me and I said, "You know what? I think I'm going to lie down for an hour or two. I'm beat."

Her eyes flicked over my face. "You look pale. Come on, I'll take your bag."

I wanted to tell her I could manage by myself, I didn't need help, but I was too tired. We climbed the stairs, found the first bedroom, and I fell on the bed. I felt her taking off my shoes and dropping them on the floor, and then I was unconscious.

When I awoke, I lay awhile looking at the room. The drapes were closed, but I could see shards of evening light filtering through. The room was small, and there was a wardrobe at the foot of the bed, allowing just enough room to squeeze between them. I stared at the ceiling, then at the bedside table with its small lamp. I decided I felt better and wondered about my conversation with Dehan. Would I have felt the same if I had been stronger? Did I want to be in on the debriefing and the interrogation?

I wasn't sure. I sat up and thought of Turner winking at Dehan, his suggestion I should take a desk job. Would they headhunt her? Would she accept? If she did, would she commute from DC to New York? Would she see much of Turner?

I thought of her behavior throughout the case, the shooting of Camacho's boys by the river, the way she had seemed to operate almost solo. Had I imagined it?

I stood up and made my way out to the landing to look for a shower. I could hear voices downstairs. Dehan laughed. Then

Turner's voice. I looked at my watch. It was six o'clock. He was early. A whole hour and a half early.

I went back to the bedroom, pulled on my shoes, ran my fingers through my hair, and made my way down. As I stepped into the living room, I saw Dehan leaning with her back against the breakfast bar and Turner in one of the armchairs, with one long leg crossed over the other. They both stared at me a moment.

Then Turner said, "He's up! How you feeling, Stone?"

I nodded. "Good. I'm fine."

Before I could say any more, he gestured at Dehan and said, "Hey, listen, I'm sorry about the misunderstanding. We'd love to have you along, but, you know how it is, bureau business . . . Some other night?"

"Bureau business?"

The easy smile. "Can't discuss it."

I looked at Dehan. Her cheeks colored and she didn't meet my eye.

"No sweat." I looked back at Turner. "I know you guys have a lot to talk about."

Turner laughed. "Have we ever! It's going to be a looong session, right, Carmen?" Before she could answer, he looked at his watch. "Listen, as the hero is up, we could get started, have a couple of Martinis while they heat up the ovens."

Dehan studied my face a moment. "Are you going to be okay?"

I felt a hot twist of irritation in my gut. "Of course I am." Then I forced a laugh. "Don't let me stand in the way of FBI business and Martinis. Or hot ovens for that matter. I have stuff to do anyway."

"What stuff?"

I held her eye a moment, then tried to hide the bitterness as I said, "Not FBI stuff. Enjoy your meeting."

Suddenly, Turner was on his feet, saying, "Okaaay, hate to break it up, guys. Shall we get going?" Dehan went to get her coat, and Turner patted me on the shoulder and winked. "We'll catch up soon, hero."

He went out, and I heard the front door open. A moment later, Dehan came back in. She sighed and looked unhappy. "I'm sorry about this, Stone. You've got it all wrong. I'll see you later, okay?"

I nodded. "Just try not to be too noisy when you get back."

I saw her eyes well and her cheeks flush. Then she turned and left. The door slammed.

I put a frozen lasagna in the oven, poured myself a whiskey, made a decision, and climbed the stairs to retrieve my laptop. While the lasagna cooked, I searched for flights that night from DC to New York. I found one leaving at ten p.m. and booked a seat. After that, I found a notebook and penned a note for Dehan.

I'm catching the 10 PM flight back to New York. Tell Turner I'll forward my report to him.

Let me know when you expect to return. I don't feel great about how you handled this, Dehan, but we'll talk when you get back.

Stone

I finished my whiskey, dropped the lasagna in the trash, and called a cab to take me to the airport. On the way, I tried not to think. My mind drifted to Amy and Charlie, and how the whole thing had started, Dehan's passion for the case, the parallels she had seen between Amy's case and her own, and how it had echoed the first case we had worked together. I had thought it was that connection with Mick Harragan, with the Chupacabras, and her own parents' murders that had fueled her passion. Now I wondered if I was wrong. Was she getting itchy feet? Did she need to move on? Was the fifteen years between us beginning to tell?

I gazed out the window at the gathering evening, the headlamps coming on, and the lights illuminating the shop fronts and the cafés and restaurants. I wondered if they'd moved on from Martinis yet, then dismissed the thought.

I thought of Pamela, Charlie's mother. I wondered if anybody had informed her yet about the remains, though his identity had not yet been confirmed. I wondered whose decision that would be.

It had been a strange case: not so much a jigsaw as . . . The thought trailed away, like smoke from a snuffed candle. We'd come to the river and turned left, following the slow, steady stream of traffic. It had been like that: following one thing to another, and then another, not really fitting them together and resolving them, but following them, from the jurisdiction of the NYPD 43rd Precinct, to the jurisdiction of the FBI.

The traffic thinned and we started to accelerate. Soon we were crossing the darkening body of the Potomac again. This time, small lights were dancing on it. It seemed I had only just arrived, and now I was leaving; but I was keen to leave, keen to escape. I surprised myself by acknowledging it. I wanted to escape. Why? What was it I wanted to escape from? Who did I want to escape from?

My mind sheered away from the question toward Amy and Charlie. They had been escaping. They had been escaping from the Camachos. They had fled from Harlem to Vinton, in the Redferns' car. And there the Camachos had tracked them down and killed them. And that was where the trail ended.

Not a jigsaw, but a thread, and you couldn't tell where it was, or how fast it was moving.

We had stopped moving. The driver had turned and was staring at me. I looked around and saw we were at the airport.

"You okay, buddy?"

"Yes! Sorry! I seem to have drifted off."

I paid him and made my way into the strange, cathedral-like building. Odd sounds seemed to echo high above my head. It felt vaguely surreal, and I knew I was not yet well. A clock on the wall told me it was nine p.m. Not long to go. I went through Departures and boarded the plane.

I took my seat and closed my eyes.

I was aware of the takeoff but slept fitfully for the hour-long flight. I had sporadic, repetitive dreams of being at Ingrid Njalsen's house with the sheriff. She was talking to me all the while about jigsaw puzzles, how they had to fit. It wasn't enough that you follow the thread. In the end, it all has to fit together. She leaned forward and stared hard into my face, frowning. "It's not good enough following the thread if *it doesn't all fit together*!"

And she reached over and gently shook my arm.

"Mr. Stone?"

I opened my eyes.

"We've arrived in New York. Are you all right, sir?"

I smiled at the pretty air hostess, who looked nothing like Ingrid Njalsen. "Thank you. I was just tired."

An hour later, I pulled up outside my house on Haight Avenue. I paid the cabbie and stood looking awhile at my front door. The dull amber from the streetlamps made thick shadows of the trees against the walls. The scuff of a foot on the sidewalk made me turn and look. There was a small, thin man with a hunched shoulder approaching me. He looked lost and a little anxious.

"Excuse me," he said. "I seem to be lost. Are you local?"

"Sure. I live right here. How can I help?"

"I'm looking for ten thirty-two, Clarence Avenue."

I pointed past him, where he had come from. "Take the first left up there, then your second right. Ten thirty-two is near the end."

He smiled. "Thank you so much. I hope I'm not too late!"

He hurried away on old legs into the shadows. I pushed through the gate and made my way to my front door. As I slipped the key in the lock, I became suddenly aware of how accustomed I had become to having Dehan with me when I arrived in the evening and left in the morning.

I pushed in and looked at my watch. It was fifteen minutes after midnight. I wondered briefly how Dehan's evening was going, if they would be back at the house by now. If Turner had offered her a job and if she had accepted it. I dismissed the thought, poured myself a stiff Bushmills, and carried it upstairs to bed with me, still hearing Ingrid Njalsen nagging at me in my head:

"It is not enough to follow the thread. In the end, it all has to fit together!"

I lay down and closed my eyes and slipped almost immediately into deep oblivion.

When I next opened my eyes, it was eleven o'clock in the morning and I felt like I had spent the night making lots of red blood corpuscles. I had a long shower, dressed in fresh clothes, and carried my bag down to the washing machine. I put bacon on to fry and coffee on to brew and stood looking out the window at the warm, dappled morning.

In my head, I was having a conversation with Dehan where I was telling her that just because a string of events were connected in space and time, it didn't mean that they shared a common meaning. In my mind, she raised an eyebrow at me and tied her long hair behind her neck in a loose knot. I felt a stab of adrenaline and wished she was there, hoped she would not leave. You wouldn't find the meaning, I told her, until you connected the *meaning* of each event. You had to connect the *meanings*, not the events . . .

And in that moment, I saw it. I froze, staring out at the plane trees. The coffeepot began to gurgle. The bacon began to crisp. I turned off the cooker and went and sat in the living room, staring at the rugs on the floor. It was crystal clear in my mind. I just had to confirm a couple of things, but I had no doubt at all that I had seen how it all fit together, just like a jigsaw puzzle, *not* a string of events. I burst out laughing.

I switched on my cell to make a call and saw that I had a missed call from Dehan at nine p.m. the night before. I also had a voice message and four WhatsApps. I hesitated, then called the chief.

"John! Are you back? What the devil is going on?"

"Ah, yes, sir, kind of, Dehan is still in DC..."

"Good lord!"

"Yes, sir, I agree. Sir, do you recall the Redfern case?"

"Of course I do. I have been reviewing it..."

"Can you check for me if Karl had a rap sheet?"

He was quiet for a moment. "Well he had, John, we *know* he had. But it was petty stuff. Small-scale violence, couple of bar fights, couple of domestics. Typical thing, she wouldn't prosecute, charges were dropped."

"Yeah, thanks, sir, that's what I thought."

"So, what on Earth is going on with Dehan?"

"Debriefing and questioning the witnesses. I was injured and came home."

"Injured? Nothing serious...?"

"Nothing serious. I should be on my feet by Monday."

I hung up, and my next call was to Sheriff Rod O'Brien of Benton County. That call wasn't as quick or as friendly, but after I had explained what I wanted, he became interested and said he would get back to me.

I hung up and looked again at the missed calls. Finally, I played the voice message. There was a moment of silence, then, "What the hell, Stone? I just got back and you're gone? What the hell is wrong with you? In the three hours I was out, you booked a flight and ran? You couldn't wait to say goodbye? And what's with this *fucking* note? You know what? Screw you!"

Nine o'clock.

I opened the WhatsApps. The first was at ten fifteen: *I guess you were at the airport and that's why you didn't pick up. I get you're not well. But this is a crap way to treat a partner, not to mention your wife!*

The next was at eleven: *I'm sorry I said screw you. But you really upset me. What the hell is going on?*

Twelve o'clock, when I was arriving home, with my cell still switched off from the flight: *You know, I don't know what I did, but whatever it was you could have told me, Stone. We could have talked. Was it what happened at the river? Or was it since the warehouse? Something I did there?*

One a.m.: *I guess you have your cell switched off. You should know I am not happy at the way you treated me. Just give me a call when you get this.*

I went back to the kitchen and ate the cold bacon, drank the tepid coffee, and thought about Dehan and what an asshole I'd been.

TWENTY-FOUR

I called Dehan after I had cleared my breakfast things. It went to voicemail.

"Hey, Dehan. I'm sorry. Looks like we had a communication breakdown. Delayed shock and painkillers. I wasn't thinking straight. I miss you. When are you coming home?"

I hung up and read through her WhatsApps again, thought about them, and sent a single reply. *My bad. Put it down to red blood cell deficiency. From my POV we're solid. Please don't read anything into it. When do you get back?*

I sent it, read it through, and thought it sounded like a fifteen-year-old, thought about deleting it, and decided she would see the deleted message and that really would look like a fifteen-year-old. Then I said aloud, "What the hell, Stone! Get a grip!" and startled myself by how loud my voice was.

And how quiet the house sounded afterward.

I spent the rest of the morning and early afternoon making a beef stew for my corpuscles, dusting, vacuuming, washing clothes, and having existential conversations with myself. At three p.m., the Jag rolled up outside my house. Two clean-shaven young men in jeans and denim shirts climbed out, smiling.

I went to meet them, and after they asked me for some ID,

they gave me my keys, shook my hand, and told me she was a sweet ride. A dark SUV rolled up, they climbed in the back, and I watched them drive away.

When I went back inside, my cell was ringing. It was the sheriff of Benton County.

"Good afternoon, Sheriff."

"Afternoon. You weren't wrong, Stone, and somehow I'm getting the feeling that's something you hear a lot."

I sighed. "There are some cases it would be nice to be wrong."

"I hear you. You got a pen?"

I told him I did and wrote down the details. After I'd hung up, I sat for a long while, staring at the slip of paper in front of me. I looked at my cell. My message to Dehan still hadn't been read. I thought about calling the bureau in Washington but decided that would be a bad idea. I called her instead and left a message.

"Hey, Dehan, listen, I really need to talk to you. Not just about . . . what happened, but something else you need to know about. Please call me . . ." I hesitated. "I know you're mad, and you have a right to be. I behaved like a jackass, but call me anyway. Please."

She didn't call. I sat in the backyard drinking a mug of beef broth and watching the shadows of the rooftops grow long with the dying sun. The air turned chill. The tail end of summer was withdrawing at last. Fall was in the air. I stepped out onto the front porch and saw that the orange moon, in its first waning, was rising over plane trees and the chimney pots.

I went in and looked at my cell on the table.

I had no appetite, but I forced myself to eat. Then I went inside and tried to read. After reading the same paragraph seven times without absorbing a single word, I gave up and tried to watch *The Maltese Falcon*. That didn't work either.

At eleven o'clock, I checked my WhatsApp. She still hadn't read my message. I tried calling, but this time I didn't leave a message.

I slept badly and fitfully, maybe a total of four hours. At six I got up, showered, and had a quick breakfast of coffee, toast, and liquid iron, then I booked a ticket on a United flight to San Francisco at ten twenty that morning. I threw a few things in a shoulder bag, locked the door, and went to my car. It was seven thirty. I dumped my bag in the trunk and called Dehan on the phone. Behind me, I heard a voice from the street. "Good morning."

I turned. It was a man in his late forties or early fifties, slight, with oddly gentle eyes. I said, "Good morning..."

"Your new neighbor from down the road. My morning constitutional. Wife not with you today?"

I nodded and smiled. "No, she's away..."

He returned the nod and made his way slowly down the street.

Finally, I checked my WhatsApp again and saw that she had read my message. I immediately sent another. *Call me. It's urgent.*

I sat on my trunk, staring at the phone. After a full minute, the two ticks turned blue. I waited. The phone startled me with a loud ring.

"Dehan?"

"Hey..."

"How are you doing?"

"M'okay..." she said, and after a moment, "You? How's your wound?"

"It's okay. I've been better. Look, where are you? You still in DC?"

"Yeah."

"When do you get back?"

"I'm not sure. A day or two."

"We really need to talk."

"Sure."

"I'm going to San Francisco."

She was silent a moment, then asked, with a frown in her voice, "What's in San Francisco?" I hesitated a second too long and she said, "Look, Stone, I have to go. I'll call you when I get back."

"Wait! Look, I wanted to say . . ."

She sighed. "I know. I can't now. I'm at work. I'll call you."

And she was gone.

―――

I LANDED at San Francisco International Airport at one thirty that afternoon. We disembarked in a slow, shuffling procession, and, after almost half an hour, I eventually made it to the Blue Line and from there to the rental car center, where I hired a Dodge Charger from Hertz. Finally, by three p.m., I was accelerating onto the Bayshore Freeway, headed north, into San Francisco.

San Francisco is probably my favorite town—at least in the U.S.A. But on this visit I made no detours into Chinatown or Fisherman's Wharf. I let the freeway carry me onto the Oakland Bay Bridge and across the water into Emeryville. I had the windows open, and the sun was brilliant on the waves beneath me. I had inside me a strange sense of exhilaration, which I didn't really understand.

At the Emeryville interchange, I turned north and followed the Grove Shafter Freeway through the Caldecott Tunnel, through Orinda and the green fields of Lafayette to Walnut Creek. That took me the better part of half an hour, and I became vaguely aware that I was feeling hungry, and I knew that in my anemic condition I ought to eat, but I told myself it was just half an hour more, and drove on, climbing through rolling parkland along the Ygnacio Valley Road until at last, at Pittsburg, I joined the California Delta Highway headed east, and five minutes later turned off the highway onto A Street, in Antioch.

From there, it was a short cruise down 18th and left into Noia Avenue as far as Harlow Drive. There I stopped and sat looking at the street. I liked it. It was clean and tidy enough not to be a slum, but shabby enough to be comfortable—a home. I studied the house on the corner, shaded by the vast pine tree that grew just inside the wooden fence. It wasn't a white picket. It was almost six feet and made of unpainted, treated wood. The lawn outside was overgrown, with shrubs and grass, and a couple of trees I didn't recognize, though I thought one might be a jacaranda. Parked in front of it was an old, late-'90s Jeep Cherokee.

I climbed out of the car. The street was quiet, and the bleep of the lock was loud and jarring. There was sporadic birdsong in the russet afternoon. I crossed the overgrown patch and peered over the fence. There was a woman in jeans and a loose T-shirt hunkered down on a well-tended lawn beside a long trough of turned soil. She was transferring the seedlings from a dozen small plastic flowerpots to the soil. Her long, fair hair was tied into a loose ponytail with an orange, chiffon scarf. I moved to the front porch. The door had two frosted panes of glass, and after I had rung the bell, I watched a figure appear and warp as it approached. Then the door opened and the woman from the garden was half frowning, half smiling at me. I figured she was in her late twenties or early thirties. She had a cute spray of freckles across the bridge of her nose and slightly guarded eyes in an open, friendly face.

"Yes?"

"Mrs. Freeman?"

"Yes." Now she was more guarded than smiling.

I pointed at the Jeep and asked, "I have a passion for pre-millennium Jeeps. Is that one yours?"

She gave a small laugh. "Yes, but I am afraid it's not for sale."

I gave her what I hoped was a cheeky smile and asked, "Would your husband agree? Could I ask him?"

She paused, and the amusement drained out of her face. "Just a moment. How do you know my name? How do you know I am married?"

I nodded. "I apologize. I am a serious collector of certain vehicles. I happened to see it the other day, thought I'd like to buy it, and checked the registration." I smiled again. "Nothing sinister."

She hesitated. "Well, all the same, it's not for sale."

She went to close the door. I asked, "How much would make it for sale?"

Now her frown deepened, but it was tinged with curiosity. "You're serious."

"The late-nineties-model Cherokees are going to be worth a lot of money for my children and grandchildren. They were unique cars in their day. Like I said, I am a serious collector." I gave her my most honest, genuine smile. "How high do I have to go?"

Now she laughed more easily. "How high *will* you go?"

"Well, so long as the condition is good on the inside and there are no later parts added . . ." I studied her face carefully. She raised her eyebrows in inquiry. I said, "Five grand?"

"Tempting, but still not for sale."

I grinned. "Is the car yours or . . . ?"

"It's my husband's, but if you've checked the registration, you already know that, Mr. . . . ."

"Stone. John Stone, from New York."

"You're a long way from home, Mr. Stone. You don't have Jeeps in New York?"

I shrugged. "I had to retire early, and this is my hobby. It's an excuse to travel, and San Francisco has always been one of my favorite towns. So, here I am. I'm prepared to go a little higher if you'll let me talk to Mr. Freeman."

"He's at work."

"Can I come back?"

She looked at her watch. "He'll be back in about ten minutes if you want to wait."

"As long as I'm not intruding."

She studied my face for a long moment, then shook her head. "No, you're not intruding. Come on in." She raised her hand and waved across the road at the house opposite. "But if you don't mind, we'll leave the door open. We run a pretty tight neighborhood watch here, and if Maggie sees the door close, she'll call the cops."

I nodded. "Smart. I wish more people in New York did that kind of thing."

She led me through the house to the backyard, where she had a round table on the lawn under a parasol. "Can I offer you anything, Mr. Stone?"

"Nothing at all, thanks."

She sat, and I sat too. "You been in Antioch long?"

"All my life."

"It's a nice place. Quiet. A haven. The birthplace of Christianity as we know it."

Her eyes were making small, darting movements over my face. "Do I know you from somewhere, Mr. Stone?"

I made a face and gave a small laugh. "It's possible, I suppose. They say that only five people separate any two people on the planet, don't they?"

"You seem to know a lot about me."

"Well, as I explained . . ."

"And Antioch . . . ?"

"I don't understand."

"As a child, I used to dream of Antioch—the first Antioch—as a place of safety and protection, as the place where Christian compassion and salvation were born."

I nodded. "I see."

"Your comment . . . coincidence?"

"Or synchronicity."

"Your face is familiar."

"I travel quite a bit. I suppose our paths may have crossed. Have you ever been to New York?"

She hesitated. "Yes, I was there once."

"In the Bronx? I used to work in the Bronx."

"Really? You said you were retired. What did you do?"

"I was a cop. A detective at the Forty-Third Precinct."

A bird had started chattering in the pine at the corner of the lawn. She looked up for a while, as though searching for it. She asked, still staring into the branches, "How long have you been retired?"

"Six years."

She relaxed back into her chair, glancing at her watch. "What happened?"

"Oh, long story . . . Colleague of mine was shot. He'd been investigating the murder of a couple on Ellis Avenue."

She winced and frowned. "Oh, I'm sorry . . ."

I gave a small laugh and a snort. "It was random. One of those random events. Had nothing to do with the case he was investigating. He happened to go into an all-night store on his way home . . . Bang, got shot."

She was looking at her hands, removing soil from her fingers with her thumb. "But he was investigating something else."

"Yeah, it was an odd case. It was like two cases in one."

"What does that mean?"

"There was a double homicide, and there was also a double disappearance, and what was driving us all crazy was, was it a quadruple homicide with two of the bodies missing, a triple homicide and one of the disappeared characters was the killer . . . we couldn't make head nor tail of it. Finally, the case went cold."

"That must be frustrating."

We sat in silence for a while, listening to the chattering bird in the pine by the fence. Finally, I said, "I met your aunt Ingrid, Amy."

There was very little change. Her cheeks colored a little, but nothing else. After a moment, she looked up and met my eye.

"Clearly you're not here for the Cherokee."

"No."

"What do you want?"

"You stole the Jeep and abandoned the Impala. That was clever. Perhaps cleverer than you realized at the time. It was found that night, burning, but nobody ever connected it with you—

until a few days ago. Then it was assumed that you had both died in the crash, murdered by the Camacho gang. Because the two occupants of the car had been shot."

She took a deep breath, bit her lip, and sighed.

I went on, "But here's what I am asking myself now. If the occupants of the car were not Amy Redfern and Charlie Albright, who were they? And who killed them? I need to know that, Amy."

A voice came to us from behind, and over to my left. It was a pleasant, affectionate voice, calling, "Honey? You know the front door is open? Where are . . . oh . . ."

I turned and smiled at him.

"Hello, Charlie. Perhaps you'd better close the door and come and sit down. We need to talk."

TWENTY-FIVE

He came out onto the lawn and stared at me. He was very like his photograph, a little older, stronger in the shoulders than he had appeared. He was wearing jeans and a light leather jacket and had car keys hanging from his right hand. There was a pair of aviators perched on the top of his head.

"Who are you?"

"Detective John Stone, of the NYPD. I head up a cold-cases unit at the Forty-Third in the Bronx, and I am investigating your disappearance, and the murder of the Redferns."

"You have to leave."

"I can't do that, Charlie. Right now, all I want is some answers. And believe me, you are better off talking to me unofficially than to the NYPD or the FBI officially, and they are both interested right now."

"Why are you here unofficially?" He shifted his gaze to Amy.

She said, "You better sit down, Charlie. Let's hear what he has to say."

He approached the table with hesitant steps, like he thought it might suddenly jump at him. He went to pull out the chair and asked, "Are you alone?"

"Yes."

He pulled out the chair and sat.

Amy said, "If you are expecting a confession from us, it will never happen."

I shook my head. "That's not what I want. All I want is to understand what happened." I drew breath. "I think I do understand. We were on completely the wrong track, but it came to me this morning. We had been so caught up in where you were going, we forgot to think about where you were . . ."

I trailed off, aware suddenly that I was talking gibberish and they were both staring at me like I was insane. Amy said, "So what *did* you think happened?"

I turned to Charlie. "We tied it up with your mother's friend, Feliciano. We thought there was some connection with drug trafficking."

Unexpectedly, he smiled. "Seriously?"

"Two of his men showed up dead just before you disappeared. We discovered you had asked Feliciano for help, and he had put you onto . . ." I thought for a moment. "Adolfo, Adolfo and Mateo. Six months later, they showed up dead. At first, we figured you approached them because you wanted to push drugs in your neighborhood . . ."

His eyes went wide, and Amy sat forward. "*Us?* Are you *crazy?*"

Charlie was shaking his head. "Do you know how much we hate that shit?"

I nodded. "I am beginning to get an idea. But all we had to go on were the traces of evidence you left behind, either on purpose or by accident. We didn't even know whether you had been murdered and your bodies disposed of for some reason, whether you had been abducted, or whether you had managed to escape from whoever had murdered Amy's parents." I spread my hands. "Then we stumbled on the missing Impala. Where was it? Why had your aunt not reported it missing? And that took us to Garrison, where we found the Impala, and the corpses. Right now, the DNA tests are being carried out . . ."

Charlie spoke up. "They won't find anything. The bodies are too badly burned, and the jaws are too badly damaged for dental records..."

"You saw to that."

"Yes." He glanced sidelong at Amy, and she gave her head a small shake.

I went on as though I hadn't noticed. "We assumed that the bodies were yours. I found the gunshot wounds..."

"That's a lie." It was Charlie again.

Amy sighed. "Don't talk, Charlie."

I smiled at them both. "They had been shot through the eye with a small-caliber handgun. There was no exit wound, which meant the slug had stayed in the cranium and melted." I shrugged. "So as we were working on the theory that you had stolen something from the Camacho brothers, that the Camachos had killed your mom and dad, and that you had been escaping from the gang, it made perfect sense that we had found your bodies, in the car, dead."

I stopped and sank back in my chair.

Amy was frowning at me. She asked, "So?"

I laughed and shook my head. "So we chased the Camachos, the Camachos chased us, and then we chased them back again, all the way from the Bronx to Arizona and Mexico..." I stared up at the sky and shook my head. "And the only thing they ever said about you was that you were nothing. You were insignificant, you didn't exist." I turned to Charlie. "They remembered your mother, but you, and Amy? You were nothing. That didn't ring true at all. You steal from the Camachos, the Chupacabras, and you may be many things to them, but the one thing you are not is insignificant. And yet, apparently, they chased you to Iowa, and murdered you there." I stared down at the grass, aware that I was feeling slightly light-headed. "It was like there was this sequence of events that were connected in space and time, but had no shared meaning..."

I frowned at them and was surprised to see that they were frowning back, curious, even interested.

"Then it struck me," I said. "You both shared a lot of things in common." They glanced at each other and smiled. I smiled too. "Amy et Charlie contra mundum. One of the things you shared was addictive parents. But Karl, as well as being an addict, had a record for violence and, most important, domestic violence. It was so obvious, it had been staring us in the face from the start, and when I understood that, I understood everything. He used to beat you up, didn't he, Amy? And your mother."

She sighed, and she and Charlie sat awhile, staring at each other as though they were in silent, telepathic communication. After a bit, she drew breath and said, "I need some ginger tea. Let's go inside."

She stood, and I followed her and Charlie into the cool shade of the house. She went through a sliding door into a small kitchen, and I heard the tap hiss as she filled a kettle. Charlie leaned on the doorjamb and watched me as I looked around.

The living room ran from the front of the house to some French windows at the back. Most of the furniture was IKEA, and old. There were posters of paintings by Van Gogh on the walls and a couple of small bookcases with an eclectic mix of novels and books on natural food, Reiki, and UFOs. There were no fresh flowers. Those were all in the garden, but there was an earthenware vase of twigs.

Charlie asked suddenly, "Are you going to arrest us?"

"I told you, I'm here unofficially."

"But you were talking about you and your partner investigating Felix and his brother..."

I sighed and sat in an armchair by the French window. "Yeah." I sighed deeply. "She took down the gang, with the help of the FBI. The truth is, what I said to you earlier isn't exactly correct. As of a couple of days ago, nobody is looking for you. Everybody assumes you're dead. I just need to know, to satisfy my own professional curiosity." I laughed and gestured at him. "You're alive! So there can't be many explanations for what happened. Right?"

Amy came out of the kitchen with a bamboo tray holding a fat terra-cotta teapot and three matching mugs. She filled them, gave one to Charlie, brought one to me, and sat on the sofa with her feet curled up underneath her. She started speaking suddenly, with no particular inflection.

"Karl was a violent drunk. He expressed his violence in many ways, by beating us, shouting at us, breaking things, threatening us . . . The list goes on and on. When I was very small, he would beat Christen and just scream at me, but as I got older, he would beat me too." A small smile twitched her mouth and she gazed out at the backyard. "Older." She said it like it was a ridiculous word. "I mean six or seven years old." She blew on her tea for a bit, then sipped it. "People talk about hell. I have been there. And I can tell you that the key element of hell is that you cannot get out. Everything else is just pain. Hell is when you're trapped.

"And oddly enough, the worst bit was not the beating. It wasn't even watching my mother being beaten until she bled. The worst bit was when they made up. You cannot imagine . . ." She paused, shaking her head. "You cannot *begin* to imagine, how much I hated him every time she forgave him, and I lay there in my bed, bruised and hurting, listening to him grunting next door, and her calling him 'baby.' The hatred I felt, aged six and seven, was something so deep and black I can't describe it."

She was quiet awhile. Her gaze was lost. Eventually, she blinked and seemed to return from somewhere. "Their reconciliations were disgusting, horrific, but mainly because somehow I knew, instinctively, that one day he would want a reconciliation with me." She looked me straight in the eye when she said it, to make sure I understood.

"But there was something else as well. I remember, time and again, being beaten so that I was bruised on every inch of my body except my face and my arms. I felt tiny and brittle in his huge hands, and when he turned on Christen and started beating her, I held on to the belief, the faith, that now, after *this* time, she would hate him as much as I did, we would leave, she would take me away from him." She stopped, gazing out the window. "But every time, without fail, they would have their grunting, disgusting reconciliation, and every time the despair I felt would be deeper and blacker. In spite of what he did to her, in spite of what he did to *me*, she still loved him more than she loved me. Unless you have lived through something like that, you cannot imagine it."

Charlie moved over from the kitchen door and sat in the other armchair. He seemed to be transfixed, listening to her as though he had never heard the story before.

"Meeting Charlie, when I was at school, was the only thing that kept me more or less sane. He gave me somewhere to hide. And the hope which Christen had robbed from me, he gave me back. It went on for years, Mr. Stone. And then, when I was in my teens, they started doing coke. A 'friend' introduced them to it. They couldn't afford it, but whenever they got together a bit of cash, they would blow it, if you'll forgive the pun, on coke. Once he started snorting that stuff, he turned from an animal into something . . ." She seemed to withdraw into herself, her face expressed disgust, and her eyes were hard. She shook her head. "Something subhuman. I tried to stay away from the apartment as much as I could, but one night I came in, I saw Christen bruised and sobbing on the sofa. He was naked and he went for me, tried to rape me. I escaped and ran. I went to Charlie and told him what had happened."

I asked her, "Was this in March?"

"Yes, I think so."

I turned to Charlie. "So you tried talking to Feliciano Camacho, your mother's friend."

"I had to do something. I had nowhere to take her where she would be safe. The cops couldn't do anything. We couldn't prove that he had committed a crime. I could smuggle her into my room for a few days, as long as my mother was drunk she wouldn't notice, but we couldn't do that indefinitely. I had to do *something*."

"So you asked them to put him in hospital."

"Yeah. That ass Feliciano thought I wanted to do business. He wouldn't listen. He fobbed me off onto Adolfo and Mateo. I told them what I wanted. I was going to pay them, but they said it was a favor to my mom."

Amy's voice had taken on a sudden warmth. "The next six months were the happiest I had ever known. Christen came back to life. She started making cakes and cookies. We talked and spent time together, went shopping. Charlie came over for dinner, didn't you?"

They smiled at each other and he nodded.

"I begged her not to take him back. I *begged* her to move, or change the lock, get an injunction—anything. She promised she would."

I said, "But she didn't."

She shook her head. "No. When he was released from hospital, she said she would just nurse him back to health and then make him leave. We both knew it was a lie. I guess I had known all along."

I nodded. "Because you and Charlie were stashing money away. You were planning to leave. You had a bank account out of state . . . ?"

Charlie said, "Here, in San Francisco, as Mr. Freeman."

"So what happened?"

He narrowed his eyes. "If you try and prosecute us, you will never be able to prove any of this."

"I don't want to prosecute you, Charlie. I told you that already."

Amy said, "They had one of their parties. Having a party meant they bought beer and vodka and coke, got stoned out of their skulls, played loud music, and in the end, he beat her up and then they had noisy sex. I got home when the party was in full swing. He went for me. He was gripping my wrist, slapping me, and telling me . . ." She faltered. "He was telling me what he was going to do to me, and what he was going to make me do to him. We struggled. I kicked him in the balls and ran."

"What was your mother doing while this was going on?"

"She was screaming at me to do what Daddy says, not to fight him. It was what she always did. I ran. I ran back to Charlie."

I turned to Charlie. "And you went and killed them?"

He nodded. "I waited till they were asleep. Then, when I saw the lights go out, I went in . . ."

"How?"

"I waited till I saw a neighbor coming in. They all knew me, and we went in together. When he'd gone upstairs, I used a screwdriver to dig away the wood around the lock and lever back the latch. When I got inside, he came out of the bedroom. He was still drunk and stoned. He asked me what the hell I was doing there. I said I'd come to see Amy. He told me she wasn't there. He thought she was with me. Then he asked me if I wanted some coffee and asked me what time it was. I told him yeah, I'd have some coffee. I think I told him it was twelve or something—not as late as it was. I remember he was filling the kettle, telling me Amy was probably out fucking some guy, and I should slap her around a bit from time to time because women appreciated that in a man.

"I was standing behind him. I reached over, took the large kitchen knife from the block, and stabbed him in the kidney. The blade went all the way in. It was a very strange feeling." He stared at me, frowning. "I didn't enjoy it. I could feel his whole body go into spasm through the knife. I pulled it out again quickly. He turned to look at me, but he must have been hemorrhaging badly, because he was sliding down. I found his fifth intercostals and pushed the knife home. That was harder, but I think he was already dead by then."

I sat for a while, studying his face. There wasn't a lot to study. Neither of them was very big on expressions. After a moment, I said, "Why Christen? Why the frenzy?"

He stared down at the carpet for a while. "On one level, Mr.

Stone, I told myself I wanted to make it look like a sex attack, as though somebody had targeted Mrs. Redfern and Karl had been the unfortunate who got in the way. But actually, I think, unconsciously, I was harboring deep resentment toward Mrs. Redfern, partly for the way she had betrayed Amy, but also I think maybe I was projecting my own frustration against my mother onto Amy's mother."

I nodded. "You've been seeing a therapist?"

"Yes."

I stared out at the garden. I could feel their eyes on me. My tea had grown tepid, but I could smell the ginger in my nostrils. I shook my head and sighed. "There are still a couple of things I don't understand."

Amy said, "We have been more than cooperative, Mr. Stone."

I looked at her, smiled, then turned to Charlie. "Why did you kill Adolfo and Mateo?"

He shrugged. "I hate violence, Mr. Stone. More, I detest it. But once you get involved in that world, it sucks you in and you have to fight to survive. After they had beaten up Karl, when he got out of hospital, they wanted to blackmail me. I realized that was why they hadn't taken payment in the first place. I don't think Felix knew about it. I don't think he would have tolerated it. But I couldn't be sure. My mother is worth quite a lot of money, so they thought they could get a nice regular income from us. I agreed, told them to meet me by the fish market, took my father's nine-millimeter, and shot them."

I frowned. "You did it like a pro. It was one of the details that put us on the wrong scent."

He made a face like he was trying to explain something to a person with only half a brain. "I am not emotional, Mr. Stone. I guess I process my emotions in a different way. I knew when I shot them, just as I knew when I stabbed Karl, that I had to see them as cardboard cutouts, targets." He shrugged. "I'm a reasonably good shot, they were not far away."

"And you were the last person in the world anyone would suspect."

"I guess."

I sat and stared at my tea awhile.

Amy smiled and said, "It's not poisoned, Mr. Stone. We don't need to kill you. What Charlie said is true, you would never be able to prove any of this. Besides, we promised ourselves when we got here and changed our names, we would never kill again. We have left all of that behind."

I gave a small laugh. "No, it's not that, Amy. I have pretty much what I came for. I understand what happened, and why. I believe you're right; even if the cops could bring a convincing, circumstantial case, I am not sure they could persuade a jury to convict. No, I guess I am done here." I put the tea down on the coffee table and turned my head to look at Charlie. "There is just one last question I have, and then I'll go and leave you in peace."

"What question?"

"Why did you lie about killing Christen Redfern?"

TWENTY-SIX

There was a deathly silence in the house. Far away, a car accelerated and was lost in the silence. A bird chattered, but the sounds seemed to belong somewhere else, to another reality, and simply slipped over the face of the silence that inhabited the room, without disturbing it.

Finally, he said, "I don't know what you're talking about. I think it's time you left."

I didn't move, but after a moment, I said, "The lock was picked after the murders, Charlie."

"How can you know that?"

"Because if you had had a screwdriver in your hand, you would not have needed a knife to stab Karl in the kidney. You forced the lock to make it look as though somebody had broken in, because you had a key. You didn't bust the outer lock because it was too risky, but you picked the inner one so the cops would think Amy had been abducted and possibly killed. But above all, so they would not suspect she had been present at the killing."

He sat up straight, and all the color drained from his face. "No!" He shook his head. "No, no! You're wrong. You're right about the lock. She gave me her key. I was going to kill them both in their bed while they were unconscious. But Amy was not there."

I turned to Amy. She wouldn't meet my eye.

"You both went along," I said. "Your intention from the start was to kill both of them, take the Impala, and disappear. You'd already set up the new identities, the bank account . . . it was all perfect, except that Charlie's clinical style of killing was never going to satisfy you, was it? Not all that rage that you had inside you, all those years of hell, all the betrayals, all the beatings you took while she looked on and did nothing. And above all, like you said, the way she forgave him and called him baby, after what he had done to you. That deserved a knife in the heart. In fact, it deserved between fifteen and twenty knives to the heart, for all the knives in the heart that you had received since you were a baby."

She was silent, looking into her mug, tipping it this way and that. Finally, she said, "So now you know. What are you going to do with this knowledge?"

I put my hands on my knees and made to stand. "Nothing. You will never see me or hear from me again."

I stood. They stood with me and followed me to the door. There I hesitated and turned back to Charlie. "Who were the two unfortunates in the Impala?"

He almost smiled. "You may not believe it, but it is God's own truth. We bought them from a hospital morgue in Chicago. You'd be amazed what some people will do for a thousand bucks. Especially if a pretty girl asks them to do it."

"You did *what*?"

"We were desperate, Mr. Stone. We needed to die and disappear. We needed those bodies to be found in the Impala."

"Why'd you shoot them in the eye? What was the point in that?"

He sighed. "It was a small-caliber pistol. We needed a through and through so we could take the slugs away. I didn't want to risk it being traced. We didn't realize they would melt in the heat." He shrugged. "As it was, even through the eye, there was no exit wound and they stayed in the brain."

Amy said, "I have a question for you. How did you find us?"

I smiled. "It was remarkably easy when everything fell into place and I realized Karl had been beating you. I asked the sheriff of Benton County if any cars had been stolen at the time the Impala was burned. Of course there had been, a Jeep. The rest was a bit of a hunch, but Pam had told me you were always talking about Antioch. So I had the sheriff contact California DMV and see if the Jeep had been reregistered there. And it had, six years ago, in Antioch."

She nodded. "Clever."

Charlie looked me in the eye. "Karl had to be stopped, Mr. Stone, and after Amy had killed Christen, she had to be taken somewhere safe. I would do it all again today if I had to. You do whatever you have to do for the person you love. I believe that as firmly today as I did when I was a kid and met her."

"May you always believe it, Charlie."

I opened the door and stepped out into the late afternoon and made my way to my car. There I sat on the hood and stared down the green, leafy street and felt the gentle touch of the sea air. I told myself it was not for me to judge if they were right or wrong. No man, no woman, no human had the capacity to judge a situation like that. Charlie was right. He loved, and he had done what he had to do to help the woman he loved. If there was a god, let Him or Her or It judge. If there wasn't, so much the better. Let them live out their lives in whatever peace they could find.

THERE WAS an American Airlines flight next morning at eight, which got me into JFK at 4:48. So I phoned the Best Western, booked a room for the night, and spent what was left of the afternoon strolling around Fisherman's Wharf, riding trams and doing all the things tourists do in San Francisco. Eventually, I wound up at Pier 23 and had a cheeseburger and a couple of beers, staring out at the lights on the bay, telling myself that everything was going to be fine when I got home; that everything would return to normal again.

After that, I collected the rental car and made my way to the Best Western, where I spent the rest of the night staring at the ceiling and replaying my last conversation with Dehan over and over in my head.

I SAT on the hood of my Jag at JFK and switched on my phone. It told me I had a WhatsApp. It was from Dehan. It said, *Where are you?*

I smiled, cautiously, and wrote, *I'm at JFK. Just got back. Where are you?*

I saw the two blue ticks, and after a moment, she started typing. *@ home. U coming over?*

On my way.

I crossed the Madison Avenue Bridge and burned rubber all the way along the Bruckner Expressway, weaving in and out of the traffic at well over the speed limit. What was the tone of her messages? Was it conciliatory? I had assumed it was and felt a pleasurable heat in my belly, but perhaps she was mad. Perhaps the tone was brief and curt, and she was going to tell me I had crossed a line, or worse. The thought made me feel vaguely sick.

I eventually peeled off onto White Plains, made Morris Park in record time, and next thing, I was rumbling down Haight Avenue toward our house. In the west, the sun was low over the trees. I looked for signs of her in the house. But it looked dead and quiet.

I climbed the steps, pulled out my key, and went to the door. It was open—just an inch. I frowned and smiled. Part of my mind told me that was out of character for Dehan. Part of it told me she was unpredictable and that was why I was crazy about her.

I pushed open the door and stepped in. "Dehan?"

The house was silent. I closed the door and looked around. Nothing was disturbed, except that her bag was on the sofa. I called out louder, "*Dehan?*"

The silence was heavy. It was growing dark. I flipped on the lamps and my cell pinged. I pulled it out of my pocket. A WhatsApp from Dehan read *Upstairs* with a winking face.

I frowned hard. Had I missed something? I thought about our last conversation, how mad and cool she had been, how she hadn't contacted me since. I climbed the stairs to the dark landing. Our bedroom door was ajar. The last of the evening light lay in a thin strip across the wooden floor. I went to the door, placed my fingertips on it, and pushed.

Nausea turned my stomach. My skin went cold and prickled. Dehan was there. I could recognize her silhouette against the window. She was sitting on a straight-backed chair, staring at me with no expression at all on her face.

"Dehan?"

She spoke without inflection, like an automaton. "Go away."

"What the hell, Dehan?"

"Go away. Get out of here."

Then I saw him. I saw his shadow, not him, leaning on the doorjamb of the en suite. He was small, slight. The failing light from the window caught his hands. They were delicate. One held a Glock 19, the other held a long, silver blade.

I said, "You're the *sicario*."

He gave a small snort. When he spoke, I recognized the voice. "You were expecting a kung fu killing machine?" He wheezed a strange old-man laugh. "You thought El Indio was the *sicario*? He looked like a killer, with that big scar. He was just an accountant, there to cook the books for the Bodegas. You don't need to be an athlete to kill, Mr. Stone. All you need is to be willing."

"You asked me for directions the night I got back."

"My job was here. Why would I be in Sonoita?"

"And then . . . you told me you were our new neighbor. You were watching our house . . ."

"Here is how we are going to do this, Mr. Stone. You both need to accept that you are going to die this evening. There is no way around that. You first, then her. The choice you have is this: she dies fast and relatively painless. Or she dies slow, in lots of pain."

He waited a beat to let the facts sink in. Dehan snarled, "Take him, for fuck's sake, Stone! What are you waiting for?"

He pointed at the bed. "Take your clothes off and get in the bed."

I looked at the bed, then back at him. My breathing was loud in my ears. Dehan half screamed at me, "*Don't you dare! Don't you dare, Stone!*"

"Okay, Stone. Hesitate another couple of seconds and I give her a Colombian necktie."

"No!"

I took a step forward, holding out my hand.

He went on, "You know what that is? I cut her throat under her chin, I pull out the tongue, and I cut it off. That's how we begin. It only gets worse after that." He stepped over to her, slipped the Glock in his waistband, and took hold of her hair in his left hand.

Her teeth were clenched and her neck swollen. "*What the fuck is wrong with you, Stone? Take the motherfucker!*"

"Bleeding out, if the blade is real sharp, can be a beautiful experience, real peaceful. You want her last hour on Earth to be hell? A hell of pain and grotesque, nightmarish amputations?"

I shook my head. "No."

He jerked his head at the bed. "Take off your clothes and get in the bed. You will die as lovers—jealous passion? Suicide pact? Who knows? You will kill each other, in each other's arms. Nice."

I looked at Dehan. He had her head pulled back. Her eyes were wild. I knew I would not be able to put her through the nightmare of torture he was describing. I said, "I'm sorry," and pulled off my jacket. I had no gun. I had not taken it to San Francisco. It was across the landing in the safe. To the *sicario*, I spoke in a pleading voice, "Please don't hurt her. I'll do anything you say, just please don't hurt her. What about my gun . . . ?"

He glanced at my body, looking for the holster. It was as good as it was going to get. In the fraction of a second he was distracted, I lashed my jacket like a whip around his arm, yanked savagely, and jumped at the same time.

He didn't flinch. The knife came at me, slashing at my throat. I raised the jacket and it deflected the blade. In a single, fluid movement, he pulled back the knife for a lunge at my belly. I threw the jacket in his face and kicked hard. It caught him in the chest and threw him against the wall. I went after him, but he lashed at my ankles. I didn't think. I grabbed the big duvet from the bed and threw it over him. Then I fell on him, pinning him down under it with my knees. I wrenched back bedding to expose his head and began pounding him savagely, right and left. His left eye was purple, his nose was bleeding, and his lip was swollen.

Dehan was shouting at me: "Stone! *Stone!* Stop! Don't kill him! *Stop!*"

My fist was raised. My heart was pounding high in my chest. There was a dark rage in my head. I looked at her face.

She said, "He's had enough. Put your fist down. Take his gun, and untie me."

She was right. I lowered my fist. I pulled back the duvet. The knife was on the floor by his side. I pushed it away into the bathroom, threw the duvet back on the bed, pulled his Glock from his belt, and slipped it in my own. My fingers felt thick, and my hands were trembling. He had bound her to the chair with a couple of my ties. I managed to undo them and release her.

"Are you okay?"

She nodded. "Call it in and help me get this son of a bitch downstairs. You got cuffs?"

"Downstairs."

I dragged him to his feet while she made the call. He had trouble standing, but we maneuvered him across the landing and down the stairs with the Glock stuck in the back of his neck.

Halfway down, he rolled his eyes. His pupils were very dilated and he muttered, "No, not like this, please . . ."

Dehan sat him on the sofa and stared at me. "Cuffs?"

My head was reeling. "In my jacket, where are yours?"

"In the drawer."

I crossed to the dresser, opened the drawer, and pulled out her cuffs. I handed them to her. She squinted at me. "Stone, get your goddamn piece, will you?"

"I have his."

"That's going into evidence. Get with the program, big guy. Get your .45."

I was struggling to stay focused. My stomach wound was hurting bad and I was suddenly feeling weak. I handed her the Glock and went back up the stairs, opened the safe, and pulled out my Colt, made sure it was loaded and strapped on the holster.

When I got back to the door, the *sicario* was sitting with his head in his hands and his wrists cuffed. Dehan was covering him, though he didn't look very dangerous. He said, "I need to be sick. I have bad concussion."

I pulled my weapon and cocked it. He slowly groped his way to his feet and walked unsteadily to the kitchen door. I opened it and he stepped out into the backyard. There he bent double and vomited profusely onto the lawn. He stayed leaning like that for a moment, panting. The cool breeze moved his thin hair. The moon, now waning, was casting a dim glow across the grass.

Dehan was behind me in the doorway. Her voice came disembodied. "Okay, now you've been sick, let's go." She came up beside him. "The patrol cars are on their way."

She didn't see the blade because it was in his right hand and she was on his left. He didn't turn at speed. He didn't do anything to alert her. He turned deliberately, and in the same movement thrust the blade low, toward her belly. The whole thing took no more than a couple of seconds.

But I had seen it. I shouted and lurched forward, thrusting my body between hers and the knife, grabbing at his wrist with my left hand and clubbing at his head with the Colt. I felt the blade bite and tear at my side and then we were falling through the dark, through the cool air, and I could see the sky and the stars moving, turning above me.

The impact of the ground was jarring and agonizing. Shards of pain like glass pierced my belly and my lungs. For a second, I couldn't breathe. Then air rasped noisily into my lungs. I clawed at the grass and dragged myself to a sitting position. The *sicario* was on his hands and knees. I looked up at Dehan. She was looking down at her belly. Her hands were red with blood.

I made a horrific, rasping noise and rushed the *sicario*. He still had the knife in his hand, but I didn't care. He slashed at me. I grabbed his wrist and he sawed at my arm with the blade. The pain didn't feel like pain. It felt like a release from the agony in my chest and my belly. I pounded his face with my fist and he staggered back. I rushed him again. He was disoriented. I grabbed his knife hand in my left and his throat in my right and we fell to the ground again. I felt him writhing and struggling underneath me. His left hand clawed at my arm. His feet thrashed and kicked. I looked up at the fall moon, saw Dehan in my mind, standing, staring at her own blood, and cried out, as the moon touched my hands, the blade drove home, and beneath me, the *sicario* stopped moving.

EPILOGUE

I sat on the sofa, watching the TV. It wasn't my parents' sofa. It was a new one I had bought, big, cream, and overstuffed. The news item described how federal agents had busted the Camacho gang's network of heroin and cocaine smuggling, based in New York and Arizona, and arrested over a dozen gang members, including the two brothers themselves. The agent in charge of the investigation, Detective Mike Turner, based in Washington, had made a statement.

I didn't want to hear his statement, so I switched off the TV.

There was the sound of a boot kicking the door. I got up with difficulty. I had a lot of bandaging and a lot of stitching on my belly and on my left arm. I went and opened the door. Dehan stood there squinting at me slightly in the late September sunlight. She had her shades perched on top of her head and looked disturbingly attractive. Her arms were full of grocery bags. "You look like you died of your wounds and you went to purgatory."

"You brought wine and tequila. How nice."

"I thought we could celebrate. You going to move your great lunking self out of the door so I can come in?"

"Of course." I stepped aside. She pushed past me and went to the kitchen. "What are we celebrating?"

"The *sicario* is out of intensive care and will live."

"That is something to celebrate?"

She was unpacking steak wrapped in greased paper, potatoes, avocados . . . "Sure. This way he will testify, and you won't have to stand trial for killing him."

"I thought he had killed you. You were standing there with blood all over your belly and your hands."

She stopped unpacking and smiled at me. "'I thought he'd killed my wife' is not a defense to a charge of homicide. Besides, it was your blood all over me, not mine. You have to stop getting stabbed in the belly."

She set about unpacking and putting away again. I said, "He didn't stab me, it was more like sawing from the outside in."

"Nice." She put the bloody steaks on a plate in the fridge.

"I thought I had lost you," I said, after a moment. "Not just to the *sicario*, to Washington, the bureau . . . Turner."

She stared at me for a long five seconds, holding the fridge door. She was smiling. It was a nice smile. "You big dumbass," she said. "I'm going to put it down to the loss of blood and the painkillers. How the hell could you think something like that, Stone?"

I shrugged. "I guess it was cumulative, from the moment you shot those two men. I felt . . ." I shook my head. "I didn't know who you were. Suddenly you seemed to be running the case alone, and then it was you and the Feds, and Turner winking at you, taking you out to dinner on federal business . . ."

She sighed and looked sad. "Yeah, my bad. I should have told him to get lost sooner. He offered me a job, tried to come on. I told him to go to hell and was really looking forward to seeing you when I got back. But you'd gone all hormonal on me and left."

She came over and kissed me. Then she grabbed a big old terra-cotta bowl and started making a salad.

"I thought you liked him."

"You're crazy. You need to read about Bowlby's styles of attachment. You may have a problem."

"Really?"

"You want a beer?" She didn't wait for an answer. She pulled open the fridge and took out two beers. She cracked them and handed me one. "So what about San Francisco?"

"I found Amy and Charlie there. They're alive and well."

"You son of a bitch!" She picked up the lettuce and threw it in the bowl. "I *knew* that's why you'd gone! And you say *I* was running the case on my own!" She shook her head. "You never did buy they were dead, did you?"

"Not fully. He killed Karl and she killed Christen. She was being abused. She and Christen. It's a long story. I won't testify. I'll lie in court if I have to. I won't let them be prosecuted."

She took a swig and studied my face awhile. "Look at you. What happened to the rule of law?"

"I guess you perverted and corrupted me."

She chuckled and took another pull. "Badass rule-breaker. I like that. Hey . . ." She reached out and poked me on the chest. She was laughing now. "What did you think? Be honest. What did you think when the *sicario* sent you that message, *I'm upstairs*?" She laughed out loud and staggered a couple of steps back toward the fridge.

I was laughing too, but less. I shrugged. "Hell, I don't know. I didn't know what to think."

"You thought, didn't you. You thought I was going to be up there, in bed, in black lace, with strawberries . . . Admit it, Stone. Go on!"

I shrugged again. "I don't know. I knew a week away from me would have you clawing your way up the walls, but I was worried about my stitches. Every Mexican woman I was ever with ended up tearing out my stitches!"

"In your dreams, *pendejo*."

She went back to making the salad, still chuckling.

I said, "Carmen, is this the end of it now?"

She went very still, staring down into the salad. "End of what?"

"The campaign of vengeance against the Chupacabras and Mick Harragan. And keeping secrets from me. Is it over?"

She came to me and put her arms around my waist, squeezing gently with her head on my chest.

"Yes," she whispered. "It's over."

Don't miss BLOOD IN BABYLON The riveting sequel in the Dead Cold Mystery series.

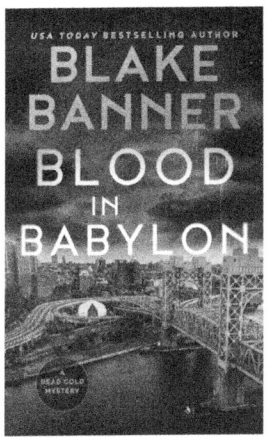

Scan the QR code below to purchase BLOOD IN BABYLON.

Or go to: righthouse.com/blood-in-babylon

NOTE: flip to the very end to read an exclusive sneak peak...

DON'T MISS ANYTHING!

If you want to stay up to date on all new releases in this series, with this author, or with any of our new deals, you can do so by joining our newsletters below.

In addition, you will immediately gain access to our entire *Right House VIP Library,* which includes many riveting Mystery and Thriller novels for your enjoyment!

righthouse.com/email

(Easy to unsubscribe. No spam. Ever.)

ALSO BY BLAKE BANNER

Up to date books can be found at:
www.righthouse.com/blake-banner

ROGUE THRILLERS
Gates of Hell (Book 1)
Hell's Fury (Book 2)

ALEX MASON THRILLERS
Odin (Book 1)
Ice Cold Spy (Book 2)
Mason's Law (Book 3)
Assets and Liabilities (Book 4)
Russian Roulette (Book 5)
Executive Order (Book 6)
Dead Man Talking (Book 7)
All The King's Men (Book 8)
Flashpoint (Book 9)
Brotherhood of the Goat (Book 10)
Dead Hot (Book 11)
Blood on Megiddo (Book 12)
Son of Hell (Book 13)

HARRY BAUER THRILLER SERIES
Dead of Night (Book 1)
Dying Breath (Book 2)
The Einstaat Brief (Book 3)
Quantum Kill (Book 4)
Immortal Hate (Book 5)
The Silent Blade (Book 6)
LA: Wild Justice (Book 7)

Breath of Hell (Book 8)
Invisible Evil (Book 9)
The Shadow of Ukupacha (Book 10)
Sweet Razor Cut (Book 11)
Blood of the Innocent (Book 12)
Blood on Balthazar (Book 13)
Simple Kill (Book 14)
Riding The Devil (Book 15)
The Unavenged (Book 16)
The Devil's Vengeance (Book 17)
Bloody Retribution (Book 18)
Rogue Kill (Book 19)
Blood for Blood (Book 20)

DEAD COLD MYSTERY SERIES
An Ace and a Pair (Book 1)
Two Bare Arms (Book 2)
Garden of the Damned (Book 3)
Let Us Prey (Book 4)
The Sins of the Father (Book 5)
Strange and Sinister Path (Book 6)
The Heart to Kill (Book 7)
Unnatural Murder (Book 8)
Fire from Heaven (Book 9)
To Kill Upon A Kiss (Book 10)
Murder Most Scottish (Book 11)
The Butcher of Whitechapel (Book 12)
Little Dead Riding Hood (Book 13)
Trick or Treat (Book 14)
Blood Into Wine (Book 15)
Jack In The Box (Book 16)
The Fall Moon (Book 17)
Blood In Babylon (Book 18)
Death In Dexter (Book 19)
Mustang Sally (Book 20)

A Christmas Killing (Book 21)
Mommy's Little Killer (Book 22)
Bleed Out (Book 23)
Dead and Buried (Book 24)
In Hot Blood (Book 25)
Fallen Angels (Book 26)
Knife Edge (Book 27)
Along Came A Spider (Book 28)
Cold Blood (Book 29)
Curtain Call (Book 30)

THE OMEGA SERIES
Dawn of the Hunter (Book 1)
Double Edged Blade (Book 2)
The Storm (Book 3)
The Hand of War (Book 4)
A Harvest of Blood (Book 5)
To Rule in Hell (Book 6)
Kill: One (Book 7)
Powder Burn (Book 8)
Kill: Two (Book 9)
Unleashed (Book 10)
The Omicron Kill (Book 11)
9mm Justice (Book 12)
Kill: Four (Book 13)
Death In Freedom (Book 14)
Endgame (Book 15)

ABOUT US

Right House is an independent publisher created by authors for readers. We specialize in Action, Thriller, Mystery, and Crime novels.

If you enjoyed this novel, then there is a good chance you will like what else we have to offer! Please stay up to date by using any of the links below.

Join our mailing lists to stay up to date -->
righthouse.com/email
Visit our website --> righthouse.com
Contact us --> contact@righthouse.com

facebook.com/righthousebooks
x.com/righthousebooks
instagram.com/righthousebooks

EXCLUSIVE SNEAK PEAK OF...

BLOOD IN BABYLON

CHAPTER 1

It was Al's birthday. That gave him an air of importance as he made his way south down Virginia Avenue from the Hugh J. Grant Circle. It wasn't just any birthday either. Joy had told him that. He was sixty. Sixty was a big number. It was an important age. An age when a man should do important things. He'd been through several important ages: Harvard, Mexico, Brazil. Twenty had been real important, but he couldn't remember much about twenty. That was like another life. Forty had been important too. That was when he'd started to go wrong.

The sun slipped behind the trees and the rooftops, casting long winter shadows across the road. The temperature dropped and Al shuddered. It was getting dark, and he wanted to be home. He wanted to be safe.

Dr. Epstein and Joy had been nice to him. They were always nice to him. They'd made him feel special. They'd given him a cake and laughed with him. That had made him shy, but it had also made him stay too late, because he didn't want to leave. Now the darkness was closing in, and he did not like to be out in the street when the darkness closed in.

He hurried with big, jerky strides, holding his birthday card with his hand in his pocket, gulping breath through his mouth, because when he hurried, he couldn't breathe through his nose. He hurried past Newbold Avenue and tried not to look up at the towering apartment blocks on his left. They always made him feel like they were looming over him, like angry judges watching him. Joy and Dr. Epstein had told him it wasn't true, that apartment blocks could not watch you or judge you, but he knew, inside, that they could. So he kept going, with heavy, hurrying steps, gulping air through his mouth, even when he heard the shout. When he heard the shout, he ignored it and just kept on going.

"Hey! Freak! Weird ass! I'm talkin' to you!"

Al didn't look. He didn't need to look. He knew who it was. He quickened his lumbering pace. He felt a strong hand grip his heart, making it harder to breathe. He became conscious of the wheezing and gasping in his throat. He also became conscious of the running feet behind him: not sprinting, not a charge, just running to catch up. Instinct made him hunch his shoulders. He could see the green shop front of the upholstery store on the corner with Ellis Avenue. He was almost home.

"Hey! Freak! I'm talkin' to you, bro!"

The voice was much closer now, right behind him, and he could hear laughter across the road, high-pitched, screeching laughter, as though they were all being strangled by invisible wires. It was what they deserved. The thought brought on a sudden rush of fury, but he knew better than to confront them. He kept lumbering forward, tried to control the croaking in his throat, kept his eyes on the darkening blacktop in front of him.

A voice, at his elbow now. "Hey, man, why you make that noise when you walk?" More laughter from across the road. Now the speaker was smiling too. "What is that? You sick or something? Or you just singing yo'self a song while you walkin' along?"

The laughter was now like shrieks. Al prayed silently that they should become real shrieks of pain. He had reached the upholstery store and started across the road toward it. A hand plucked at his shoulder. "Hey! I'm talkin' to you! You don't disrespect me, you motherfockin' piece a' shit!"

Al broke into a stumbling run, grunting as he went. He heard his own voice saying, "No! No . . ."

The door of the upholstery shop opened. A small group of men and women emerged, talking. Two men and a woman stood at the door of the deli next door, going in. He almost collided with them. One of them half shouted, "Whoa! Look where you're going, pal!"

He ignored them, hurrying on, listening. The voice came again, more distant now. "Wait up, freak! I wanna talk to you!"

He kept going. His heart was pounding in his chest. His breathing was loud, like the roar of giant waves. He passed the apartment block, the gated alley behind it. He lumbered on, passed 1929, passed the house next door with its pretty wrought iron porch, and then he was at the gate of his own house.

Now he could hear feet, lots of them, running in earnest. His hands were shaking badly and he fumbled with the latch of the gate. His gasping breath turned to a whimper. He pushed through the gate and stumped up the four steps to his door. His whimpering turned to sobbing as his fingers, large and clumsy like sausages, struggled with his keys. Behind him, feet skidded to a halt: four, five, six pairs. He dared not look.

"Hey! Freak! I'm fuckin' talkin' to you! We got questions for you!"

The key slipped in. Behind him, the gate clanked open. He pushed in, wrenched the key from the lock, and slammed the door. But it did not close. Instead, there was a terrible scream of pain. He wrenched the door open and slammed it again, putting his full three hundred and ninety pounds behind it. Another scream, and again he pulled it open and slammed it. This time, it closed and locked.

He backed away, sobbing violently. Outside, he could hear screeching, shouts, furious voices, judgment, hatred: a great tidal wave of hatred washing over his house, and him. He turned and stumbled into his small kitchen area. There he grabbed for the phone and called Dr. Epstein. Joy answered and he cried out, an inarticulate noise of relief and love, and grief and fear.

"Al? Is that you, baby?"

He tried to say it was, but a primal grief deep in his gut would not let him shape the words out of the awful noises in his mouth.

"What in the *world* is wrong with you? Now you take a moment and breathe . . . that's right, you just take one good, big old breath and relax. Good, and another . . . Now first off, you tell me right now if you are okay."

His breath shook, but the tightness in his chest eased. "Yes . . ."

"So what has you so upset?"

"They were waiting for me."

"Who were, honey? You sure it wasn't somebody you imagined . . . ?"

"No." His voice was clear, educated, articulate, strangely at odds with his huge, graceless body. "No, it was that boy, and his gang. They wait for me. They call me a freak. He says he is going to cut me. And they make dark waves that come at me from the street."

"Now, honey . . ."

"I am *not* hallucinating. You can't see it. But it comes when they close in on me. It overwhelms the house. I don't know *how* they do it, but they do."

"Are they still there?"

"No, they've gone. But they might come back. They always come back. Joy, I think they followed me from Mexico. I saw them in Mexico, but they were farther away. But if they have found a way into my dreams, if they can get in during the night . . ."

"Okay, baby, now here is what I am going to do. I'm going to call the police and I'm going to have them swing by and make sure you're okay. Can you tell them what these boys look like?"

"I never look at them. You mustn't look at them. That's how

they followed me. But I know his name. I hear them call him Ned."

"Ned? You sure about that?"

"Yes, I'm sure about that."

"Okay, good. So you be sure to tell that to the officers when they come by. And Al? Remember, these are not evil forces, they are just stupid boys whose momma was too soft on them. If I take my belt to them, they gonna find out what good manners are *real* quick!"

That made him laugh, and she laughed too. They spoke a moment longer, till she was sure he was okay, and then they both hung up.

After that, he did the rounds of the house, keeping the lights off, peering through the darkened glass at the empty, lamplit streets outside. The windows had bars. He had insisted on that when Joy had got the house for him. Dr. Epstein had thought it was a good idea. He had said it was good to see him making important decisions like that.

The kitchen door out to the backyard was locked and had two heavy dead bolts. The windows here also had bars. He stood awhile, transfixed by the shadows cast across the floor by the lamps in the parking lot beyond his backyard. One of those lamps was behind a tree, and the shadows of the leaves tossed slightly in the pool of light on his floor.

He went to his living room and stood for a long while, staring out at the empty street. He still had his birthday card in his hand. When he was satisfied there was nobody there, he went and closed the drapes. Then, he lay on the sofa and covered himself with the blanket he always kept there and switched on the TV. He had it set up and ready. He was starting *Murder She Wrote* from episode one for the thirty-fourth time. As the music started to play, he hummed along, and as the dialogue started, he spoke it silently with the characters. His eyes closed, as though of their own volition, and he drifted into sleep.

Everything was safe. Jessica would take care of everything.

When the hammering on the door came, he didn't know how long he had been asleep. Episode two was almost finished. He walked stiffly into the hall and stood holding the living room doorjamb, staring at the door. It hammered again and his heart jumped and started pounding.

Then the voice. "It's me! Open up!"

He went to the door and unlocked it. He smiled. "Hi, I was watching TV... Come on in."

He led the way into the living room, pointed at the TV, and smiled. "I like Jessica. She makes everything okay." He turned to smile at his visitor but frowned instead at the large, silver blade of the kitchen knife. It entered swiftly and with precision, slipping between the fourth and fifth ribs on his left side, slicing through his lung and his heart in one smooth thrust.

His body briefly went into spasm. His consciousness endured for a few seconds, enough for him to be aware of the strangeness of the feeling, and to reach back for the sofa. But as the blood drained from his brain, darkness enfolded him and he crashed to the floor.

I FOUND Dehan doing a dangerous mixture of yoga and tae kwon do in the backyard. She smiled at me, winked, and delivered a devastating side kick to an invisible foe who, judging by the height of the kick, must have been seven feet tall. I withdrew to the kitchen and made coffee.

She came in just after the coffee had started to gurgle and the rich, dark aroma had wafted out to the backyard and hooked her by the nose. She was panting, flushed, and perspiring slightly, dabbing her face with a towel. I sighed and wondered, not for the first or last time, what I had done in a previous life to earn such good kama.[1]

---

1. *Kama* in the original Pali, *karma* in Sanskrit. Stone is of course aware of this.

She stopped dabbing her face and stared at me. "What?"

I shrugged with my eyebrows and shook my head.

She continued wiping. "I know, I look a wreck, but I want that third dan, and that's hard work."

"You want coffee?"

"Is the Pope a Catholic? What's wrong? You look troubled."

"I'm in a kitchen with a beautiful woman who is flushed and breathing heavily. Naturally, I look troubled."

She smiled and fluttered her eyelashes. "Okay, smart-ass, you got your brownie points. Now pour me some coffee and tell me what's really on your mind."

I poured. She sat at the kitchen table, and I rested my ass against the sink. I sipped and said, "Aloysius Chester, otherwise known as Al."

She nodded. "What about him?"

"I just wrote the prologue."

She grinned. "That's amazing. Can I read it?"

I shook my head. "Not yet. And I'm not sure I'm going to write it."

She frowned with her cup halfway to her lips and set it down again. "Why not? You said it was perfect."

"I thought it was."

"You stood right there and told me it was insoluble, so you could build a whole set of fictional circumstances around it. Perfect for your first attempt at writing . . ."

"I know. I know what I said, and that was what I thought."

"So . . . ?"

"I think it should be our next case."

"You just told me you know what you said. What you said was that it was insoluble. That means 'can't be solved.'"

I raised an eyebrow at her. "Stop being a smart-ass and listen to me. Just reading the case file, reading the reports, trying to imagine what it was like—for *him* . . ." I trailed off. "It's hard to explain, Dehan, but hell! Bottom line is, whether I write the book or reinvestigate the case, I'm going to be doing the same damned legwork! And I just feel this guy deserves justice. Let's look into it. What's the worst that can happen?"

She shrugged and made a face to go with it. "We get our first unsolved cold case."

I pulled out the chair and sat at the table, leaning forward on my elbows. "Who came to the door that night? Can you imagine how he felt? He must have been terrified. Why would he open the door? If it was the kids who'd been harassing him, he would not have opened the door."

"Are you sure he did? The forensics were inconclusive. Somebody might have picked the lock."

I grunted. It was one of the many—too many—unanswered questions shrouding the case. "You've seen the crime scene photos . . ."

"Many times."

"He didn't *look* as though he'd . . ." I hesitated, not liking the vagueness of what I was about to say. "There are questions I want to ask about those photos."

She nodded. "Sure, I get that. Me too. There are a couple of things that don't make a whole lot of sense. But it was twelve years ago, and those questions are not questions anybody can answer anymore. Sometimes the truth just . . ." She made little explosions with her fingertips. "Fades away. Even when the trail was still warm, they were hard to answer. Now . . ." She shook her head.

I sighed, sipped, and watched her. "What can I say? I have a feeling, Dehan. Something in my gut just says there is *something* there, something in what happened that night. Something," I repeated, "maybe, in the photos, that we can use. I don't know how else to say it. Al *deserves* that we should make the effort. Poor guy, you know?"

She smiled, not unkindly. "That is sentimental reasoning, Stone, and has no place in police work."

"I know." I nodded. "But at the end of the day, it's why we do what we do." I sat back. "Well, what do you say?"

She spread her hands. "Frankly, personally, I think it's a waste of valuable police resources on a case that is probably never going to be solved. Having said that, you know I'll back you up, whatever you decide to do."

"See? That's why I married you. That and the whole . . ." I gestured at her with my open palm. "The whole flushed cheeks, heavy breathing, slightly perspiring thing you have going on there. It really works for you."

She leaned back and gave me the kind of smile that should be against the law but, thankfully, isn't. "Does it work for *you*?"

"Kind of does."

She stood and winked at me. "Well, I'm going to take a nice, looong, hot shower. You can be gathering up your case notes, and maybe prepare a salad for lunch."

She took her big grin upstairs with her. I sat a moment, staring after her. Then I rose, opened the fridge, and stood staring at the lettuce and the tomatoes, till I heard the hiss of water from the shower. Then I closed the fridge and went upstairs.

CHAPTER 2

The shadows were growing long across the lawn. There was a slight breeze, and thin wisps of smoke, with an occasional, lazy trail of sparks, drifted over the grass to be lost among the rosebushes. Rosebushes my mother had planted, I had neglected, and Dehan had brought back to life.

She stepped out from the kitchen onto the patio, holding plates, cutlery, salt, and pepper. Her hair was still wet from her second shower, hanging long down her back, making damp marks on her summer dress. I watched her, feeling the heat of the barbeque on my back.

She set down the load, grabbed a bottle of wine by the neck, and stabbed the cork with a corkscrew. As she began to twist, she said, "The guy was crazy, right?"

I nodded. "But don't let the thought police hear you saying things like that. He was diagnosed with schizophrenia and also paranoia."

The pop of the cork echoed in the early evening. She set the bottle down and pointed at it with the corkscrew. "Now you have to let it breathe for at least an hour."

"No kidding. Where do you learn that stuff, Dehan?"

"Some guy who was coming on to me. I forget his name. So he had a psychiatrist who he was seeing for his meds and stuff..."

"Indeed, Dr. Epstein."

She leaned down, pulled two bottles of beer from a bucket of ice, and cracked them both, then handed me one and sat. I took a pull and continued.

"His practice was, and still is, at 1910 Benedict Avenue, just off the Hugh J. Grant Circle. A short walk from Al's place. In fact, he had just been to see Epstein the night he was killed. According to Epstein's statement, Al was not great at keeping up with his meds, but he always made a point of turning up on his birthday, November twenty-third, because they always made a fuss of him and brought him in a cake."

"Cute. That's nice. I should go crazy so people would do nice things for me."

I ignored her and went on. "It seems he stayed a bit late that day. Apparently, he would just sit in the waiting room, or chat with the staff. By all accounts, he was a pleasant kind of guy, polite, well educated, so they didn't mind him hanging around."

Dehan was frowning. "Seriously?"

"I know. It sounds odd to me too, but that is what we have at the moment. So he hung around and then left, intending to go home. What happened next isn't one hundred percent clear. It was pieced together from eyewitness accounts. He crossed the Hugh J. Grant Circle, as he would have to to get home, saw a couple of people who knew him and greeted him. Then he made his way down Virginia Avenue, toward his place on Ellis. It's not a long walk—two hundred yards from the Circle to Ellis, and another fifty to his house."

She was frowning at me over the rim of her glass as she sipped. "Is that relevant? You seem to be stressing it like you think it's relevant."

"I don't know yet. The thing is, as he is walking those two hundred and fifty yards or so, some kids start hassling him. As I said, this is put together from accounts of people who saw or heard things as he walked past. Remember, he had been in the neighborhood for a long time, and he was known as a kind of local character. According to what they were able to piece together in the original investigation, this gang . . ."

I hesitated and Dehan said, "You don't mean like a real gang, like the Chupacabras . . ."

"No, not at all. It was just a gang of kids, sixteen to eighteen, who used to hang around and make a lot of noise. But there was one of them, Ned, who, according to local gossip, kind of had it in for Al, used to call him the Freak, and anytime he saw him he'd give him a hard time, shout abuse, call him names . . ."

She leaned back in her chair. "Is there any record of physical violence?"

"Yes and no. Ned was always getting into fights, was known to carry a knife, and he was certainly on the radar. There is no record of his ever having physically attacked Al . . ."

"That doesn't mean it never happened."

"No, it doesn't, but neither do we have any record of Al suffering from any kind of injury that might have been inflicted in a fight. So if there ever was a physical confrontation, it didn't lead to much."

"Okay, so that evening, these assholes start giving him a hard time. What happens next?"

"He panics. He was seen by several people passing the upholstery shop and the deli on the corner of Ellis and Virginia, and all of them reported him as being in a very agitated state. Apparently Ned was right behind him, seemed angry and aggressive, and Ned's pals were holding back, but laughing. The witnesses watched Ned and his friends follow him to his house and go into his front yard. There was a slam, like a door slamming, a lot of screaming, and the kids left. The people at the deli said it looked like Ned had hurt his hand. They thought about calling the cops but felt the whole thing had blown over."

"So presumably, Ned then became the prime suspect and was easily traced because he has a bruised, swollen hand."

I smiled, removed the tinfoil from the two T-bone steaks I had beside the barbeque, and sprinkled them with Maldon sea salt. Then I dropped them onto the iron grill over the burning coals. Flames leapt three feet high around them, licking at the herb-seasoned oil I had soaked them in.

I swigged my beer and went on. "Unfortunately, it is not quite that simple. Al telephones the surgery. Judging by the time of the call, it must have been almost as soon as he got in. The call was taken by one Joy Jones, Dr. Epstein's receptionist, assistant, and general factotum—his words, not mine. According to her testimony at the time, he was practically incoherent. She managed to calm him down and he told her, more or less, what the detectives at the time managed to piece together, and I have just told you. Except that he added in a fair old dose of paranoia about tidal waves of darkness engulfing him and his house, and evil beings who had followed him from Mexico. She told him she'd call the precinct and ask for somebody to pass by and make sure he was okay."

Dehan frowned. "And did she?"

I flipped the steaks. "No, she didn't. In her statement, she said she thought about calling the cops, but decided against it. She knew that Al imagined things. She also knew there was a bunch of kids who used to call him names, but she was pretty sure they were not dangerous. She didn't feel it was right to waste police time, so she left it at that. Martinez, that was the investigating detective at the time, said she was devastated when she discovered what had happened."

"So what did happen?"

I took the scorched steaks and put them onto our plates. Dehan poured the wine, and we sat and ate in relative silence for a while, broken only by Dehan making small noises of visceral pleasure. When she had got halfway through her steak, she sat back with her wine and smiled. "Man, love a good steak."

I nodded and returned the smile. "What happened? That's the million-dollar question. Here's what we know. He didn't cook. He didn't make himself any food at all. He didn't turn on any lights. He closed the drapes in the living room and put on a DVD from a box set of *Murder She Wrote*."

"I love that show."

"Who doesn't? He obviously did. According to Dr. Epstein, he had watched the entire series more than thirty times."

"Wow, that's intense." She started cutting into her steak again.

I continued. "He wasn't found for three days. Joy Jones got worried when she didn't hear from him and he wouldn't answer his phone. She doesn't live far from his house, so on the way home from work, she went to see him. There was no reply when she knocked, and, when she questioned the neighbors, nobody had seen him since his birthday. So she called the cops."

She stuffed the last piece of steak in her mouth and spoke around it as she chewed. "They found him on the living room floor, with a stab wound to his heart."

I drained my glass, refilled hers and then mine. "That misses all of what Holmes would call the most interesting features, my dear Dehan. First of all, the place had been trashed, turned upside down, though nothing was broken. Second, he was, as you say, killed by a single stab wound to the heart, but the blade of the knife was exceptionally long and broad, consistent, according to the ME, with the blade of a large kitchen knife. He was lying on the living room floor, beside his sofa, with the TV still playing Jessica Fletcher on repeat, over and over."

"That's kind of creepy to think about."

"There were shots fired."

"What?"

"Three shots. Nobody heard them. That is not surprising in itself: residents of the Bronx have a peculiar deafness where gunfire is concerned. However, the nine-millimeter rounds traveled from the living room through to the open-plan kitchen and shattered various items: the kettle, a stack of plates, and a radio sitting by the sink. The radio had a clock, so the lab was able to establish at what time the power was cut off."

"So we have time of death . . ."

"Ten thirty on Friday night, the twenty-third of November, 2007."

"Good. So what happened?"

"The first thing Martinez did was haul Ned in for questioning. He had a very badly bruised right hand with two broken fingers. At first, he said he got his fingers caught in a car door. That's what it says on his medical report from the ER department. But later, he admitted that it was Al who had slammed his front door on his fingers when they were, and I quote, 'messin' with him and just trying to scare the old guy a bit.' They didn't mean no harm."

"So they charged him?"

"No, he came up with an alibi. He was with his friends all that weekend, nursing his hand, and he didn't go out. His friends were willing to testify that they were with him every hour of every day from Friday lunchtime to Monday morning."

"So the son of a bitch got a false alibi."

"Perhaps; either way, they were unable to shake it or make anything stick. Forensic evidence was very thin on the ground. There was not a trace of DNA evidence, not a single thing to link him to the scene of the crime *at the time* of the murder. They had to let him go."

She sat forward with her elbows on the table. The light from the flames in the barbeque bathed her face and danced in her eyes.

"Well," she said, "there is no mystery to this case, Stone. Making the evidence stick may be a problem, but you and I both know exactly what happened. Ned was having some fun tormenting this poor guy. Maybe he got pissed because he didn't like the way Al answered him, or maybe he got mad because Al ignored him. Whichever. You know—you don't disrespect a bro from the hood, know what I'm sayin'? You feel me, dude?"

"I feel you, man."

"Assholes like that don't need an excuse. They smell your weakness and they go after you. So things get out of hand and they try to force their way into his house. He slams the door. The guy was big and heavy..."

"Six three and almost four hundred pounds."

She grinned. "So when he says, 'I'm gonna close the door here,' he closes the door. Only this time, he closes it on Ned's fingers. Ned goes away to nurse his hand but comes back a few hours later with a nine-millimeter, picks the lock, and goes in planning to shoot Al dead. Al freaks out and panics. So Ned has four hundred pounds of panicking crazy to contend with. He panics too and fires. The shots go wide. Maybe Al snatches the gun or knocks it out of his hand." She shrugged and spread her hands. "So Ned stabs him."

I took a deep breath and swirled the wine around in my glass. I took a sip and sighed.

"That is pretty much word for word what Martinez concluded."

She nodded and snorted. "But you have some pain in the ass Sherlock Holmes observations which make it impossible, my dear Watson."

I shrugged. "Not impossible, but they are, as he would say, features of interest. For a start, when questioned, Ned was asked if he had a knife. He admitted that he had a switchblade. It was a barely legal folding knife with a five-inch blade. More than enough to kill a man with."

"So...?"

"Well, the blade was much smaller than the one that was used to kill Al. So, make the movie in your head. What happened? He went home from the hospital, sore as hell. He packed a nine-millimeter pistol, which we assume he had, though it was never found, and, even though he had a lethal knife, which he carried everywhere with him, he also went and took his mother's huge, cumbersome kitchen knife, just for good measure?"

Dehan grunted. "Maybe he used one of Al's knives."

"Wait, we're not there yet. Assuming still that he took the kitchen knife with him for some reason—that knife has, at the least, an eight-inch blade, maybe three or four inches wide at the base, plus it has a four- or five-inch handle. If he already has a gun and a knife, why does he burden himself also with this very large knife that he doesn't need? Where does he carry it?"

"And what for?"

"Exactly: What for? And when the gun is knocked from his hand, does he wrestle this short sword from his jacket pocket?"

"Point taken. So now can you answer my question? Did he use Al's own kitchen knife?"

"No. The one knife he had that might have fit the wound had only his fingerprints on it, and those had not been smudged by latex gloves or anything of the sort. Plus, there was no trace of Al's blood on the knife, not even in the grooves by the handle. To have been cleaned that thoroughly . . ."

"The prints would have gone too. Okay."

"There is another point, which is quite important."

"What?"

"Have you ever had a broken hand?"

"No . . ."

I laughed. "It hurts. A lot. The last thing you want to do with a broken hand is fire a gun. If he's shooting left-handed, then that might account for the shots going wide. But the knife wound to the chest did not go wide. That was precision engineering, powerfully executed, dear Dehan. That blade was placed and thrust without a second's hesitation. And with considerable force. That was not done with a broken hand, or left-handed."

"Son of a gun."

I nodded. "No, I don't like Ned for this. I have a feeling somebody else went to visit Al that night."

"But what motive could anyone possibly have to kill him? The guy was harmless."

I made a protracted "hmmm" noise. "I don't know if he was harmless." I shrugged. "He may well have been. But there was a rumor, which most people paid little or no attention to, that said he'd had a pretty wild, shady life and kept a vast sum of money in his house, in a paper bag or a carton or some equally stupid container."

"Oh . . . and the place had been ransacked."

"Yup, and when you look at the photographs . . ." I sighed. "I don't know, it looks to me like a search that somebody has tried to disguise as a fight or a struggle."

She laughed. "How the hell can you tell that?"

I hesitated. "Nothing is broken. That struck me as odd. When two people thrash around fighting, they break things, but not necessarily when they are searching. And every time I look at the pictures, it strikes me as more odd. Why is nothing broken?" I shrugged. "And naturally, no trace of the money was ever found."

"You think he really had a stash of money?"

"I shouldn't think so for one moment. But it may well be that somebody in Ned's gang thought it was worth exploring the possibility."

"Did they pull in the other kids?"

"They asked them questions, but they were all each other's alibi. So the case stalled."

She gazed at me for a while. Then she spoke suddenly and emphatically, nodding her head. "No, that is a really interesting case. It has, like you said, interesting features. But, Stone, how the *hell* do you plan to crack it? Where do you begin? It *is* insoluble."

"I know," I said, and smiled. "That's why I want to solve it."

CHAPTER 3

Next morning, we dropped in on Dr. Epstein's practice on the way to the precinct. We approached through heavy morning traffic via the Metropolitan Oval and peeled off into Benedict Avenue, where I managed to find a space for my ancient, burgundy Jag, right outside his block. By the time I'd climbed out and slammed the door, Dehan was already on the sidewalk, doing little jumps on her toes. It wasn't cold, but there was enough chill in the morning air to bring out pink flushes on her cheeks. That made me smile. She ignored it and said, "So, you want to tell me what it is you hope to find out here?"

We entered the lobby. There was a thick, dark green carpet, there were wood-paneled walls, brass lamps, and a mahogany desk for a porter. But there was no porter, the lampshades were flyblown, and the thick green carpets were worn thin from years of being trodden on by increasingly cheap shoes. I pressed the button to call the elevator and shoved my hands in my pockets.

"I hope to find out," I said, "what it is I hope to find out."

"Have you been reading annoying books on Zen philosophy again?"

I closed my eyes. "I *am* annoying Zen philosophy, Dehan. You godda be de watter, Ritoo Glasshopper."

The elevator doors slid open and we stepped in. I pressed the button, and as the doors closed, I said, "Let me explain: somewhere in this apparently insoluble case, there is one small, loose end, but we don't know what it is yet." We began to climb. "So if we are busy looking for fingerprints, but the loose end is a handkerchief with blood on it, we may never find it, because we are looking in the wrong place for the wrong thing."

"So?"

"We must look nowhere—and *everywhere*!"

She smiled with hooded eyes. "I bet you used to watch all those shows and movies, didn't you?"

The elevator stopped and the doors slid open. "What shows and movies?"

She followed me out to the landing. "You know, Bruce Lee, kung fu, *Karate Kid* . . ."

I spied Dr. Epstein's brass plaque and headed for it, speaking over my shoulder. "Never heard of them. It seems to me, however, young Dehan, that you are quite familiar with *all* of them! Here we are . . ."

I tapped lightly on the door and stepped through to a comfortable reception area while Dehan muttered something behind me. The walls were plain cream with half a dozen unobtrusive prints hanging. There were chairs and a couple of small sofas that had been new not so long ago, but weren't anymore, and there was a coffee table with lots of magazines on it. Opposite the door, and slightly to my right, there was an old oak desk, and behind it there was an attractive woman in her late thirties or early forties. She had large, humorous eyes and a mouth with generous lips and very white teeth that found it hard not to smile. When she spoke, her accent said she had once been from Barbados, but she was now from the Bronx.

"Good morning, what can I do for you?"

We showed her our badges. "I'm Detective Stone, this is Detective Dehan, of the NYPD . . ."

She was already shaking her head and laughing. "Oh, I know you're cops, darling!" She laughed and flapped her hand at me. "You got that written *all* over you! But tell me what I can do to help you."

I smiled. "We'd like to see Dr. Epstein."

She glanced at her watch. "He's got his nine thirty in twenty minutes." She eyed me with a hint of mischief. "Procrastination, but he is always late!" She screamed with laughter and flapped her hand. I heard Dehan snort behind me. She picked up the internal phone and pressed a button, still chuckling. "Procrastination . . . always late. I swear it's true . . . Dr. Epstein. I got two beautiful detectives from the NYPD here to see you . . ." She paused, watching us and nodding, then said, "Twenty minutes, but you know he's *always* late . . . okay."

She pointed to a mahogany door across the room and said, "That door. He's noisy, but he's a good man."

"Thanks for the heads-up."

She winked at Dehan, and I went and knocked on the door.

"Come!"

I opened the door and we stepped in.

Dr. Epstein was on his feet, rising from his large oak desk, gesturing at us with a huge hand. "I told her to send you in. Why do you need to knock? If she tells you to come in, it's like *I* told you to come in! Sit down. What do you want?"

He was a big man, though not tall. He had a white shirt with thin brown stripes and a burgundy tie. His hands were large and hairy. He had a large, gold wedding band, and the nails of his right hand were long. Those on his left were short. He used gold cuff links.

The office was comfortable, more like your favorite uncle's study than a place of work. It was elegantly shabby, well used, and smelled of pipe tobacco. The bookcases, the oak desk, and the sideboard were all genuine antiques, and the books on the shelves were an eclectic mix of leather-bound tomes and well-thumbed paperbacks, filed according to the nearest available empty space system.

I assimilated this in the time it took him to swing his arm from pointing to the door to pointing to the ancient leather armchairs across from his desk.

"Sit down," he said again. "You'll be more comfortable sitting down than talking on your feet." He dropped into his own huge leather chair and we sat. "When you stand too long, all the blood drains from your brain to your feet, makes it harder to think. That's a joke, but it's also true. So what do you want?"

I let him finish, smiled, and waited in case he was going to start again. After he didn't, I showed him my badge and said, "You were Aloysius Chester's psychiatrist, back in 2007, when he was murdered?"

You read about people's faces darkening. Epstein's actually did. He frowned, and his tan seemed to take on a deeper hue.

"I was. I saw him the very day they say he was killed, in fact. It was his birthday . . ." He waved his hand vaguely toward reception. "We did a little thing for him." His eyes shifted from Dehan to me. He looked like he wasn't sure whether to be mad or not. "He liked the attention, the affection. It made his load a little lighter." His face darkened further, into a scowl. "He was a kind, loving person trapped in a damaged body, and a damaged brain."

I drew breath to ask my next question, but he barked suddenly at Dehan, "I hope you're not one of those people who spout trite little Facebook wisdom bites, like, 'Everything happens for a reason'!"

I saw her repress a smile and raise an eyebrow. "Excuse me?"

He waved a dismissive hand at her. "A pet beef of mine. You know them? Those people who greet every damned tragedy in life with that trite little phrase, 'Everything happens for a reason.'" He looked at me, hunched his shoulders, and narrowed his eyes into incredulity. "*What?*"

I was about to tell him I hadn't spoken, but he said it again. "*What? Excuse me?* I mean, what does it *mean*? Everything happens for a reason! Yeah, your husband got killed and the *reason* was, he stepped in front of a goddamn car! Children in developing countries die of malnutrition. The *reason* is human beings are sick and corrupt! Six million Jews were exterminated in German death camps. The *reason* was that the Germans elected Hitler to power! These are the *reasons* bad things happen, not because of some goddamned benign, all-knowing Universe!"

Dehan smiled. "We're cops, Dr. Epstein, not philosophers. We just want to ask you . . ."

"It's like those people—I want to shoot them—somebody says . . ." He sat forward and rearranged his ass. "Somebody says, 'Hey, did you hear? John's got terminal cancer.' And some asshole always says, 'Oh my God! His *poor* wife!'" His face collapsed into an exaggerated gape. He showed it to Dehan, then to me. "Excuse me? What? No! *John* has cancer, not his goddamn wife! Poor *John*! Am I right? Am I right or am I wrong about that? I mean, it's *John* who has cancer, right? So poor John!" He flopped back in his chair. "I can't stand that. Compassion is for the person who is dying, right?"

Dehan tried again. "Dr. Epstein, we really just wanted to . . ."

"Dehan? You're Jewish, right? I can see it in your eyes. You're always asking questions that can never be answered. We don't have a cross, right? We're Jews. But if we had one, that would be it. The eternal questions. Godda love the stereotypes."

"Dr. Epstein?"

He turned to face me.

"We are taking another look at Al's case. We have the full report, obviously . . ."

"Obviously."

"But it would be really helpful . . ."

"You wanna hear it from the horse's mouth. Of course you do. What do you wanna know? What happened that last day? How he looked? Did he seem worried about anything? Preoccupied . . . ? Who'd know, if not his shrink?"

I sat back in my chair. "Yes, all of that, and anything else you can think of."

He dilated his nostrils and took a long, deep, noisy breath.

"What can I think of . . . ?" His eyes became abstracted. "He was a beautiful person. Kind, humane, compassionate." His eyes locked onto mine for a second. "Brilliantly intelligent. Highly, *highly* intelligent. A seeker for truth. But . . ." He tossed his right hand, like he was throwing away something that had once had promise but had since been found wanting. "Like so many young people of his generation, he thought the way to wisdom was to burn your candle at both ends." He paused and smiled at Dehan, studying her face. "My candle burns at both ends;" he quoted, "It will not last the night; but ah, my foes, and oh, my friends—it gives a lovely light."

I sighed loudly and made no effort to hide it. "If we could get down to concrete . . ."

"Facts! It is a fact that Aloysius Chester was a brilliant student. Wellington College prep school, in England, Marymount High School, New York, Harvard Medical School. He had a glittering career all lined up at the top of his profession as a heart surgeon. But unlike his family, the man had a heart. He had a soul! He *cared* and asked *those* questions . . ." He eyed Dehan. "He wasn't a Jew, but we haven't got the monopoly on searching questions, right?"

"Right."

I asked, "What are *those* questions he kept asking?"

"Why? Who? How? He asked how a lot, but mainly, why?"

I sighed again. "Dr. Epstein, we really haven't got time . . ."

"You think I'm being facetious, but I'm not. He really did ask those questions. And it was the asking of those questions that shaped his life. Now, he was twenty years old when he was at Harvard. I'm talking about the late sixties. And we all know what was going on—*and what was going down*—at every campus in the U.S.A. during the late sixties. And there . . ." He gestured with his open hand at the middle of the floor. "Right there, was Tim Leary telling us all it was okay! Am I right?"

"So you're telling us that..."

"And big, powerful brains like William Burroughs, Allen Ginsberg—you know?—telling us this is good! This is spiritual evolution. And these were no intellectual slouches! Not like Jack Kerouac, who was, if you will forgive me, intellectually lazy *at best*. So there we were, at the dawn of a new age, being offered the fruit of the tree of knowledge. I was a bit younger than him. He was there right at the start, and who could blame him?"

Dehan said, "For being there at the start?" And frowned.

"No, for experimenting with LSD and mind-altering drugs. He was pretty wild, unafraid. And, you know, at that time, we were all reading Carlos Castaneda, *as well* as Ginsberg and Leary and the Beatles. Everywhere you turned, there was this message, 'Get high! Turn on! Blow your mind...'"

He went quiet, staring at nothing, seeing his memories.

"I met him once, you know that? Castaneda. Interesting guy, mild-mannered, polite, very academic. It was all true, what he wrote about. He told me."

"Al...?"

"Yeah, so he dropped out of college, went to Mexico, met a shaman, just like Castaneda. He did the whole peyote mescalito thing. His family were horrified. They disowned him. He didn't care! He didn't give a good goddamn. He was on a mission, brother!"

He threw his head back and roared out laughing, intoning in a booming voice, "*He was on a mission, brother!*" Then he subsided into chuckles. "A mission to find the Truth, with a capital *T*. From Mexico, he went to Brazil, in search of a shaman who could teach him to use ayahuasca." He sighed noisily through hairy nostrils and shook his head. "It wasn't enough. He never found the Truth. The *Truth* is never *out there*, is it? So, he came back, deeply disillusioned with Latin America, believing now that we in the West were closer to the answer. This was Our Time, he thought. We were searching, in our collective unconscious, for the ultimate illumination. And for this reason, we had created LSD. He used it immoderately, recklessly, and it drove him into a doddering, ineffectual, *infantile* psychosis. He was made *stupid* by his own, wild search for Truth."

I leaned forward and raised a hand. "Let me just take this one step at a time, please, Dr. Epstein. You are telling me that Al's schizophrenia was caused by his abuse of hallucinogenic drugs?"

"I thought I had made that clear."

"And that he, Al, came from a privileged background..."

"I was also under the impression that I had made *that* clear."

I struggled for a moment, trying to see the implications of this new information. Dehan scratched her throat with her index finger, narrowing her eyes.

"You said his family disowned him, and please, don't say you'd made that clear."

"Oh yes, the Chesters are one of the great families of New York. They are so privileged that nobody has heard of them. Anonymity is the true mark of class..."

I smiled. "Like the British royal family."

"Exactly, vulgar German upstarts. The Chesters were among the first settlers in New York, long before the War of Independence. Since then, they have produced a string of eminent medical practitioners, particularly surgeons. Every generation has produced at least one eminence. It was widely thought that Aloysius would be that eminence in this generation. But his soul burned too bright."

There was an edge of impatience to Dehan's voice when she said, "So they disowned him."

He shook his head. "Not at first. His mother had died when he was young. I have no doubt this affected his attitude to life—and women. She was, perhaps, the answer he was forever seeking, but was doomed never to find. Be that as it may, he was raised most of his life either at boarding schools or, on the rare occasions that he was at home, by nannies. He had very little contact with his father. But while he was in Brazil, his father died. He did not return for the funeral, but he did return shortly after that for some kind of Harvard reunion. His brothers and his sister met with him and gave him an ultimatum: toe the line and take up your position as head of the family, or we will disown you."

I couldn't help giving a small laugh. "What does that mean? What would be the consequences of being disowned?"

He viewed me a moment, then nodded a few times. "You mock, and perhaps in some cases you would be right to. To be disowned by the Chester siblings would mean social ostracism. His clan, his class, his social peers would all disown him. They would all turn their backs on him. He would be cast adrift, and his old school tie would be of no use to him whatsoever. That can—and did, for Aloysius—have very serious consequences, professionally and financially. The well of privilege suddenly dried up!"

I nodded, aware that he was telling me something that was important, though I wasn't exactly sure why. "But this case was different in some way?"

"Oh yes, very. Because when Aloysius got back from Brazil, it soon became apparent that he had suffered serious neurological damage. So not only did they disown him, but then they had him diagnosed as suffering from paranoid schizophrenia. He effectively lost control of all his wealth overnight. His shares in the family company were put in trust . . ."

I frowned. "In trust?"

He snorted. "In *trust* . . . ! Meaning that his brothers and his sister administered his shares in the company, *and the proceeds from those shares*, and I was appointed by the court to be his guardian. It was up to me to oversee his care, watch over him if you like, and also to make sure his siblings did not abuse the trust too outrageously."

Dehan asked, "What is the family company?"

"Their father, Isembard Chester, invented a small, visually insignificant, yet medically essential valve which is used in every cardiology department in the world. He founded the company,

Chester Cardio-Valves, and now they all live like kings on the proceeds. They were always rich, now they became insanely rich. And Aloysius had inherited twenty-five percent of the shares in that company. When he was diagnosed as suffering from paranoid schizophrenia, the siblings requested a court order to enable them to administer his share of the company. Then they disowned him."

I said, "So he lived on an allowance from the family?"

He shook his head. "The company paid him a director's salary every year. It was far less than the other three received, because they claimed he had no input into the firm. His shares were worth millions—a king's ransom! But he was not allowed access to it because they claimed he was a danger to himself—a statement you could hardly argue with."

"And once he died?"

He shrugged. "That was where my involvement ended. Everything reverted back to the estate. He had no heirs, nor could he make out a will, because he was not of sound mind. So his brothers and his sister got everything."

Dehan's eyebrows shot up, but she didn't say anything. I stared at Epstein a moment. "You talk about him and his family as though you knew them..."

He spread his hands, flopped his head on one side. "He was in my care for a long time. I liked him. He was a couple of years ahead of me at Harvard. He didn't know me, but I saw him around and I admired him. I admired his relentless *search*! It was fortuitous that later in life he would be put into my care."

His internal phone rang, and he snatched it up. "Yes!"

He listened a moment, then hung up without saying anything. To me, he said, "My patient is here. Joy might be able to tell you more. She was more directly involved with Al on a day-to-day basis. Talk to her."

I pointed toward reception. "Is that Joy?"

"Not anymore. She opened up and let you in this morning, bless her. But now she's at the church. Mondays she volunteers to combat the encroaching darkness of Babylon. Right now you'll see her daughter, Mary. Dim, IQ of about ninety-eight point five, but willing. She'll tell you how to get to the church. Now, go, please."

Scan the QR code below to purchase BLOOD IN BABYLON.
Or go to: righthouse.com/blood-in-babylon

Printed in Dunstable, United Kingdom